What p[...]
Jenn[...]

MW00943197

"A fun, sassy read! A cross between Erma Bombeck and Candace Bushnell, reading Jenny Gardiner is like sinking your teeth into a chocolate cupcake…you just want more."

--Meg Cabot, NY Times bestselling author of *Princess Diaries, Queen of Babble* and more, on *Sleeping with Ward Cleaver*

"With a strong yet delightfully vulnerable voice, food critic Abbie Jennings embarks on a soulful journey where her love for banana cream pie and disdain for ill-fitting Spanx clash in hilarious and heartbreaking ways. As her body balloons and her personal life crumbles, Abbie must face the pain and secret fears she's held inside for far too long. I cheered for her the entire way."

--Beth Hoffman, NY Times bestselling author of *Saving CeeCee Honeycutt* on *Slim to None*

"Jenny Gardiner has done it again--this fun, fast-paced book is a great summer read."

--Sarah Pekkanen, NY Times bestselling author of *The Opposite of Me,* on *Slim to None*

"As Sweet as a song and sharp as a beak, *(Bite Me)* really soars as a memoir about family--children and husbands, feathers and fur--and our capacity to keep loving though life may occasionally bite."

--Wade Rouse, bestselling author of *At Least in the City Someone Would Hear Me Scream*

SOMETHING

IN THE

HEIR

by Jenny Gardiner
(book one of the Royals of Monaforte series)

Copyright © 2014 by Jenny Gardiner

Chapter One

EMMA Davison had a date with a prince. Well, not really a date, but yes, really a prince. Calling it a date would be a bit of a stretch, considering she would only be within breathing distance of the man by dint of her professional skills. Emma had been hired to photograph His Royal Highness Crown Prince Adrian William Philip Nicholas Winchester-Westleigh, future King of Monaforte, in a series of grip-and-grins with wealthy donors at a Washington, DC charitable event. For Emma, this was a perfect night out with a man: one for which she'd get paid, and only for her skills. Professionally-speaking, that is. It was about as much of a pseudo date with a guy as she'd expected for the foreseeable future, since she'd sworn off men for a while after a series of dud relationships.

And while it was hard not to fleetingly fantasize about being swept off your feet by royalty, the fact was, those types of princes only came in fairy tales, and Emma wasn't a big subscriber to that sort of fiction. Having already tossed back into the swamp more than her share of warty toads over the years, she knew that at the end of the day, even a prince was just a man. And in her world, men hadn't exactly panned out. Besides, she'd seen the tabloids: this pretty boy was a player, a new woman on his arm in every city, rumor had it. As far as she was concerned, they could keep him. *Prince-schmince.* She sure wasn't looking for another love 'em and leave 'em type in her life. She was here to do a job, and the sooner she did it, the sooner she could go home and take a nice hot bath with a good book and a glass of red wine.

As she awaited the arrival of the guest of honor while hovering just inside the cordoned-off velvet rope section in the palatial Great Hall of the Library of Congress, Emma mentally ticked off the essentials she needed to keep in mind for the shoot. She'd thoroughly reviewed the protocol handbook with the palace's press secretary earlier in the week. All forty-six pages of it. She'd been told a curtsey would be a nice gesture, and warned not to shake the man's hand, which sort of seemed annoying, as if her own wasn't good enough or something. No vulgar language in his presence, which made her laugh, since under other circumstances she'd maybe have to show a bit of restraint in that area, but she figured she could refrain from an f-bomb for an hour or two.

Emma had actually practiced how to address the prince for a good while in advance of the event so that she wouldn't come across like a complete country bumpkin in his presence, repeating in front of the mirror, *"Pleased to meet you, sir"* till she could say it no more. She was ready. She'd even straightened her shoulder-length chestnut curls for the occasion, thinking straighter hair lent her a bit of gravitas. Yeah, she kept telling herself, she didn't care one bit about impressing even a prince.

She'd brought along her assistant and best friend Caroline McKenzie, whom she knew wouldn't screw up—though it was a crap shoot whether she'd hit on the man herself. Caroline, a green-eyed redhead with a penchant for serial flirtation, was known for her ability to pick up pretty much any guy she wanted without batting an eye. But Emma knew even she had her limits and would, with any luck, respect royal protocol, in deference to her friend's career.

Tonight Emma would remain on the VIP side of the velvet rope as she set up to shoot the prince alongside all sorts of deep-pocketed D.C. dignitaries, with the President of the United States thrown in for good measure. Lately she'd found it hard to remain too starstruck in her line of work, shooting famous people as regularly as she did. But a prince *and* a president? As much as she wanted to play it cool, even she had to admit that was none too shabby.

Caro, standing just behind Emma, squealed in surprise when the prince's arrival was announced with blasts from those long royal trumpets draped with crimson flags bearing the Monaforte royal crest. It was straight out of a Disney movie when Prince Charming's arrival was heralded to the guests at the ball. As soon as the trumpets fell silent, a deep blue velvet curtain parted and the prince, followed by his right-hand man, stepped forward to the thunderous applause of the audience.

Emma was close enough to see that he had mesmerizing bright blue eyes. She was a sucker for blue eyes.

Just then a quartet struck up a tune and the music shattered her momentary reverie. She knew she had all of about two minutes to greet the prince and then get started with the host of images she needed to capture. There were titans of industry, political bigwigs and a collection of pandering celebrities already queued up, desperate for their own eight-by-ten glossy with famous royalty that they could mount on their wall like some taxidermied bear head. She had no time for gawking.

The prince walked slowly down the line, greeting one by one the organizers of the charitable event and members of the Monafortian embassy staff, all standing in the VIP zone near Emma. Everyone seemed to do a perfectly fine job with his or her allotted three seconds of undivided royal attention, making casual chitchat with the prince. Until it came to Emma. Because as soon as the man approached her, she felt as if her tongue had become a sandbag weighted down in her mouth. And while a curtsey wasn't mandatory, it was what she'd planned on, until that very moment when her eyes made contact with his deep, sapphire ones, and she knew for certain she'd face-plant on his expensive royal bespoke Italian shoes if she dared try any tricky maneuvers.

Emma tried to give him a discreet once-over, but it felt awkward, like gawking at a stranger's tattoo, or trying to read the T-shirt message on the chest of a person walking by. She definitely wanted to avoid coming across like a sad-sack groupie, and had planned to play it cool. But then she found herself focused on his thick, wavy black hair, which led to a fleeting fantasy that involved burying her fingers in it while he was busily...*Oh, stop!* She tamped down that betraying thought, dismissing it as some stupid latent celebrity crush, all the while recognizing that her darned body was selling her out and swooning over the guy despite her strong inner protestations.

So when Prince Adrian stopped before her, bent his head down but raised his gaze and continued to fix it on Emma's eyes only, reaching both hands out for hers — totally defying that whole handbook of royal protocol — she simply stammered. And when he pressed his lips to the top of her hand, she could only gulp as she tried to clear what felt like a giant hairball lodged in her throat.

"Peas to greet you, slur," she said, failing miserably to just mouth correctly those five simple words, turning about fifty shades of red in the process. She felt certain she was going to be fired on the spot.

But instead of calling for his royal bodyguards to toss her out into the cold December night on the grounds of complete idiocy, he clasped her hand in both of his for a moment longer, his eyes continuing to hold hers, and smiled broadly. Emma could feel her heart beating in her throat, and she wondered for a minute if he was only holding onto her hands until someone else could grab them and haul her away. In handcuffs maybe.

"The pleasure is all mine. And please, call me Adrian," he said in what seemed barely a whisper, adding with a wink, "Oh, and by the way, I'm most pleased to greet you as well."

Emma was so glad she wasn't prone to throwing up because if she were, that would've been the unfortunate outcome of her moment in the spotlight with her "date." Instead she let him cling to her hand a second longer while she trembled just a bit and hoped to God her palms weren't sweating too badly.

The spell was broken when Caroline elbowed her, blurting out, and not in her inside voice, "Oh, my God. His accent is orgasmic. And did you get a look at that friend of his?"

Adrian and Emma's heads followed her friend's pointing finger, which led right to the tall, handsome brown-eyed blond man standing beside the prince.

"Who? Darcy?" Adrian said, waving his hand dismissively. "He's hardly anything to write home about!" He laughed as he gave him a friendly smack on the back.

"Don't listen to a word he says," Darcy said. "He's just jealous that women always choose me over him."

Which meant those women must have been certifiably insane, if they didn't want Adrian to keep for all eternity. Emma wondered if she could stuff him in her camera bag and no one would notice. And then she could have him all to herself. To join her in that bubble bath even. Which was an insane thought, considering she'd just met the man minutes ago. But he was obviously so good at charming the pants off of a girl, how could she not maybe at least ponder having her own pants charmed off, at least for a second or two?

By the time Emma snapped out of that delusional fantasy, the prince had finished greeting the receiving line and was engaged in conversation with some member of Congress. That was her cue to get to work, so she raised her camera up to her eye, her other hand turning the zoom on the lens to frame the shot, and started taking pictures.

A short while later, a syrupy-drawled senator approached and glad-handed the prince with a too-firm grip and slap on the back. So much for diplomatic decorum.

"You gonna tap that one?" he said to Adrian, his booming voice resonating. He nodded in Emma's direction, rubbing his paunchy belly like he'd had a satisfying meal, as she snapped the two of them in conversation. He might as well have been licking his chops like a starving dog. It wasn't the first time she'd been exposed to obnoxious good-old-boy comments from an old fogey politician. Such crassness seemed to be elevated to an art form in this town.

"You mean our lovely photographer?" the prince said, playing along. "Actually, she's the woman I'm going to marry." He gave her a wink, assuming she'd be complicit in his joke.

5

Something in the Heir

Instead Emma blanched, mortified that they were discussing her as if she was a slab of meat they were choosing off a hot grill, all for their boys-will-be-boys amusement.

"Yeah, in your dreams, buddy," she said in too loud of a voice as she continued to snap pictures, handily obscuring her face and thus her emotions. Her royal subject squinted his eyes at her and pouted, as if she'd hurt his feelings, and she immediately regretted her words. It made no sense to be annoyed with the prince; he was simply defusing the obnoxious comment made by the senator. But it was too late. Within a minute he had his arm draped around the sexy trophy wife of a well-known lobbyist, and so Emma did what she always did to hide from the world and resumed snapping pictures.

"I'm so ready to get out of here," Caroline said as they sipped sparkling water while taking a five-minute break. "These old geezers around here with those gold-digging bimbos on their arms are giving me hives. Maybe I can kidnap blondie over there and make a run for it. Think his friend would notice?" Once again she pointed toward Darcy, who was dominating the conversation in a circle of women nearby.

They'd been notified by the event coordinator that the president would be arriving shortly, so Emma was taking advantage of a momentary break to run to the bathroom and double check that her equipment was ready for the big moment. Despite an encroaching sense of ennui about her job that had settled in recently, she was feeling anxious about shooting the president and wanted to be sure she got off all the shots she needed.

When she returned to Caroline's side, they worked their way back toward the front of the crowd to get in position for the president's arrival. She noticed how Caroline's gaze rarely left

Darcy.

"Forget about him," Emma said, nodding toward the prince's assistant. "This place is crawling with Secret Service, at least until the president's gone. If you try to bag that one, you'd be hauled off for interrogation by Homeland Security, never to be heard from again."

Her friend shrugged. "You know, some of those Secret Service guys are pretty hot."

"You do know you've got a one-track mind, don't you?"

Caro shook her head in dismay at her friend. "At least there's something going down my track. Ever since that last derailment with Richard what's-his-name, yours has been a whole lot of nothing. No train ever stops at your station."

"Please," Emma said, annoyance flickering in her hazel eyes. "I do not need to be reminded of that regrettable relationship. The jerk still owes me five hundred dollars I lent him. Not to mention my dignity, which he took off with along with that stripper from his buddy's bachelor party."

"Pretend I didn't even mention him," Caroline said, holding her hands up in defeat. "I totally forgot I promised I'd no longer resurrect your litany of painful break-up stories. At least not while at work. Although, you gotta admit," she said, wrinkling her nose as she held back her laughter, "it was sort of funny to watch him on YouTube jamming fifties in her g-string. Just think how romantic it is that one day they'll be able to show their grandchildren the video of the very moment they met."

Emma made a grumbling sound. "At least I figured out where my money went."

"And it was money well spent, darlin', if it meant finding out the truth about that one. Way cheaper than alimony."

"Which I'd have had to pay since he couldn't keep a job for more than six months." Sometimes Emma wished there was a punching bag nearby, just to get out her aggression toward the loser.

Their conversation was interrupted by the unmistakable

sound of drums and bugles that precede "Hail to the Chief." Emma snapped one wide shot of an audience's worth of hands raised in the air, smart phones at the ready for their very own money shot with the president.

The president parted the velvet curtains, waved to the crowd, then greeted the prince and his entourage while Emma clicked away on her camera. After a brief, five-minute address, he was whisked away by a coterie of security guards, *tout de suite*.

Once the headliner was gone, the crowd began to dissipate. Emma managed to pop off a handful of shots with other guests and the prince, and finally the embassy press secretary thanked Emma for her service and dismissed her.

She scoured the room in search of Caroline, who'd taken another bathroom break, just to let her know she was off the hook and could leave. She found her friend chatting up a cute bartender.

Emma tapped her on the shoulder, trying to draw her attention away from tall, dark and hottie, who seemed intent on slinging mixed drinks to impress, shaking cocktails atop his head like he was go-go dancer from the sixties

"I'd tell you that you can leave but it looks like you don't want to have a reason to slip out quite yet," she said.

Caroline startled and gasped. "You scared the crap out of me!"

"Just wanted you to know you're technically off-duty in exactly T minus ten seconds," Emma told her, pointing at the time on her cell phone. "Obviously you can feel free to stick around and latch onto some useless guy, but if I were you, considering the caliber of this crowd, at least I'd aim a little higher."

"Thanks for the sage advice, relationship expert that you are." She laughed at Emma. "But seriously, you know I'm not looking for the guy with the deepest pockets," Caroline said. "I'll take the hot bartender with the smooth moves any day," she said, pointing over to the guy pouring her drink, "— over some snooty, rich country club-type who wouldn't abide my less-than-uppity ways." She lifted the tip of her nose with her pointer finger as she said that, her long, straight red hair falling into her face.

Emma laughed and mussed her friend's hair. "Whatever. Have fun, and don't do anything I wouldn't do…"

"That leaves my options wide open," she said, holding her thumb and pointer finger up in an "L" shape to her chest. "How about just to prove you're not a complete loser, why don't you see if you can snare that cute prince and get your wild on?" Not that there was a chance of that anyhow, as the prince and his entourage had already taken their leave.

Emma fake-glared at her. "Thanks, but I'll take a pass on the Cinderella fantasy. Though he was pretty easy on the eyes. I'm surprised you didn't already commandeer that friend of his."

"Sadly, once I got finished wiping the drool from my chin, he'd disappeared."

"Leave it to you to not miss out on the eye candy, whether he's your basic bartender or a royal footman," Emma said, pausing to contemplate the thought. "Is that what you call them? Footmen? Do they do something with their feet, or have a creepy foot fetish? Sort of weird name, isn't it?"

"Probably more like henchman is my guess. Back in the day his footman would've cut off the enemy's head. Am I right? Ah, well, clearly we weren't born into that world, so I'm not gonna bother even fantasizing about it, not to mention decipher the terminology."

"Yep. Besides, imagine how high maintenance a prince would be. Sheesh!" Emma stuck out her pinky finger while pretending to pick up a delicate china teacup. "Spot of tea, Mummy? Oh, royal knave, fetch me my slippers!" she said with an exaggerated accent.

The two women practically fell over laughing, until Caroline's mixologist cleared his throat at an elevated volume, trying to rein in his audience.

"Okay, then. Looks like Bartender Ben over there wants

your undivided attention," she said, aiming her thumb over her shoulder at the guy. "I've got no shoots scheduled for the next week, which means I won't be requiring your assistance, so have fun mixing it up with this one."

Caroline's eyes grew wide and she mouthed "Shut up!" to Emma, then turned back to her man of the moment.

Emma took a final quick glance around the room as she packed up her camera bag. After working more hours than she cared to count with her feet wedged into a torturous pair of black stilettos, she wanted nothing more than to peel off her floor-length, black satin sheath, lose the strapless bra that was cutting off the circulation in her mid-section, and tug on her favorite oversized sweatshirt and yoga pants. Then she'd finally pour that very full glass of Chianti she'd been craving, and return to her natural slothdom.

The party was still going surprisingly strong, but since she was only contracted to do grip-and-grins of Prince Charming, there wasn't truly a reason to stick around much longer. Hell, she'd likely get pressed into service with the wait staff if she wasn't careful. Not like she had anyone she could hang around and chat with anyhow, with Caroline being preoccupied. That was the thing about her work world: being a worker bee at the ball wasn't really much fun, even if the top-tier champagne was flowing freely and the passed canapés probably bore a per-piece price tag that exceeded her daily meal budget.

For Emma, being an outsider at an insider's party was losing its luster; she was getting old enough to appreciate that it wasn't what it was cracked up to be. Sure, she got to share proximity with some of the world's elites, but since she wasn't a member of that rarified universe, it didn't rank a whole lot higher than being the one polishing the silver at the palace. It wasn't as if she could chat up the guests, comparing notes on their winter holidays in Aspen, shared vacations on Necker Island with Sir Richard Branson, or summering on Nantucket. The closest Emma got to summering (and when did that become a verb?) — not counting Caroline's annual skee-ball smackdown on the boardwalk in Ocean City, Maryland, which didn't quite elevate vacationing to the next level — was escaping to her parents' beach house in North Carolina every August.

Okay, she had to clarify this a bit: her job sure beat working in a windowless cubicle. And tonight's venue, The Great Hall, on a scale from one to wow, was no doubt a wow. Picture every little girl's fantasy of taking that Cinderella descent down a grand marble staircase, garbed in a luscious tulle ball gown twinkling with crystal beads, with the man of your dreams (like maybe that Adrian guy) waiting at the bottom to clasp your outstretched hand and pull you into an intimate dance. Throw in that two-story tall Christmas tree, which would put the famed Rockefeller Center version to shame on grandeur alone, and, well, this was where that dream would come to life. That is, if that was the kind of fairy tale you could somehow work out for yourself. Good luck there. Nevertheless, she attended interesting events, met fascinating subjects, and did so in some pretty spectacular venues. But for some reason this wasn't thrilling her the way it used to.

As Emma was working her way toward the coat check, she spied the obnoxious senator pawing at what looked to be a Capitol Hill intern, judging by the badge dangling from her neck. Emma quickly opened up her camera bag, pulled out her camera, and began snapping pictures of the senator in a clinch with the girl, his hand squeezing the young woman's butt.

"Hey, Senator," she shouted over the din of the crowd. "Wonder what your constituents would think about you tapping that."

She moved the camera away from her face and gave him a big thumbs-up as he quickly detached himself from the girl, who had to be fifty years his junior.

Gotcha.

With that, camera still slung over her shoulder, she grabbed her coat from the coat checker, handed the girl a buck, and slipped out a side door, never to be missed by those inside. Now to get back to the car, cross the bridge into Virginia, and be home in twenty-five minutes, tops.

Chapter Two

HIS Royal Highness Crown Prince Adrian was one very ticked-off man. He paced the floor of the private office-slash-holding room in which he was holed up as if he had somewhere to go. Only he didn't, since somehow his driver had yet to arrive to usher him back to the embassy. Although he might, soon enough, right on down the aisle, what with his mother force-feeding him a heaping helping of Lady Serena Elisabeth Montague, Duchess of Montague, like a fat spoonful of that disgusting, overpriced caviar that girl seemed to be on a steady diet of.

Despite Adrian's repeated entreaty to the contrary, his mother the queen had deemed Serena to be "ideal marrying material," via yet another text message to her son, and palace efforts were now under way to ensure the fulfillment of her wishes, regardless that they were in direct conflict with her son's own desires. Certainly it hadn't helped that Serena's mother, Lady Sarah, a close consort of the queen, had been touting the glories of her daughter to his mother for years now.

"*Serena Montague.*" He said, growling her name, swatting away his equerry and trusted confidante, Lord Darcy Squires-Thornton. "Despicable would be too generous a word to describe that manipulative witch. I'd no sooner wed that scheming, conniving—"

"Adrian," his aide said, stopping him with a hand against his chest and a stern look in his eyes. "The walls have ears."

Adrian glanced around the room, remembering that there were indeed others nearby whose discretion wasn't guaranteed. It wasn't easy always having to worry that what you said could be broadcast publicly and not in a good way. Ridiculous, really. He was starting to feel almost imprisoned in his life of privilege, what with the extreme limitations on his privacy, his freedom, and, point in fact, his choice of life partner. He never chose to be an heir to a dynasty; rather, it was thrust upon him thanks to that outdated primogeniture nonsense. Who was to say he was any more deserving of the throne than his siblings, or even Darcy, for that matter? It all might have made sense a few centuries ago, but now?

He was beginning to wonder if being a relic of days gone by wasn't more of a strange curiosity that ought to be relegated to sideshow status or somehow set up as a tourist attraction to sustain the royal needs, of which there were plenty.

"Besides which, she's a complete drunk!" he whispered in his friend's ear.

"True, but you have to admit it was kind of hilarious when she took that spill down the grand staircase at your father's birthday party last month. Without that you'd have been left to listen to a string quartet as your only entertainment."

Adrian laughed. "Would have been preferable. And here I thought seeing her tumble head over heels down a flight of steps would have been enough for my mother to finally realize the woman's a total lush. Instead she bought into the whole excuse about Serena's blood sugar dropping so quickly, and Mother swoops into care for her. *Bah!* Maybe if she'd eat a meal once in a while, she wouldn't be so embarrassingly smashed every time I see her."

"Obviously, she's head over heels for you," Darcy said, smiling. "What better way to prove it to you than quite literally showing you?"

Adrian moved into a smaller office within the confines of the larger one in which he was pacing, seeking a moment's solace from onlookers. He pulled Darcy close to him.

"Darc, I can trust you, no matter what, right?" he asked, his brow knit in concern.

"We're mates, Ade," Darcy said. "But you already know that!"

"And you don't want to see me stuck with Serena for the rest of my life, do you?"

"Are you kidding me? I'd practically marry her myself just

to spare you," his friend said. "Although, honestly, I couldn't be that devoid of self-respect, so sorry, she's all yours." He chucked him in the arm, a sign of friendship he could only display amongst their closest of friends lest the "hired help" look like more. That whole propping up the royal stature thing really bugged Adrian, but Adrian was grateful that Darcy didn't mind at all.

"I need some space, Darcy," Adrian said. "I need time to think. And maybe to give my mother reason to care more about me as a person rather than a mere branch of the family tree that needs to be spliced together with what she deems to be an appropriate mate. I'm more than a glorified version of one of my mum's beloved horses, set out to stud to sire racehorse-quality offspring.

"I can't even stomach the *concept* of spending the rest of my life with Serena, let alone the reality of it. I'd give up my royal status and take a job waiting tables in a dingy pub before I submit to my mother's demands on this one."

"Good luck with that. You know your mother always gets what she wants. She's the queen, for God's sake."

"Maybe the queen needs to realize her once-little boy is a man now, capable of acting on his own behalf. And I'm going to start that right now."

"By?"

"By slipping away from here, unannounced. Getting out. Going somewhere. Doing something. For once not being led around with a bit in my mouth and a crop at my flanks. I need to get away, Darcy. And I need it now. I can't hide in Monaforte. But I can easily get lost in America. Think about it — it's a brilliant idea. Disappear for a while, see what it's like to actually live a bit."

"So you're running away from home then?"

"Don't make it sound so childish. It's nothing of the sort."

Darcy stood back and stared hard at his friend, his hands in his pockets, his shoulders back, his closely-cropped blond hair in direct contrast with the shiny black waves Adrian sported. He leaned forward and fixed his brown eyes to Adrian's blue ones.

"You're really serious about this, aren't you?"

"I think it's the first decision I've been serious about my whole life. I'm tired of living the life everyone expects of me. I need to see what it's like to just be *me* out there, Darcy. I really need you to help me escape. You can hold everyone at bay when they start asking questions. I know I'm asking a lot of you, but I swear to you I'll be safe and I will return, soon. But not before I discover who the hell I really am."

His friend stood, lost in thought for a few minutes, rubbing his chin with his thumb and forefinger, staring off into space. Finally he looked back at Adrian.

"You really think this is what you should do?"

Adrian nodded his head. "Look, not to slight you, but I don't think you can totally appreciate where I'm coming from. You're a marquess. If you decided to quit me, you could go back and lord over your father's estate and manage the family business. You aren't stuck as an appendage to the institution of the palace. You aren't carrying the weight of a country on your shoulders."

"You know one day I'll have no choice in that matter," Darcy said. "Once my father's gone." He looked down, and Adrian was sure he hated that idea, since he adored his father.

Adrian waved his hands, dismissing that concern. "Your father's healthy as a horse. It'll be years till it's your problem to deal with."

"We can only hope," his friend said. "Though yes, you're right, I don't have to partake in the dog and pony show of being the heir to the throne that you're stuck with. I get that. And you know I'm only here for you because it's you. We've been best friends since we met on the train on the way to boarding school when we were five. Hard to turn down a bloke I've known since his voice squeaked like a mouse."

"At least mine deepened into a man's voice," Adrian said, chiding him.

"Oh yeah? You think I still sound like a little girl?" Darcy

16

said, making his voice go as high as possible.

The men laughed.

Darcy shook his head. "This goes against my better judgment. The queen would about kill me if she knew I was going to do this. Make that she would *actually* kill me. With her bare hands. But your wishes take precedence over hers for me," Darcy said. "If for no other reason than to spare you a lifetime of high-maintenance, low return-on-investment Serena, I'll do it."

Adrian looked puzzled, like he'd just been awarded a huge prize. "Seriously? You'll actually go along with this? You're not going to try to talk me out of it?"

"Christ, Ade. You and I practically finish each other's sentences. I've seen what your life is like. I know a lot of it is fun and games, beautiful women, fawning attention, but I also know how much pressure rests on you to always be perfect, to never fail your family, your adoring public, and your family."

He put air quotes around that "adoring" part.

"Yes, well, I do have a lot of adoring fans," Adrian said, mocking himself. "What with all those little old grannies who give me crocheted booties, begging me to produce a royal heir."

"Good lord, the last thing you need right now is a royal heir, particularly minus a royal bride. And I can promise you, Serena is *not* going to fill that void on my watch."

Adrian grabbed his friend by the shoulders. "You think we can make this work?"

Darcy buffed his nails on his chest as if showing off his prowess. "Are you kidding? With me as the brains behind this operation?"

"Perfect. Then how are we going to pull this off?"

"We? I thought this was your plan!"

"I don't have a plan, simply a need. I hadn't thought through how to implement the thing," he said. "How about we just work our way out of this holding room and I sneak out some back door, unnoticed. How hard could that be? There must be another way to slip out — maybe an employee entrance?"

Darcy chewed on this idea. He looked over to see a computer on a nearby desk. "Hmmm, let's see here," he said, walking over to the computer to see what he could find.

He typed in a bunch of keywords, trying a variety of searchable words until he finally found what he was looking for — a map of the building indicating various exits and detailing all rooms and spaces within.

"So much for national security. You can find pretty much anything on the Internet these days," Darcy said, shaking his head. "Looks like you can work your way down this back staircase. Along this long corridor there appear to be a series of rooms. One would think there should be an unlocked room or two along there you could pop into to remain undetected, in case a security guard comes down that hallway. If nothing else there's always the loo." He pointed to the men's room sign.

He reached into the breast pocket of his cashmere overcoat.

"Here, take this," he said. It was his wallet, containing plenty of cash and credit cards.

"These are what you call dollars in America," he said with wink as he opened it wide to reveal a thick wad of bills.

"Ha-ha. Very funny. I'm not stupid, you know."

"So you like to tell me. But it's not like you've been out painting the town red on your own before."

"I'm not planning to paint anything red, or blue, or purple for that matter. That would draw a bit of attention, don't you think? Besides which, I'm not Zander."

Sometimes he wished he could be his brother Alexander, famously known as Zander, last year caught by paparazzi while cavorting naked in a Las Vegas swimming pool with a bevy of equally unclad, very young and very hot women. Seems could get away with just about anything if weren't the heir to the throne, and the worst that happened to you was a little tongue-lashing from Mother, once the tabloids had their fill of splashing the overexposing pictures across their front pages. And Zander could hardly have cared less.

Darcy shook his head.

"Just having at it with you, boss. Listen, I'm giving you my credit cards. The cash is from the palace anyhow — it's what I use as mad money when you need it. I don't want to give you the palace credit cards as they'd find you immediately if you used them."

He fumbled around in another pocket.

"Oh, and you'll want this." Darcy handed Adrian's passport to him. "I know you wouldn't be daft enough to leave the country, but it's always a good idea to have this on you just in case of an emergency. That way if you have to prove you are the future heir to the throne, maybe they'd actually believe you.

"Right now, I'm going to provide some pass interference for you. I'll tell the bodyguards that there's a woman involved and the two of you need some privacy, just to keep them at bay. I'll escort you to a lavatory and give you a chance to be out of the line of vision for enough time.

At that point, you need to follow this path, and get out fast. Once you're out, hail a taxi — you do know how to do that, right?"

"I think I can figure it out." Adrian rolled his eyes.

"Once you're in a taxi, you need to figure out a way out of town. You've got two phones on you: your official palace one, and your own private one that I lined up for you. You'd better hand over the palace version or else they'll find you in no time."

"You're so organized, you'll make a great mum someday." Adrian grinned.

"Please. I've got my hands full enough being your de facto governess. And that's why you're paying me the big bucks." He raised his eyebrows and pointed to his friend. "This is the most important thing: stay in touch with me. I am ultimately responsible for your well-being, so you owe it to me to keep the lines of communication open. You can call, you can text. Whatever you do, keep me apprised of where you are going and whom you are with. And most importantly, be wise about who you fraternize with."

"Fraternize? I'm going to find myself, not find a hook-up. Trust me, I sure as hell don't need to complicate things even more by adding a woman to the mix. Particularly an American one who lives thousands of miles away from me and hasn't a drop of royal blood—not to mention Monafortian blood—in her. Wouldn't my mother just love that?"

"Might be better if she at least has less liquor in her blood than Serena. Oh, I nearly forgot the most important thing. Just in case." He reached into yet another pocket. "Whatever you do, take these. The palace can't afford to have unwanted princelings popping up in the States nine months from now." He tucked a wad of condoms into Adrian's palm.

Adrian rolled his eyes. "Unnecessary optimist. Besides, I'm pretty sure I can keep my pants on for a few days."

"Well, I wouldn't be much of a friend if I didn't wish for you to get laid, now would I? Now, go, before I change my mind about this completely ill-conceived escape plan."

Chapter Three

NIGHT had long since fallen by the time Emma left the building. The breathtaking grandeur of the Library and the Capitol dome set against the darkening cobalt sky was something she never tired of. That, combined with twinkling Christmas lights from charming nearby row houses on Capitol Hill, made the view so beautiful that she decided to lean against a tree and just take in the scenery for a few minutes, enjoying the simple beauty of the moment.

She pondered what it was that had her so agitated about her work these days. After all, what better setting to work in? And what fascinating subjects, barring such exciting shoots as the morticians association annual meeting, which was coming up in a few weeks. Maybe it was just that feeling of wanting something more in life, maybe even someone to share it with. Though, ugh, so far sharing with someone hadn't exactly worked out, what with her last three boyfriends backfiring so spectacularly. Thank goodness Caro hadn't even brought up Gordon, bless his heart, who insisted he wasn't gay even after she found out he and his boyfriend had shared her bed when she was out of town last year.

Emma blew a tuft of hair out of her face, heaved a sigh, and pushed herself away from the tree.

She rifled in her purse for her keys, as she had a long walk to her car and liked to keep her keys at the ready just in case she needed to poke a mugger in the eyes unexpectedly. While she shook her purse trying to unearth the things, a hand closed over her mouth and an arm around her waist.

She gasped, ready to scream her lungs out, when a familiar accented voice whispered in her ear. "Peas, peas, be quiet. It's me, Adrian. Whatever you do, don't scream. Please, don't scream."

Her heart raced like a hummingbird's. The only thing

keeping her from fainting in fear was the recognition of that voice and her stupid comment being thrown back at her from earlier in the evening. But why? What? Huh?

"I'm so sorry. Believe me I'm not going to hurt you at all. I need you to turn around very quietly, please. I need your help desperately," the voice whispered, his breath so close to her ear she could feel her hair shifting with each word he spoke.

"Just turn around casually and pretend I'm a friend who surprised you, in case anyone's watching."

She knew no one was watching. She'd walked out a back exit to a virtually empty street just moments beforehand, save the occasional taxi cab speeding past. Her breath came fast, even as she told herself surely she was safe. It was only the prince. The prince? *The prince!* What would someone like him need from her? And why was he standing out on the street, alone, begging for her help?

She turned around and his hand slipped away from her mouth, though he then moved it down to clasp his other behind her back, securing her body close to his. If these were other circumstances and she wasn't being accosted by the guy, she'd almost think he was about to kiss her. Which wouldn't have been so objectionable, were she not still feeling a bit terrified.

"Would you mind telling me what the hell you are doing, your *highness*?" She put extra emphasis on the word, just to be sure he knew she was pissed. "You're lucky I didn't kick you in the family jewels. Considering your family, that might have been considerable." She laughed nervously at her own bad joke.

He rolled his eyes. He'd heard that family jewels joke about, oh, a bazillion times over the years. He did, after all, attend boarding school full of rambunctious and completely idiotic boys.

"Please forgive me, I'm so sorry. I said those words because I knew you'd immediately recognize me and not turn and spray mace in my eyes or something. Or kick me in a delicate location. Future Monaforte generations thank you for that, by the way. But truly, I'm so glad it's you I encountered out here."

Under what life circumstances would a handsome, wealthy,

and famous young prince be glad to see her? She glanced around, expecting to have cameras filming this for some reality series, waiting for her to say something even more stupid than *peas to greet you, slur*, or whatever boneheaded thing lifted off of her tongue at that fatefully humiliating moment. *Definitely need to consider brushing up on conversational skills, lady.*

"And you're glad it's me because?"

"God, it's a long, long story. It has to do with Serena and my mother and I can't tell you everything now, but you need to know I have all of a few precious minutes in which to slip away before they send the hounds out after me, and I very much need your help."

"Hounds? And here I thought they were goons, those two apes lurking around you this evening."

He laughed quietly. "Yes, apes indeed. That's what my life comes down to, being followed around by a wall of human flesh to ensure I don't break the boundaries at all."

If she were a therapist, right about now she'd suggest he pull up a couch while she handed him a box of tissues. This story sounded like it could get good.

"So you want out, then?" she asked.

"That would be an understatement. I need to get away for a few days. I've got to figure things out, decide what I should do next, before the rest of my life is handed to me on a silver platter, like it or not."

"And I suppose this Serena chick has something to do with the silver platter?"

"Unfortunately, this Serena chick has a lot to do with it. Only make that a tarnished silver platter, in her case." He sighed. "As you can imagine, it's not so easy to be a public figure and attempt to find privacy. And right now, I very much need privacy. I know we don't know each other—"

"'*I know we don't know each other*'...If that's the most spot-on phrase of the night," Emma said. "Except for maybe that rockin' witty comment I blurted out earlier with the peas."

He laughed. "Oh, that was a good one. Believe it or not, people often say the stupidest things in front of me. Not that what you said was stupid. Okay, actually it was sort of stupid." He paused, and gave her a wink. "But people invariably become befuddled in front of royalty for some mysterious reason. They refuse to realize that we are human beings too, we eat the same way, we put our pants on the same way, we just happen to be—"

"Privileged?"

"Yes, privileged. I freely admit that. But enough of this now. I need to get somewhere, anywhere. I really don't care where. Just as long as I can get away and get some time to think. Any chance you'd be willing to help a stranger in need?" He batted his eyelashes at her, as if that would work on her hardened heart.

"Men," she said with a huff, rolling her eyes. "Honestly, the minute you want something you turn on the charm, and we're supposed to drop our pants for you?"

Adrian squinted his eyes in confusion. "I'm not asking you to—"

"I know, I know. Just an expression. My point is, dammit, I was so looking forward to going home and chilling out and not having to think. And now not only am I going to have to think, but I'm going to have to do it for two of us."

He looked at her, lower lip pouting out, eyes wide like a sad beagle.

"Oh, all right. Then let's get a move on. We've got to hoof it a few blocks if you want to get to my car before anyone recognizes where you are."

"I owe you, Miss—"

"Emma. Emma Davison. And no, you don't owe me anything. Consider it a humanitarian gesture for a new friend. Or welfare, for royalty." She reached out to shake his hand, in open defiance of that silly royal handshaking cooties rule. He extended his arm toward her, and they clasped hands for a moment, the warmth of flesh on flesh standing out against the cold night air. His fingers on hers were giving her flashbacks to their earlier meeting. And not in a good way. In a way that spelled trouble for

24

a girl who was avoiding heartbreaker types.

"Emma, I'm most peas to greet you, yet again," he said, bowing with an exaggerated flourish, extending his arm out to the side. "And please, call me Adrian."

"Time to blow this popsicle stand," she said, handing him her camera bag. She reached down and pulled off her shoes, taking a heel in each hand. "If we're going to make any good time, these have to go. But you are going to so owe me a foot massage for this, buddy." And she wondered in what world would she have ever have expected to tell a royal houseguest that he needed to service *her*. How was that for role reversal?

She grabbed his hand and they began to run, and he ran as if his life depended on it, would even have taken the lead if only he knew where they were headed. But somehow he knew he was in capable hands with Emma in charge.

Chapter Four

WHEN Emma and Adrian arrived at her antiquated Volvo diesel, she threw her bag in the back and urged him into the car quickly.

"You ride shotgun, but you'd better duck down low, at least until we get out of the city," she said.

"Shotgun?" Adrian knit his eyebrows in confusion.

"Of course a prince wouldn't know what riding shotgun is, let alone ride there," she said as she pulled on her seatbelt. "You're probably used to sprawling out in the back of stretch limousines. Or is it horse-drawn carriages? Is that what you get around town in?"

"Actually I prefer one of those massive gilded pumpkins with solid gold wheels. Led by horses that turn into mice at midnight."

"Yeah, I suppose I'd ride in one of those if I had to, but I'm not a big fan of pumpkin pie, and I'm afraid that smell might get to me. But then again, probably beats the smell of weed you get in some of our local cabs."

He laughed. "I'm afraid I'm out of my league with that one. The closest I've come is the overwhelming scent of incense they love to douse us with at high church functions we have to attend."

"Incense," Emma said, plugging her nose with her fingers. "I had a roommate in college who burned patchouli incense all the time. I'd take a rotting pumpkin carriage smell over that any day. For that matter, I'd take the combo weed-infested cab with rotting pumpkin odor before volunteering to inhale the scent of patchouli ever again."

Adrian looked at her as if she was speaking Portuguese.

"You haven't a clue what I'm talking about, do you?" she said. "I can tell this is going to be interesting, bridging the cultural gap between royalty and commoner."

"I could think of worse ways to fill the time. For that matter, I could think of even better ones." He wiggled his eyebrows in jest.

Emma shook her head. She was so not going to go there. But then again, maybe she could. After all, he was awfully handsome. And he kissed her hand. That was pretty darned charming. No question about it, Richard never kissed her hand. Only thing he seemed to kiss was her ass, when he was caught betraying her.

"I tell you what," she said. "Let's deal with getting you someplace safe and undetected, and then we'll worry about exploring some sort of cultural norm.

"In the meantime, let me extend a blanket apology for anything rude or crass or thoroughly idiotic I might be about to say. I appear to have only two settings when it comes to royal conversation: total bonehead or complete smartass. My mother always told me I could never woo royalty with this mouth. If only she knew how right she was. Forgive me, in advance?" She scrunched her brows together, flashing him a woeful look.

Emma pulled out of her space and onto the road, taking a quick glance around in case anyone was paying much attention to them, and pushed Adrian's head down lower for good measure.

"No need for an apology," Adrian said. "I suppose I deserve it. After all, I did attempt to kidnap you."

"It was hardly a kidnapping," Emma said. "More like a hijacking."

"Semantics. Thank God I found you standing out there. I have no idea what my next move would've been otherwise. I just knew I had to get out fast."

"Fleeing a burning building?"

Adrian rolled his eyes. "More like running away from a fate worse than death."

"Ooooh, that does sound serious. So not being threatened

Something in the Heir

by the rack, or beheading, or poisoning, or any of those normal ways royals meet their deaths, then?"

Emma merged onto the highway, following the signs toward Northern Virginia.

"Ha, ha. You're a funny girl," he said. "No, nothing quite so dramatic. It's just that I have a very imperious mother."

"Well, she is imperial."

"Yes, that. My mother's best friend, Sarah, has a daughter named Serena. And the two of them have conspired to force Serena on me as if I'm a sire on one of my mother's stud farms or something."

"I hate it when that happens."

"Don't we all?" He laughed. "My mother let it be known that she expects me to marry Serena and won't take no for an answer."

"Surely she can't be all that bad," Emma said. "I mean she's your mom's BFF's daughter! Apple doesn't fall far from the tree and all."

"Believe me she's worse than bad. First of all she's manipulative. And sneaky. And dishonest. And never to be trusted. And she's a complete lush. Plus I don't doubt she's warmed more beds than your average house cat. Imagine if I were to marry her, would that ever be fodder for tabloids."

"Yikes."

"No kidding. So you see why I could never marry her. Not only do I not love her, I don't even like her. She's absolutely dreadful."

"I bet she eats puppies for breakfast, too," Emma said with a wink. "So then what's your plan?"

"Plan?" Adrian shrugged and looked around him. "I haven't got one. Seems this is my plan."

"Running away from home?"

"You sound just like Darcy. When you put it that way it sounds so childish."

"Really? Good. Cause I meant to make it sound childish."

"I see what you mean about that smartass tendency."

28

"Sorry. I'm trying to curb it in deference to your title."

"No, no. Don't hold back. I wouldn't want you to be someone you're not on my behalf. You go right on about your business. I'll adapt."

"Well, if you can adapt, then did you ever think maybe you could get used to Serena, then? Surely she's not so bad?"

"Impossible She's worse than bad."

"Bad enough they have a wanted sign with her face on it at the post office?" She glanced over her shoulder and switched lanes.

"I've seen those movies, I know what you're talking about. And no, she's not an armed robber or a terrorist. Though, actually, she is a terrorist now that I think about it. She's terrorizing me."

"So you just decided to sneak out of a cocktail party with several hundred prominent guests, thinking no one would notice you missing? What about your security detail? I'd think they're going to be in just a little bit of trouble once word is out that their charge has skipped town."

"I've got it all under control. Darcy's going to deal with all of that."

"Ah, you mean the blond one? The guy Caroline was drooling over?"

"Caroline?"

"My friend who was helping me at the shoot. She comes along to a lot of my jobs. Or at least when there will be cool people attending."

"So I'm cool?" he gave himself an exaggerated pat on the back.

"The guests."

"Then I'm not cool?"

"Jury's still out on that verdict."

"So, she was the redhead?"

"Guess you weren't paying attention."

"I was too busy trying to decipher what it was you were

trying to say to me. That whole peas thing confused me terribly." He smiled.

"Ha-ha. So funny I forgot to laugh. But getting back to business here. So you tell Darcy you need to get away, and he buys it?"

"Pretty much. He's my closest friend. We've known each other our whole lives, practically. He's got my back."

Emma swerved slightly to avoid another car as she moved into the right lane of the highway. God, the last thing she needed to do was get into an accident with this guy in the car.

"And that means he's good setting you free in the wilds of Washington, D.C., and hoping it all works out fine?" She put on her blinker and took the next exit off the highway. "Do you have any idea where you could've ended up if you'd taken a wrong turn in your wanderings? Does drive-by shooting ring a bell?"

"Well, when you put it that way… But really, Darcy has complete faith in me. Besides which, I'm perfectly capable of fending for myself, it's just that—"

"You've never had to do so."

"But that's not such a big deal. So I stumble around for a few days while I find my way. That's part of the plan. Besides, I'm a grown man. What's going to happen that can't be fixed?"

"Your country is taken over by a marauding group of marauders?"

Adrian crossed his arms and scratched his chin, as if contemplating such an event. "Don't see that on the horizon."

"You get beaten up and your lunch money is stolen from you?"

"You can't live in fear of that, now can you?"

"I dunno, no lunch money, no chocolate pudding for dessert. That would be tragic."

"I do love my desserts."

"Now you're talking my language."

His stomach growled.

"Perfect timing. I don't suppose we can find something more substantial to eat than those microscopic tidbits of food I never got to touch tonight?" Adrian asked.

"Yeah, just wait till you see everything I've got in my food pantry at home. Probably about enough to feed a small mouse. I haven't been to the grocery store in ages. Besides, I'm pretty sure what food I have in my pantry is petrified by now. But I'll find you something. In the meantime we've got to come up with a plan."

She turned on her blinker as she arrived at her neighborhood, one of those old post-World War II communities with run-down brick ramblers sitting next to overwrought replacement homes designed by style-challenged people who thought it was a good idea to mix Tudor style with Southwestern contemporary. Nothing like a stucco wall and dying cacti (and some unwarranted optimism about the plant hardiness zone) surrounding a half-timbered home with a turret. Although at least the turret will make him feel at home. Surely his palace has one or two of them.

She pulled into her driveway and hit the garage door opener, never more thankful that her dad installed an opener for her own safety. This way she could get her hitchhiker inside without raising any local eyebrows.

"So," she said, dusting off her hands as she ushered him inside. "Welcome to the 'burbs. It's not exactly a palace, but it'll have to do."

"All good. I'll be perfectly fine without a palace."

She nodded. "Good, 'cause you won't be seeing one anytime in the near future, it seems. Nor any presidential suites, either.

"This," she said, stretching out her arms as they walked into her living room, "is my ever so humble abode."

Adrian glanced around at her cozy home. A small Christmas tree stood in a corner, looking a bit forlorn with about five ornaments dangling from it, while an overstuffed L-shaped sofa took up much of the main room. Adrian's gaze stopped in front of the couch on the far side, where a large round hoop on a pedestal stood, with some sort of blanket stuck inside of it.

"Interesting decorator touch," he said, nodding toward it, wondering what the use of it was.

"Oh that?" Emma pointed at a standing quilt hoop. "It's a quilt I'm working on. It's my relaxation. This one is really just a labor of love, nothing I ever plan to actually need."

"Then why do you work on it?"

"My grandmother taught me how to quilt when I was just a girl. She and I made them together sometimes. This one was her idea, and she was still at it when she passed away last year."

"I'm so sorry—"

"It's okay," she said. "My grandma lived a long and happy life. She was ninety when she died, and had good health up until the end."

"So why wouldn't you want to use this when you finish it? It must hold sentimental value."

Emma waved her hand in the air, dismissing that notion. "It's not that I won't use it. It's just that I won't need it, technically speaking. I'm sentimental about it because it's something we made together. But this is a particular pattern, known as a Double Wedding Ring. Grandma had hoped that it would be in my trousseau."

"Now there's an old-fashioned word you don't hear much."

"That would be my grandma, for you. She had tucked away all sorts of linens and things for when I got married. Not like I don't have plenty of them myself. She wasn't satisfied that I could simply stock up on dishtowels at Target whenever I needed more. So she made a slew of needleworked ones that are too beautiful to ever get dirty, truthfully. This quilt was to be her crowning glory—excuse the crown reference there.

"Anyhow, Grandma insisted that no self-respecting young woman could marry without a completed Double Wedding Ring quilt, and this is it, nearly completed," she said. "It was her wish that I would finish it in her memory, so I'm doing that. But I have absolutely no intention whatsoever of marrying anyone, ever, so I guess I'll just have to suck it up and use it to keep me warm on those long, lonely spinster nights." She stooped over and pretended to be a old lady walking with a cane.

"Come off it—I can't imagine you don't already have someone special in your life," he said.

"Most definitely not. And you're just being chivalrous because that's what princes are supposed to be. Thanks for the kind words, but I'm well aware that at the age of twenty-six, my chances of finding a useful mate are dwindling. But after having sampled one too many bad offerings in the men department, I've decided to just steer clear altogether."

Adrian shook his head. "Look at us, both the same age, with you taking yourself out of the running, and me hiding out in fear of being forced into it a relationship. Though at the risk of defending the wrong men, we're not all bad, you know. Maybe you shouldn't write off the entire gender just yet."

A loud trill sounded in Adrian's pocket. "What the—?" He said, patting his pocket randomly. He reached inside and pulled out his cell phone. He looked at the text message his friend had posted: *Adrian—it's me, Darcy. Listen, you might want to put some greater distance between us if you want to succeed. Pronto.*

"Huh," Adrian said.

"Trouble at the palace?"

"Apparently," he said. "That was a warning from Darcy, who thinks I need to get out of town. I don't suppose you'd have any great ideas as to how I could do that, like now. And without any fanfare?"

Emma stared at her quilt in the hoop frame and pondered their options.

"Hmmm…It probably wouldn't be right for me to go and stick you on a Greyhound bus. Too much culture shock for one day. Can't fly anywhere; they'd know you right away going through airport security—passport would be a dead giveaway. And hitchhiking's too dangerous," she said, crossing her arms and drumming her fingers on her bicep. She held up a pointer finger. "But I do have one place we could go, though we'd have to get in the car pretty quickly and leave while it's dark. We can throw some cheese and crackers in a plastic bag and bring that along for you to eat. If you're lucky maybe I can scrounge up some potato chips for dessert.

"I know, it's totally not an actual meal. But I'll throw whatever I have in the fridge into a cooler for breakfast. And you'll be happy once we get to our destination. Deal?"

"Sounds perfect."

"At least packing will be easy, being that you have no clothes along. We can worry about that when we get there."

"You going to tell me where there is?"

"Nope. It'll be a surprise. A good one, I promise. In the meantime let your friend know you're in good hands."

Darcy had to think hard to come up with a whopper that Her Majesty would swallow. It was a good thing he spent much of his formative years covering up his own bad behavior. And even better still that he could text rather than speak with her directly. He had enough of a conscience that he couldn't feel good about lying directly to the queen: so much easier in print form.

"I've taken ill. I'll be unavailable for a few days," he typed on Adrian's cell phone. *Ill?* What kind of excuse is that? She was going to demand he fly home immediately. Or at least see some doctor endorsed by the embassy.

"My God, what's wrong with you?" the queen replied.

"Nothing, really. No need to worry. Just a little stomach thing," Darcy typed, realizing he needed to double down on the lies in order to keep her from trying to call to talk to him. *"And my throat. I think I've caught that thing."*

"What thing are you talking about?" she asked.

"That thing, everyone here has it," he typed. "You can

imagine, I was in such close proximity with hundreds of people, all of those germs. But now it hurts to talk and my stomach is unhappy. I really just plan to take to bed for a few days."

"I truly think you should be seen by a doctor," Adrian's mother typed back.

"Of course you do. You're a mother. That's what mothers are supposed to think. Trust me, I'm fine. Just give me a few days and I'll be all good."

"Very well, but be sure that Darcy stays in touch with me so I know everything is all right. It's a good thing your schedule is open for the next several days."

"Thank Christ for that," Darcy typed, thinking that was truly his own reply, not even that of Adrian's. *"Be well, Mum. Talk in a few days!"*

"And then we'll discuss Serena," she added.

"Sorry, I'm off to sleep."

Coast clear with that one, Darcy then huddled with the bodyguards who knew, like it or not, they had to go along with the plan, or it would look as if they had lost their charge. Which they had.

Chapter Five

WHAT *I would give for that tub soak and glass of wine right about now*, Emma thought as she fought to keep her eyes open on the five-hour drive to Emerald Isle. The only place she could come up with to disappear to on short notice was her parents' beach house in North Carolina. A reasonable enough drive with an upside of listening to the tide rolling in by morning. Not a bad trade-off for missing out on the immediate joy of relaxing after a long day.

Adrian snored softly beside her as she crossed the bridge entering the island. His mouth was slightly open and a telltale trace of potato chip crumbs dusted his lips. Emma couldn't help but think how bizarre it was to have not only a complete stranger, but actual royalty in the passenger seat of her car. *Odd times we're living in when someone who has everything wants to escape from it all and slum it with the likes of me. Go figure!* And here she was taking him to the place that spoke "home" to her more than anywhere else.

How many times had she crossed over this bridge on the way to visit her grandmother, ever since she was a bitty baby? Too many to count. It was still hard to realize she'd not get to see her when she arrived. But the reality was it wasn't her grandmother's house anymore; it belonged to her parents, who had gutted the place last year and redecorated it. Not that the do-over was such a bad thing; it might make half a positive impression on Adrian now, versus when it looked like it was owned by a nonagenarian who hadn't thrown anything out in fifty years.

Emma was finally pulling the car into the garage on Spinnaker Drive as dawn broke on the horizon. She nudged Adrian to wake up.

"Huh? What?" he said, disoriented, his eyes fluttering open, a trickle of drool at the corner of his mouth. Emma was

Jenny Gardiner

pleasantly surprised to realize that he was indeed only human,
when it came right down to it. Even if he was sleeping in a handmade tuxedo that probably cost three times what her car was
worth.

"Hurry, look, over there," she said, pointing, as she pulled
him out of the car and ushered him toward the weathered
wooden walkway that cut through the dunes to the beach.
Before them, the lilac, mauve and crimson fingers of the day's
first light rippled across the cold December water, a sight that
always took her breath away.

"Welcome to your hideaway," she said, arms spread wide.

He spun around, assessing his new environment, and
nodded his approval. "To think I feared you might squirrel me
away in a below-ground bunker to keep me from being detected,"
he said. "This, I could get used to."

There was a brisk winter chill in the air, and they could see
the vapor from their breath as they stood watching the sun
gradually mount the sky. Emma rubbed her arms to generate
warmth. "Let's get inside and figure things out before neighbors
start wondering who's the James Bond wannabe wearing the
walk-of-shame tuxedo out here."

He looked at her and shook his head. "I'm not even gonna
ask about the walk-of-shame thing. But the James Bond
comparison I'll take. Though if only I could be so suave."

"Suave you've got in spades," Emma said. "The shoe phone,
I don't know about that. Wait, maybe that was Maxwell Smart
with the shoe thing."

"When you're done talking in code, you want to let me
know?"

"Maxwell Smart. From *Get Smart*. You know, it was a
famous sitcom?" Emma shook her head. "You grew up in
Europe, for goodness sake. It's not as if you were raised in a
small tribal village in New Guinea. Surely you had Nickelodeon
on cable?"

"I'm afraid I'm pop culturally deprived when it comes to

television. Mother forbade most television for us growing up. She figured if we never had it, we'd never miss it."

"Of course you probably had court jesters to amuse you, so all things considered, your form of entertainment was far more intriguing."

"You do realize that I didn't grow up in a medieval fortress? Never once did I witness a man sporting colorful leotards and a hat with jingle bells and pointy-toed slippers being forced to juggle for his life. Now granted we might have had performers at the palace periodically, but I can assure you it was nothing terribly out of the ordinary, more like the ballet, or a pianist. And I can assure you as well that my mother has never even sent anyone to the gallows. That I know of." He winked at her.

"Yeah, well, I don't have a point of reference so I'm just taking a stab in the dark. The closest I've ever gotten to royalty before you has been a flame-broiled burger at Burger King. And once I won a hand of poker with a royal flush."

"We've got a lot of ground to cover, don't we?"

"We've got all week in which to bridge that cultural divide before I have to get back to work and give you back to the real world."

Adrian helped Emma unload the few things she'd brought down for the week, including her quilt, which she set up in the bright living room before the hearth.

"I don't think I've ever seen someone travel with a massive blanket and huge wooden hoop before," he said.

"I'm weird. Get used to it."

"Duly noted."

"So I'm going to defer to the fact that you're my guest—and not that you're a prince—and give you the master bedroom," Emma volunteered.

"I'm fine sleeping in another bed. I don't want to take up your room."

"No worries," she said. "Fact is, it's not my room, anyhow. It's my parents' bedroom now, so I wouldn't sleep there regardless. I just wanted to appear a martyr to score brownie points. Plus, believe me, you'd get woozy in my room."

"And as soon as I know what brownie points are—"

"Damn, we're gonna have to educate you on Americanisms," she said. "I might even have to drag you to Walmart. Maybe we'll ease you in with Target. Don't want to break out the big guns if we don't have to."

"When you start speaking a language I understand maybe you can just send up a smoke signal or two?"

"How does breakfast sound?"

"Finally, the mother tongue. That I can understand completely. Truth be told, I'm famished. Anything I can do to help speed things along?"

"Those middle-of-the-night Hostess Sno Balls I got you from the gas station weren't enough, eh?" Emma started rifling around the kitchen to find out what food supplies were available and still edible. "Looks like between the food I brought from home and what my folks left from their last visit down here, I think we can scrape together a couple of omelets," she said, opening the freezer door. "Hallelujah. There's bacon in here. We have ourselves a meal, my friend. Now, to put you to work." She grabbed the package of frozen bacon and tossed it in the microwave to defrost.

Emma looked at Adrian, rumpled but still looking pretty hot in his designer tux. "We can't have you cooking in that thing. I'd hate for you to ruin it." She brushed some lint from the lapels.

"I'm afraid it's all I've got."

Emma stood, arms crossed, her fingernail tapping on her teeth as she pondered the dilemma. "Whatever you do, don't apologize for that. Let me think, I can't put you in my father's pants. They'd be dropped to your ankles, what with his oversized waistline." Her dad did love his desserts a bit too much. Though, hmm, perhaps not such a bad idea to have Adrian left only in his skivvies. If only she weren't so darned responsible, dammit. "Oh, wait." She held up her finger. "I've got the perfect thing."

She opened a closet door next to the kitchen and pulled an apron off a hook. It bore a human-sized photograph of Michelangelo's Statue of David from the neck down imprinted on the apron, designed for the wearer to appear to be the famous naked statue.

"Oooooh, this is so perfect!" She held it up for his inspection. "Bought it from a street vendor in Florence as a joke for my dad. Shame he couldn't even tie it around his belly. I knew it would come in handy one day!"

"You're not truly going to make me wear that, are you?" Adrian nodded his head toward the thing. "Why don't I just take off my jacket and shirt—" He began unbuttoning his cufflinks and studs, and stuffed the tie, dangling from his neck, into his pocket. "Here, much better." He slung the tuxedo jacket and shirt over a nearby chair.

He stood before Emma in nothing but his tuxedo pants, and she stood before him fairly certain her tongue was lolling from her mouth like a very hungry wolf with a fat, juicy rabbit dangled before its eyes. Clearly they had palace gyms, she thought, marveling at the definition in his abs, not simply a six-pack but something even better. A split of grand cru champagne, perhaps? Why diminish that stomach with a beer reference when you could upgrade to the good stuff? Obviously he was graced with superior genes, if that body was any indication. And plenty of warm vacations during cold winter months, probably on a very royal yacht tooling about the South Pacific, judging by the golden tone of his smooth skin. For a fleeting moment she was prepared to fling herself onto him, blaming it on a strong gust of wind maybe, even though they were indoors and that was an entirely lame excuse for her temporary lack of self-control.

"Uh, um, uh." In a moment she'd be drooling in a corner and babbling nonsensical words if she didn't get a grip. "Well, that's one way to do it. But still, it's December! You should put something on to cover up."

She didn't dare mention that her insisting that he cover up might have something more to do with her current vow of relationship abstinence and her certainty that nothing about Adrian was going to involve Emma or her newly-overheated libido, so why start any engines purring in the first place? She did wonder if it might be okay to just reach out and pet his chest, pretending it was a little kitten or something innocuous. Just for a minute.

"I'm perfectly fine as is, thanks." Adrian smiled as Emma squirmed.

"Well, great." She sighed. This was going to take some inner discipline to ignore. Make that he was going to take some inner discipline to ignore. "But why don't you at least spare those pants." She doubled back the apron so that only the lower half was showing, held it up to his waist and burst out laughing. "Oh God, I would love to have a picture of this."

Adrian looked down to see nothing but David's well-endowed endowment placed strategically over his own. It was his turn to squirm. "Really? Do I have to?"

Emma laughed. "Honey, you most definitely have to. I will remember this moment for the rest of my life, so I need to be able to savor it."

"So glad I'm amusing you. Feel free to keep on laughing at my expense." His good-natured smile was reassuring. "But promise me no pictures. If this ever got out, my mother would kill me. She's still reeling from Zander's indiscretion in America."

Emma couldn't help but burst out laughing, remembering the images of his brother's very naked royal arse spread across tabloids worldwide. What mother wouldn't cringe at that one?

"That mother again, eh? You really need to figure out how to get her under control. You're a big boy now. It's time she recognizes that fact. And I'm sure you're nothing like your mischievous brother."

Something in the Heir

Adrian sighed. "Let's not go there right now. I'd just as soon not think about my demanding mother and my irresponsible brother if it's all the same to you. I suppose it's a good thing I have a few siblings who march in lockstep with my mum, so at least she's not completely miserable with her offspring."

Emma handed him some ingredients. "Change of subject. Here. You know how to crack eggs?"

"I'm royal, not clueless. Surely I can figure that out."

"Seriously, you've never cracked an egg before? This should be amusing. Go ahead and break them into this." She handed him a bowl, then held up a wire implement on a handle. "This is called a whisk. You're gonna use it to whip them up well, like this, and then you're going to add milk till I tell you it's enough." As he cracked and whisked, she tossed in some salt and pepper to season the mixture.

Emma took another look at the David apron and started laughing again. "It's a good thing I don't have any coffee in my mouth or I'd have spit it all over the kitchen."

Adrian's eyes lit up. "Is coffee an option? Because I'm not beyond groveling for a cup." He got down on his knees and held his hands up like a desperate man.

"Ah, nothing like a man who's willing to beg. It's my Kryptonite. Your wish is my command."

She pulled the coffee machine out from a cabinet and set it on the counter, rifled through a drawer till she found the coffee capsules. "Now, I know this thing might be foreign to you, since Jeeves probably brings your coffee piping hot in a china cup. But this is how the rest of the world gets their morning Joe these days."

"Still waiting for the Little Lord Fauntleroy jokes to let up."

Emma sighed and scrunched her nose. "I promised I'd stop, didn't I?"

Adrian arched an eyebrow at her. Which made a hank of hair drift down toward his eye, lending him a boyish charm. Curse him.

Jenny Gardiner

"I know, I know. Not like you're making cracks about my mediocre suburban existence back at me. So why would it be fair for me to use your heritage to take swipes at you?"

"Now that you mention it…"

She grabbed the whisk from the egg bowl, and held it up like she was taking a vow. "I do hereby declare that I, Emma Leigh Davison, do solemnly swear to stop riding your ass." She burst out laughing, wiping a bit of egg that dripped from the whisk onto her arm. "Oops. I guess the coarse language doesn't fit with royal protocol."

"Trust me, I'm well-versed in swear words at this point in my life. Although pretty much nothing about this experience is in my comfort zone, I have a feeling I'd best accept and move on."

"The lesson of every captive: the sooner you accept that resistance is futile, the better. Now, to make the coffee: first you fill up the water reservoir, then you take this thingy here," she said, holding up the small canister containing the ground coffee, "and you stick it in here." She popped it into its holder. "You pull this lever down, it punctures holes into the coffee thingamajiggie, you press 'start' and ta-da!"

A minute later she handed him a steaming mug of coffee that smelled divine.

"Now that's the best application of inserting tab A into slot B I think I've ever seen," Adrian said, then squinted his eyes, reconsidering. "Make that *second* best."

He winked at Emma and she was certain she blushed from her toes to her scalp. She squirmed, completely unsure how to divert his attention from the insertion of various tabs into slots. Must. Change. Subject. Now.

"I've got all sorts of modern-day wonders for you, my friend. Strap on your seatbelt. You're about to learn how to be an average person." *Strap on? What the hell, Emma!*

Adrian squinted his eyes at Emma. "Should I be scared?"

"Beyond the shadow of a doubt," she said, laughing. "I'm

43

going to teach you how to be one of the rabble. First off, how to cook. You did quite well with your egg whisking. Don't think I didn't notice the wrist action. You've got a natural gift. For lesson two we'll move onto chopping. If you'll grab that cutting board over there, I'll get the knife and demonstrate how you're going to cut these veggies. But before that, we need to deal with our bacon."

She made a mental note to dope slap herself for that idiotic wrist action comment.

Emma pulled out a cookie sheet and lined it with foil from a nearby drawer.

"First, you line the pan with foil. I hate cleaning up grease, so the less the better," she said, cutting open the package. "Next you're going to take these slimy strips," she said, pointing to the raw bacon, "and lay them out side by side on the pan."

Adrian grimaced as if she was expecting him to conduct abdominal surgery. "I have to put my hands on *that*?"

"It's surprisingly satisfying. Trust me."

He reached down and grabbed a piece, which stretched as he pulled it. "It's gooey!" he said, surprised. "But I sort of I like it!"

"See, I told you. Brings out the animal in you." She winked at him. "Sometimes I like to top it with some brown sugar and cracked pepper to give it a little sweet, savory, spicy flavor, but today we'll aim for simplicity." Yeah, right. Simplicity while she was trying hard not to stare at his terribly tempting and very bare chest just inches away from her longing eyes and idle fingers. Making it all the more complicated, dammit.

"You like it hot?"

Emma blanched.

"Er, um, let's just say they don't call me Tepid Tammy for nothing." Emma looked away and pinched the bridge of her nose, instantly embarrassed by his inference and her incredibly stupid reply. Something about this guy constantly elicited the daft in her. *Tepid Tammy? What is* wrong *with you, girl?*

Adrian knit his brows, looking like he hadn't a clue what the hell she was saying.

When they finished the tray, she opened the oven door and put it in. "We set it to four hundred degrees — don't even ask me to convert that to Celsius for when you need to make this back at the palace. I'm sure you can get the palace chef to do it for you. Then, set the timer for fifteen minutes and we'll be golden. Next, onto our veggies."

She rinsed a pepper and a tomato and grabbed a shallot from a bowl on the counter, and placed the pepper on the cutting board.

She demonstrated how to dice the pepper and handed the duties to Adrian, who had all the cutting skills of a medieval surgeon.

"Hmm, that won't do," Emma said as she watched him have a near-miss on a flesh wound with the blade. "Let me help with that." She came up behind him, reaching around on either side, placing her hands atop his, showing the proper positioning, where the knife should go, how to protect his fingers. She pretended she didn't notice his warm skin as she pressed up against his shirtless back. Or the unmistakable lingering aroma of some spicy aftershave her nose couldn't quite pinpoint but wanted to keep sniffing until it did.

"Can't have that finger whacked off," she said, hoping she wasn't panting like a dog in heat. "Or else your shiny gold ring would have no home." She pointed to a beautiful ring encrusted with tiny gemstones resting on his wedding ring finger. "And please don't tell me you're secretly married and your mother is suggesting you ditch wife number one for this Serena chick."

"Oh, that," he said. "It's the royal seal, my family crest, which in my country we wear on this finger. I suppose I should have given that to Darcy to mind while I'm gone. I was in such a hurry it didn't even cross my mind."

"It's very beautiful," Emma said, admiring the tiny, glittering sapphires, emeralds and diamonds that surrounded his family's emblem. "To tell the truth, I'm glad you're not married.

I mean, not that I care if you're married. I just mean I'm glad I won't have an angry wife breathing down my neck alongside your bossy mother. Which is not to say your mother's bossy. I don't even know her. I'm just going by what you've said. Though I know it's rude to say things like that about someone's relative. I have a friend who got in a fight with her husband and bad-mouthed him and then I agreed with her and she got so mad at me for saying he was selfish, even though she'd just said he was selfish! So I take that back, you're mother isn't bossy at all. Although maybe she is, since she's trying to force you to marry an awful woman, but I won't say that."

Adrian stared wide-eyed at her and burst into laughter. "Do you always babble so much? I suspect I'll never have to ask you if the cat's got your tongue. I'm sure your mouth won't slow down enough for any feline to catch it."

Emma felt her face heat up to at least a Sriracha hot sauce level, if not that of a burning habanero or ghost pepper. "God, I'm such a doofus," she said. "Sometimes I get diarrhea of the mouth. Though that's probably not a great term to discuss while preparing breakfast, in mixed company, no less. Or should I say mixed *royal* company. Because I have one or two guy friends I'd be perfectly fine blathering on about diarrhea of the mouth with, but not with you." Ohmigod, Emma, *shut up*. "Let's get back to that ring of yours. I can't imagine having a family crest. Or a seal for that matter. Hell, I'd settle for the kind of seal that barks and swims with flippers. That would be kind of fun to have around. Though it wouldn't fit well on my finger. Plus I'd need a bigger bathtub."

Adrian turned to look over his shoulder at her, causing her to have even more contact with his bare skin. *Argh!* "Your mind does take strange turns, doesn't it?"

Emma blushed. "I have been known to go off on a tangent or two along the way, I suppose." Of course the tangent she'd opt for now would be maybe licking a path along his strong back, all the way around to that beautiful chest. Then while she was at it, following that tempting happy trail on his belly right on down

46

south…

"I'm beginning to learn that the diversions are half the fun with you."

"Enough with the sidetracks," she said, anxious to get away from any thoughts or actions that would keep luring her down the temptation trail that was this man near her.

She reached around him again, breathing in the scent of him, realizing she hadn't smelled a man this close in forever. And that she needed to dismiss that thought immediately, so instead she focused on demonstrating the rocking motion the knife should make with her hand, nestling closer to him to have a good handle on the vegetable. And grateful she wasn't demonstrating what to do with a cucumber, at least.

Suddenly she was acutely aware of his breath, moving in sync with her own, as if they were one. With her soft and shapely parts matching up a bit too comfortably with his solid, very male parts. For a minute she wondered what would happen if she reached around right there, in that perfect spot, just to see if he was feeling it as much as she was. But no, that would be such a bad idea, what with her kinda sorta chastity vow and renouncing all men and plus having nothing in common with someone of his ilk.

The word "ilk" seems a little lowbrow in reference to royalty. Though lowbrow was in keeping with where her thoughts were going anyhow, considering she kept pondering reaching down to see if he was as turned on as she was. *I am human, after all. It's a natural reaction to do that. After all, a man, a woman, alone. Throw in some food. I mean, we're hungry. It's the empty stomach talking, I know it. It's not the empty heart. It's not.* Only she didn't just mutter it in her mind, that last part, she said it loud enough for Adrian to hear her.

"Empty heart?" he asked.

"Heart? No, not heart. I said *part*. I was just talking about this bowl over here, it's empty. The empty *part*, that's where you'll put those shallots."

Lord, she needed a class on self-editing.

They finished their chopping in relative quiet, and Emma assembled her raw ingredients to complete the omelets.

"So you heat up this pan, drizzling a little bacon grease on it for added flavor," she said, rolling the grease around to lubricate the pan. "And then you pour your egg mixture here, spread it around, then put the sautéed veggies on top of it, and cover with a thin layer of cheddar cheese, like so."

Adrian watched, mesmerized, as the omelet sizzled in the pan.

"You act as if this is the first time you've ever cooked anything," she said.

"Would I betray myself as a spoiled rich boy if I admitted it was?" he asked, sounding a bit sheepish. "It must sound somewhat pathetic that I've hardly stepped foot in a kitchen, doesn't it?"

Emma turned around to face Adrian. "A culinary virgin—pathetic? Not at all. It's what you know. Why would you have done so? There was no need. Besides which, the kitchen was probably nowhere near your living quarters, I'm guessing."

He laughed. "I am further ashamed to tell you I wasn't particularly concerned about where in the palace the kitchen facilities were located, as long as good food showed up on my plate. I feel a bit out of touch with reality to admit that."

Emma put her hands on either of his shoulders. "Look, Adrian. We all come to the table with our strengths and weaknesses. So you can't cook. No big deal. We can easily rectify that. At least you're willing to give it a try; that's not such a bad thing, right?"

He shrugged. "Slight concession, but I'll take your pity vote if you're willing to give it to me."

Emma grabbed the handle of the frying pan and with a rubber spatula, deftly turned over one side of the omelet, then flipped it. "Voila!" She said, glad she didn't drop the thing in a heap on the floor.

"Bravo!" Adrian clapped, impressed at her culinary prowess.

"I've never seen something so entertaining before!"

"Oh, please," she said. "I'm pretty sure whatever royal entertainment you've had over the years eclipses a little omelet showmanship. Even if I am pretty darned masterful at it." She mockingly buffed her nails on her shirt, as if she was a pro.

"I don't care what you say," he said. "That was terribly impressive."

Emma slid the omelet onto his plate and gave him several strips of bacon. She made quick work of the rest of the ingredients and served herself.

"Now, to top it off."

She pulled out a carton of orange juice from the fridge that mercifully hadn't expired yet, then walked over to her parents' wine rack in the dining room and helped herself to a bottle of Prosecco.

"Sir, if you'll do the honors."

"Now *this* I have some skill with," Adrian said, removing the foil cover and wire basket from the head of the bottle and popping the cork. "Thank goodness I didn't just shoot that into your eye."

"I have faith that one thing you've mastered is cracking open a little bubbly. Granted, this isn't vintage Dom Perignon, but mixed with a little orange juice it's a perfect addition to our brunch."

She handed him two champagne flutes to fill with the Prosecco, and she topped them off with juice. "To adventure," she said, clinking her glass with Adrian's.

"And to my gracious hostess. Thank you for saving me from a fate worse than death," he said, tipping his glass to hers yet again. "At least for the time being."

They sat down at the tiny dining room table off the kitchen.

"As my grandmother used to say before each meal here, enjoy your vittles," Emma said, laughing. "Before you even ask, it's a country term for food. Not that my grandma was a country gal, she wasn't. She just loved *The Beverly Hillbillies*."

Something in the Heir

Adrian raised his eyebrow.

"Of course you wouldn't know that cultural touchstone. Television, from back in the dark ages. Just know that it's a classic, and if you're lucky maybe we'll watch some this week on Nickelodeon."

"I'll hold you to that," he said, digging into his first bite, his eyes opening wide in surprise at how good it was. "This is amazing." He moaned. He actually moaned.

"Huh, I don't think anyone has ever gotten too excited about my cooking," Emma said. "So glad you're enjoying it. You can take pride in knowing you contributed to its amazingness. You helped birth this puppy. Even though I'm fairly certain the food you've eaten to this point in your life is a bit more impressive than my omelets. But thanks for the vote of confidence."

"You underestimate your gifts."

"Beats being a gifted jewel thief, or a talented stripper, I guess. So tell me, besides being painfully dapper and charming, what gifts do you hold up for the world to see?"

Adrian sat in silence, pondering this question, cutting a bite of omelet and eating it, then cutting another bite and eating it as well. "I suppose no one's ever asked me that before. I'm not certain I have any gifts."

Emma shook her head. "I think you underestimate yourself," she said. "First off, you're flexible. I mean come on, twenty-four hours ago you were a pampered prince. And look at you now! You're slumming it in a statue of David apron in my parents' beach house. That's nothing if not flexible."

"So I'm on par with Gumby, then." He smiled.

"Aha! So you do have cultural references. You're familiar with Gumby."

"Who isn't? That would be like not knowing who Saint Nicholas is. Nonetheless, resiliency doesn't win me any prizes in the humanitarian department."

"And cooking a good omelet does for me?"

"Good point. But still, you give me pause to wonder what

50

I'm doing that is relevant in this life."

"Hold that thought." Emma raised her index finger, got up from the table and grabbed her laptop that she'd left near the door. She sat back down, opened it up and started typing into a search engine. "Aha, just what I thought.

"'Monaforte's Prince Adrian, at the opening of a homeless shelter in the nation's capital,'" she recited from a news story. "'His Royal Highness Prince Adrian, heir to the throne of Monaforte, visits infirmed children at a local hospital along the coastal town of Principia.' Wait, wait, here's another: 'Prince Adrian hugs a grieving mother whose child died in an avalanche in the Alpine village of Alise.'"

She threw Adrian an I-told-you-so glance. "So let's dispense with the 'I'm useless' mentality and appreciate the 'that with which we have been blessed' one, got it?"

"Okay, you win. I'll concede I'm able to use my position as a platform to help others. But I am still not convinced that I have a higher purpose. Maybe it's still to be determined. Like you, you're a fabulously talented photographer, I assume."

"Damn straight I am," she said, laughing. "Nevertheless, we're talking apples and oranges, my life and yours, though. And not like that makes me any great savior. Let's just be happy with we are who are."

"Indeed. And that you had a getaway car at just the right moment for poor, poor pitiful me. You're my savior, at least." He grinned at her.

"And I'll be grateful I have you here to help me do the dishes. So roll up your sleeves," she said, pointing to his bare arms, sleeveless since he'd removed his shirt while prepping the meal, "and let's knock this out so we can figure out the rest of your vacation."

"Deal," he said. "But, er, um, I'm afraid you're going to have to teach me how to wash pans. I haven't a clue."

"You're hopeless, you know that?"

"That's what I've been telling you."

Chapter Six

EMMA sat glued to her laptop, cranking out an email to Caroline.

"Oh, girl, you are so not going to believe what I've been up to."

She'd put Adrian on the nearby sofa and turned on Nickelodeon, figuring he'd be perfectly entertained with classic sitcoms for a while.

She proceeded to fill in the blanks on what had transpired over the past twelve hours, adding her friend was sworn to secrecy on all of the above.

"I alternate between being all fan-girl that I've got this handsome prince as my captive at the beach house, and wanting to dope-slap myself that I am even thinking of him as a handsome prince. I have no business going there in my brain. He is so far off limits for me he's practically within limits.

"Argh, maybe that's the problem. He's actually very approachable and *normal* even, yet he's never even cooked a meal before. Can you imagine? Who hasn't stepped foot in a kitchen to prepare a meal? Unfathomable what that life must be like. Although I think he's really chafing at the rules and restrictions. I guess even those with unlimited everything have limitations. It seems his mother is calling the shots on his marriage. He said she'd let him 'sow his wild oats' and now it's time to buck up and do what's right for the family. I guess it's all fine and good to sow those oats, but you can't harvest them and eat the bread from it! I can't imagine my mother telling me whom to marry! Although as we all well know, she would give up her first-born child to see me married, except that I'm her first-born — make that only— child.   Then she could stop worrying about my availability shelf-life. I swear the woman thinks I'm a tub of yogurt about to spoil. Ahhh, well, I have to run. Now that I'm royal social director I've got to figure out what to do with the guy. Other than the obvious, which is not an option. I think the first order of business is finding him something to wear. Can you picture me putting him in Bob's clothes? Somehow I can't see him donning those brightly patterned pants Daddy loves to wear. I mean they might have a certain tacky charm on my father, but how mortifying would that be for his royal highness to be tugging on a pair of seersucker pants with embroidered red lobsters all over them? I'm not sure I even want Adrian to see them, they're so far beyond what normal people in his world wear, let alone have to wear the things. I'll keep you posted. And remember, mum's the word. Don't tell a soul!"

"Well, your most princely, what say we find you some clothes to wear?"

Emma had earlier unearthed an oversized sweatshirt stuck in the back of her closet that she'd lifted from an old and mostly long-forgotten boyfriend. Great sweatshirt, not so great boyfriend. If memory served her, he was the one who ditched her because she told him that his brilliantly self-serving suggestion of a threesome with her best friend would forever be relegated to his dreams. At least the threads lasted longer than that relationship. So right now Adrian was wearing the guy's Carolina blue Tarheels hoodie and a thousand-dollar pair of tuxedo pants, along with those spiffy shoes. Somehow the look worked, in a slumming-it sort of way.

"I'm fine with this, really," he said.

"You won't be for long. Before you know it you're going to find those clothes have gotten ripe. Plus I don't want Jeffrey's creep factor to inadvertently rub off on you."

He turned to sniff his armpit. Typical male. Guess they

weren't that different the world over. "Smells okay to me," he said. "And what's this about a creep factor? Go on. I'd love to hear this story."

Emma rolled her eyes. "That is one that's better left untold." She tried to divert his attention. "Besides, I can't begin to know how to wash designer tuxedo pants. Let's at least aim for some variety. My treat."

"Don't think I didn't notice you trying to change the subject. Believe me, I will get that story out of you. Vee haf our vays," he said. "And no, you are not treating me to a wardrobe. I'm paying." He whipped out the collection of cash and cards he'd tucked away.

"In that case, maybe we can buy me a new wardrobe too. I have been known to spill my guts if the price is right," she said, winking at him. She grabbed her keys and his hand and pulled him off the sofa. "Don't want you to become a couch potato. Yet, anyhow. Speaking of potatoes, we need food. This will be your indoctrination into daily life for us commoners. It'll be fun!"

"I had considered taking you to a big box store first, but I think they're just a little too low-end from what you're used to. There's a cute little beach shop I think we'll start at. Then we'll hit a grocery store for the necessities."

"What's a big box store?"

"Giant warehouse retailers that sell everything from ride-on mowers to boxer briefs, and anything in between. Cradle to grave, in a depressing sort of way. For that matter they probably sell caskets."

"Gee, can't wait to see it."

"On the upside, there's a liquor store nearby too, so we can stock up while we're out."

"Drunken debauchery on the agenda this week?"

"Maybe not debauchery, but we are at the beach… It's a given that you have cocktails while on vacation. Even in the off-season. Even if it's not exactly a vacation, and more like a hideout."

After a short drive, Emma pulled the car into a small strip mall and they got out at *Where's the Beach?,* her favorite surf shop in town. Adrian looked skeptical but followed along obligingly.

Inside there were few signs of the season, with racks and racks of board shorts and displays of sunglasses and flip-flops and lots of surfboards.

"Hoping they do a brisk business in Christmas gifts for people jonesing for summer," Emma said. She looked into his eyes and saw the question and shook her head. "It means yearning."

"Gotcha."

"Do you sell any clothes that might offer a little wintertime warmth?" she asked the very bored-looking store clerk with tat sleeves up both arms with a semi-shorn head and a thatch of green hair covering both of his eyes. He struggled to detach his line of vision from his smart phone, but finally mustered up the effort to point to a rack of pants and sweats toward the back of the store.

"Perfect," she said. "We'll find something." She started whipping through the rack, pulling off a few sweatshirts and a pair of jeans and some sweat pants. "What do you think?"

Adrian studied the selection she held up. "A bit casual from what I normally wear, but I think these will do."

"In that case, fashion show time," Emma said, pointing to the dressing room. She was fairly certain he'd never stepped foot into a broom closet with a burlap curtain, the only thing closing the distance between his unclad self and the rest of the world. If he wasn't careful he'd expose his royal hiney to all the world — or at least her and Greenie McTatster over there.

One by one, though, he emerged from his dressing room, showing Emma the threads.

"Oooh," she said, spinning her finger around. "Turn. Be a supermodel, strut your stuff, man!"

Adrian shook his head and laughed, playing along faux-posing for her. She clapped so loud the clerk glared at her. She stuck out her tongue in defiance. After he'd returned to texting his punk rock band or whatever had him so glued to that phone.

When Adrian came out in the skinny jeans and long-sleeved cotton T-shirt, Emma did a double-take.

"Damn," she muttered.

"Something wrong?" he asked.

"Oh, God. No. I'm sorry. There is decidedly nothing wrong."

"You don't like these then?"

"To the contrary," she said. "I'm going to have to keep you hidden in the house because if any women get one look at you in that, they're going to be elbowing me out of the way to get to you. As your protector, I feel an obligation to ensure your safety from rabid females. Not that there are many at the beach in December." *Thank goodness..*

"So America is full of aggressive females willing to accost a man in blue jeans?"

"You're not exactly a 'man in blue jeans,' Adrian. More like a shining example of eye candy at its finest."

"Eye candy?"

"Yes. Eye candy. Think Gisele Bundchen, male version. With an especially nice ass." *Oh my God, did I really just say that to him?*

Adrian just smiled.

"In that case, I'll take these."

"In every color, I'd suggest," Emma said, cringing at her inability to self-edit in front of the guy. "In the meantime, just leave those on. And let's grab you a North Face jacket, which will hide at least part of you from those overly assertive women."

"You mean those rabid females?"

"I didn't mean female rabbits, if that's what you're asking." She gave him a teasing smirk.

"Man, I almost forgot," she said, snapping her fingers. "Those fancy shoes of yours are so not okay with your new duds. We'd best grab you a pair of Rainbows. I know it's cold out, but you can get by with these." She asked his shoe size and pulled a pair from the wall display. He looked leery about flip-flops, regardless of the season, but shrugged.

He finally decided on a few tops and pants, paid for them and they departed.

"I hesitate to share this with you, but now that I've got the outerwear, I still need something for underneath them," Adrian said.

She hit her forehead with the heel of her hand. "Of course! How could I forget? That means a diversion to the big box store Caro and I call 'WallyWorld'. Brace yourself for culture shock."

They made the fifteen-minute drive to the closest large town, and Emma grabbed his hand as they entered the store. "Okay, first off, you get a prize."

"A prize?"

"Yep! A sticker. Just for being you."

As she spoke, a plump, gray-haired woman with thick-lensed glasses that enlarged her eyes to an unnatural proportion handed them each a smiley face sticker.

"What do you think?" Emma asked. "Is it your lucky day or what?"

Adrian thought about that for a minute, looking straight into Emma's eyes. "All things considered, I'd say it most certainly is." Emma glanced away, too terrified to be burned by such a heated glance. "Yeah, well, we're keeping you far from that temptress Serena, so it has to be a lucky one."

They wandered the aisles, with Adrian marveling at the bizarre selection, the occasionally equally bizarre patrons, and the fact that you could buy anything from food to fertilizer to clothing to trash cans all in one place.

"Overwhelming?"

"You could say that. I'm glad I have you as my navigator. I

don't think anything about running away from my life prepared me for this place. I'd likely be curled up in a ball in the corner of the store without your guidance." He smiled at her.

"And now, not only do you have brand new sexy black boxer briefs and a toothbrush, but you've also got the knowledge of how to shop like regular folk. All good." She linked arms with his as they left the store. "Next stop, groceries!"

Once in the grocery store, they made the rounds and she grabbed essentials as they went. "Frozen pizza sound good?"

"I couldn't begin to answer that question. I've never had it. You decide."

"It'll make a decent lunch this week. We'll grab some beer, some fruit, something for breakfast — you ever have French toast? How about steaks? We'll grill out in the thirty-degree weather and pretend it's July. Let me also find a couple of bottles of wine." She continued talking to herself out loud as she gathered up the needed food items, and at the check-out she threw a copy of *People* in her cart. "A little light reading," she said with a laugh, half-wondering if she'd find Adrian or any of his peeps within the folds of the magazine. From here on out she was going to have to pay closer attention to the royalty gossip therein.

As they got in the car to return to the beach house, Emma's stomach let out a loud growl. "In case there was any question as to whether I was a classy broad, I think that settles it," she said. "But that does remind me…it's past lunch time and a shrimp burger sounds scary good right now."

"Shrimp burger?"

"Trust me, this will become your best friend," she said. Ten minutes later they were turning into the dilapidated parking lot at the Big Oak Diner, a hole-in-the-wall take-out restaurant specializing in all things fried, but especially the holy grail of grease, the shrimp burger.

"Want me to order for you?" Emma asked.

Adrian shrugged. "When in Rome…"

She ordered two shrimp burgers, a side of hush puppies, and two chocolate shakes, just to add to their clogged arteries. "You only live once, my friend," she said to Adrian, handing her cash to the clerk.

They both watched through the carryout window as their meal was prepared: a steamed bun topped with tartar sauce and coleslaw, followed by a mound of fried shrimp, and finished with a fat dollop of ketchup.

"Not exactly the royal kitchens, eh?" she said, rubbing her hands together against the winter chill in the air.

"I'll let you know once I try this thing." He reached out and rubbed her arms with his hands, willing her blood to warm her up more. His touch was remarkably toasty even through her winter coat.

"Don't think we can eat these outside today," she said. "Looks like it's dashboard dining instead."

Emma grabbed the bag as the server handed it out the pass-through window, and motioned for Adrian to get the milkshakes. She hit the unlock button on her car remote, quickly got into the driver's seat, then handed Adrian his food, setting up the hush puppies atop the center console between their seats.

"Bon appétit," Emma said. "Or as they say 'round here, dig in!"

Adrian took a bite and let it linger in his mouth for a minute. Emma watched, hoping he wasn't about to spit it out on her lap. He began to chew and then let out a moan.

"My God, this is incredible," he said, taking another bite. "And to think my mother warned me about Americans lacking in taste."

"That mother of yours sounds like she needs an attitude adjustment."

"It's complicated," Adrian said. "I'm afraid my mother is from the old school, and she's not particularly interested in keeping up with the times. She's lost perspective. She has always done as she was told, followed the straight and narrow. She expected the same of me and my brothers and sister. All while watching royalty decline in Europe, with her trying to sustain things they way they used to be. I think it's been hard for her. Times have changed, the world has modernized greatly. And while within the borders of our small nation, our family is highly regarded and appreciated, certainly in the greater world there are those who would love to see all royal ways disappear. It saddens my mother and I think she blames all this modernity for it. But I think you have an American saying, what is it? You can't fight city hall? Progress happens, like it or not. I think my mother is coming around to that way of thinking, but ever so slowly."

"Yet not fast enough to allow you to marry whom you choose, rather than the very one you'd least choose?"

"Unfortunately."

"Can you imagine how aghast your mother would be to know you're sitting with a commoner in her beat-up Volvo, in your skinny jeans and North Face jacket, munching on a shrimp burger? Poor thing, it would probably kill her."

"She'll have to deal with it."

"Not really," Emma said. "It's not as if she's ever going to know about this."

Adrian shrugged. "I can't hide forever. At some point my hand will be forced. And I'm not going to pretend this week never happened. After all, so far it's turning out to be one of the more entertaining times I've had in the past several years."

"Really? You're having a good time?"

He looked at her with raised eyebrows. "You have to ask me that? I force you to take me with you, then you're stuck practically going off the grid with me, you're introducing me to a whole new — and perfectly fascinating — world. How could it be anything but fabulous?"

Emma thought about that for a second, chewing on a hush

puppy while she considered it. "It's not exactly a yacht off the south of France, you know," she said. "Or an African safari. Or a few hundred other exciting adventures I'm sure you could be doing instead of experiencing my boring lifestyle, up close and personal."

"But it is *your* adventure that you've introduced to me," he said. "And that makes it —and your life— just about perfect. You'll never know how much I owe you for this, Emma."

"Eh." She waved her hand at him. "Owe, schmowe. This is my pleasure. I mean, how many people like me get the chance to hang with someone like you?"

"I could say the same."

"Then please, do," she said, laughing. "But really, I was in a huge funk when you accosted me. Lucky me that you've dragged me out of my pouty state."

"Pouty? You? You don't seem as if you have a care in the world."

"Trust me, I've got cares that have cares."

"Name one."

Did she really want to start moaning about her boring life to him? How could he even relate to it?

She let out a sigh. "Oh, I don't know. On paper I have it great. A wonderful job with lots of flexibility. I meet interesting people, and have plenty of variety in my work. I get access to things most people could never dream of — I mean, look! Twelve hours ago I was photographing royalty with the President of the United States! How cool is that? But I just keep feeling like there's something missing. I'm twenty-six years old. I'm a veteran of so many bad relationships I could write a country-western album about all the cheaters and reprobates I've settled for who couldn't even be bothered settling for me. Talk about feeling like a reject, when the losers don't even want you!

"I guess maybe I'm lonely. I have a nice little house. Wonderful family and friends. A great job that I'm kind of bored with — I always feel like an outsider at someone else's party when I'm at work. Maybe because I am. But I picked it, so why am I complaining? Especially since I've been so successful at it. Weird, isn't it? Sorry." She heaved a sigh. "I prattled on a little more than I ought to have. I should shut up now before I start hearing crickets, huh?"

She looked over at Adrian, who sat in rapt attention but didn't say a word.

"Well?"

He remained quiet for another minute. Talk about crickets.

"Okay, then, I guess we'll head back," she said, trying to fill dead air.

"I'm sorry," Adrian said. "I'm not ignoring you. I'm just processing all that information you gave me. It's a lot, you know."

"Yeah, I have a bad habit of oversharing."

Adrian shook. "Not that I've noticed, you don't. And while I haven't seen the photographs you've taken, I have to presume you're pretty talented. Otherwise you'd never have been hired for the kinds of things you shoot. I can assure you my embassy wouldn't have reached out to you if they didn't have complete faith in your skills. So I hope that's slight consolation, for what it's worth."

Emma shrugged in concession.

"Believe it or not, in an odd way, I can relate. I think we are both feeling burned out, perhaps unappreciated even? I've been doing what I've been doing since I had my first spoonful of porridge, I suppose. It's all I've known. And yet, what's the point? A life of pampered privilege, I go out on these dog and pony show events to promote my country, to put on a happy face. I feel like I'm in a perpetual beauty pageant sometimes. Like I'm a two-dimensional character and no one really cares about me as a person, but just about what they want from me."

"Huh." Emma never gave a thought to the life of a prince being anything but smooth sailing. But clearly there was more to this man than met the eye. "I'd never considered that, but now that you put it that way, yes. It must be hard to know who to trust, like everyone wants a piece of you."

"Precisely," he said. "Like the family heirloom everyone is tugging at because they and they alone want it in the inheritance. But I don't think very many people have even thought about me as *me*. Instead they see only me as in famous-prince-whose-presence-can-draw-an-audience." He shook his head. "But enough about me. Those useless men you mentioned before... What a loss for them! I mean look at you! You're young and beautiful—"

Emma snorted. *Nice.* "Easy on the hyperboles there, fella. Beautiful's a bit of a stretch."

He stared at her as if she'd gone mad. "You really don't see it?"

"See what?"

"You don't see what a beautiful person you are?"

"I mean I don't exactly cause eye strain if someone looked my way, but I'm not up there in supermodel contention or anything. Put it this way: at least I'm not a brown-bagger."

Once again Adrian looked puzzled.

"It's an awful term. I heard a guy refer to a girl at a fraternity party like that. He'd only take her home if he could put a brown paper bag over her head."

"Honestly. Sometimes we men need to apologize for our half of the species," Adrian said, sighing. "I'll have to keep that line in mind next time I want to be a royal asshole."

Emma burst out laughing. "Ha ha! I get it! *Royal* asshole! Who knew royalty made jokes like that? Good one!"

Adrian shook his head to redirect the conversation. "Seriously, Emma, even though you are indeed beautiful on the outside, you're beautiful in more ways than that. After all, how many people would drop everything they were doing when a crazy man implores them to rescue him from a dire situation? And if those men didn't see that in you, that's their shortcoming, not yours."

Emma rolled her eyes, not quite buying what he was saying.

"Fine, don't believe me. Go ahead and let their idiocy

control the way you see yourself, if that's what you want."

"Okay, okay, I'll take that into consideration. In the meantime, you wanna check that thing out?" She was pointing to a sign for the nearby aquarium. "My grandmother used to take me there when I was younger."

"Are there sharks?"

"Why? You scared they might get ya?"

He laughed. "I've always had a fascination with sharks. If it weren't for my overprotective entourage I'd have loved to have gone diving with sharks in a cage."

"Ooooh, how cool would that be? Sign me up."

"It's a deal. Let's plan on it, you and me together. A shark cage built for two." He smiled at her.

"I'll mark it on my calendar. Just as soon as you return to your other life, you let me know when we're going." As if she'd ever be able to afford that. "In the meantime, we'll have to settle for ogling the local variety from the other side of a glass wall."

"Fair enough. But I'll hold you to it. When I get back, things are going to change. No more Mr. Nice Guy. I'm going to stand up for myself and do what I want to do from here on out."

"You might want to keep the Mr. Nice Guy part," Emma said. "It's the best part of your personality, if you ask me."

"Seriously?" he asked.

"Believe me, it's not often I've come across a guy like you who ought to be completely full of himself, but instead is just thoroughly nice and normal. Even if you don't exactly know how to use a chef's knife."

Adrian tucked his head down, nodding at Emma. "As members of the mutual admiration society, we'll just have to enjoy each other's company more often."

Emma smiled. "I'd like that."

Too bad, she fretted, it wasn't going to last.

Chapter Seven

EMMA'S phone rang as soon as they entered the aquarium. She glanced at the caller and quickly excused herself from Adrian to take the call.

"I can only talk for a second. What's up?" she said to Caroline.

"What are you, nuts? You can't leave me dangling after that email I got from you!" Caroline said. "I mean you're kidnapped by this gorgeous guy who was all over you at that reception. All over you! But not just any guy. *The* guy. The one who's going to take over an entire country. Like one that's full of people. And land. And crown jewels stored in a royal vault."

"I really can't talk about this all right now. Adrian's waiting for me and I don't want to leave him alone. But trust me, we're just friends. I'm helping the man out. That's it."

"I'm sure that's what you'd tell your mother but this is me! Let's talk turkey here. Have you done it yet? What's he like? Are the rumors true?"

"Rumors?"

"Yes, I read in some online tabloid that he's known to be packin', if you know what I mean. Apparently an Italian stylist who was dressing him spilled that info. Can you imagine, having access to the royal crotch? Maybe you already have. I guess he's already heard the jokes about the family jewels. Hilarious! The things you just don't normally contemplate until you have to."

"Uh, can I get a word in edgewise?" Emma said. "I'm not going to ask him about his, his, his *girth*!"

"Girth? How do you know it's not length?"

"Gah! I can't believe this conversation!"

"Meanwhile, what kind of friend are you? Why didn't you hook me up with that manservant of his? Seriously, though.

What are you doing with the guy? What does one do with a prince? Shame it's December so you can't take him out on the banana boat ride. Although for all I know you're having your own banana boat ride right about now…Oh, my God, you are killing me with your silence. Dish, already, would you?"

"Honey, I haven't had a chance to say much of anything with you bombarding me with questions. Look, nothing is going to happen. He's a nice guy. He's got issues he's dealing with. And I'm not going to insert myself into all of that. Talk about a non-starter of a relationship. I am going to be content just being friends. And I'm sorry I haven't had a chance to play matchmaker to the stars for you. I've been busy."

"Fine. But promise me, if you get a chance to put in a good word for me with that blond one, you know where to find me."

"I'd like nothing more than to find you a fresh victim. I mean man. I'll be sure to give him your number. In the meantime, Adrian's walking my way. I'm going to hang up now before he hears me talking about his anatomy. Love you, you big idiot!"

"I love the interactive exhibits where you can actually feel things," Emma said. "How cool is this, touching a ray with your very hands?"

"Not exactly sure putting my hands on that thing is high on my list," Adrian said. "Don't they sting or bite or something? Isn't that why they call them *sting*rays?"

"Good point. But maybe these aren't stingrays, maybe they're some other ray. Ray of light, maybe."

"Or ray of hope?"

"Yeah, I like your optimism. Ray of hope, that sounds perfect."

"But I think I'll let you do all the touching, just the same," he said.

"C'mon, don't be a scaredy-cat. It's perfectly safe. Do you think they'd let schoolchildren stick their fingers in there if it wasn't?"

"You have a point," he said, but nevertheless started backing slightly away just as Emma pulled him closer. She grabbed his hand and directed it into the shallow water before them.

"See? Harmless! It's so smooth, feels a little gelatinous, doesn't it?"

"Perfect, just what I wanted to feel: slime."

"Watch out for that barbed tail!"

Adrian jumped back and she started laughing. "Adrian, I am sure they've done something to de-barb the thing, or whatever they do to stingrays. They're not going to let it shoot a poisonous arrow into your face or anything! Oooh, but look over there — my favorite! Sea turtles."

They investigated the sea turtles, some of which had been injured by propellers from motorboats, others tangled in discarded plastic bags, which only made Emma sad. "I think I need to go see something else because I hate to imagine these poor turtles being hurt in the water. It breaks my heart too much."

"Shows you've got a huge heart, Emma."

"Yeah, to match my huge butt," she said.

Adrian reached for Emma's shoulders and turned her around to get a closer look at her point of reference. "Granted you have a winter coat on, but I'm not seeing it," he said. "From my view it's just about perfect."

Emma blushed and changed the subject.

"So over here, this is where I got to do a sleepover when I was twelve. My grandmother volunteered here and they had some summer event where kids could come spend the night by the shark tank. It was pretty awesome. We lined our sleeping bags up right here," she said, pointing to a stretch of flooring nearby, "and every time I'd wake up there would be a shark meandering by. Suffice it to say I didn't get much sleep that night.

"And here," she said, pointing to a nearby bench, "is where I used to eat my peanut butter and jelly sandwiches when I'd come with my grandmother. Sometimes I'd stand right by the glass wall and offer them up to the sharks. They weren't amused."

"Ah, you're generous, too, I see."

She rolled her eyes. "Yeah, me offering my sandwich up to Jaws. That qualifies me for sainthood."

"You don't appreciate yourself much, do you?" Adrian asked.

"What do you mean?"

"Well, every time I pay you a compliment you deflect it instantly."

Emma shrugged. "Really? I never thought about it. I guess I'm not used to having people lavish me with attention." She wound her pointer finger in a circle by the side of her head, indicating what a nutty idea that was.

"Maybe you're selling yourself short?"

"Hardly." She sighed. "I mean I'm just not the center of anyone's attention is all. In fact, it's just the opposite. I'm usually like that planet circling the sun. That bright star is the one getting all the attention, and I'm just sort of along for the ride I suppose.

"That's how it goes in life. Besides, I don't exactly run in circles in which I find possible suitors. I don't go to an office like normal people. Not that you should date work colleagues, but still. And when I do go to work, well, I'm working, not flirting. And not like I can be picking up men while I'm on a shoot. Plus there's that little problem of me not being an invited guest. It would be tacky, to say the least."

"But don't you do anything besides work where you'd find people?"

"Of course I go out with my friends," she said, staring off at a meandering shark streamlining his way toward them. "But it's not like we're out there for the meat market aspect. We go to hang out and visit. It would be sort of icky picking up a guy at a bar anyhow. But enough about me. What about you? Where does a prince find eligible young women, aside from meddling mothers, that is?"

Adrian laughed. "Yes, the mother factor doesn't help much, does it? It's complicated. On the one hand — and I don't mean this as bragging — women are kind of beating down my door to get to me."

"Not boastful at all." She held up her hand, making a circle of her thumb and forefinger, in that symbol for "okay."

"You know what I mean," he said. "But that's not actually a good thing. It's not as if anyone is interested in me, per se. Rather they're interested in landing a prince."

"Or at least bedding one."

"That too. There was a time when that was all fine and good. I mean, I'd be crazy to turn that down."

"Yeah, right," Emma said, shaking her head. "You're a guy. You're genetically programmed to take what you can get."

Adrian paused to look directly at her. "Thanks for that vote of confidence. You do hold my gender in high esteem, don't you?"

"More like I'm a bit burned out in the men department," she said. "Been there, done that, suffered the rejection."

"I'm sorry you haven't found a man who treasures you. You deserve that and more."

"Tell me about it. I feel like I've been a magnet for the worst of the worst. Surely there must be some guy out there who isn't just crap on a stick?"

"You have quite a way of describing things," Adrian said with a chuckle. "I don't feel qualified to be a defender of all men, but I can assure you we're not all that bad. Don't give up yet."

"Oh, I don't know. I'm rather enjoying being a royal rehabilitator instead, anyhow. Much more interesting," she said. "Might be a whole new career for me. Got any more of your type you can send my way to indoctrinate into Americana?"

"Yeah, I'll send my brothers over next. If you're lucky my

sister will show up sometime. You'd have a fun time with her."

"I'm good with that, but whatever you do, please don't send your mother my way. She terrifies me and I hardly know a thing about her."

"No worries. I love my mother dearly, but we're steering clear of her for now. Maybe someday you can meet her and you can find out she's really a delightful woman. When she's not matchmaking and imposing her will on others."

"I'll take your word on that," Emma said. She glanced at her watch. "While wearing a bulletproof vest. You ready to head out of here?"

Just then Adrian heard his phone ding, which startled them both. "Hmmm. Let's hope the natives aren't getting restless."

He opened up a text message from Darcy.

"Do you have any idea how persistent your mother can be?" Darcy asked. "She's got you in her crosshairs, but I've been playing her like a violin. So far, so good. I think you'll have a few days respite from her."

Adrian typed back. "So she bought your story? Thank God."

"Don't think she suspects a thing. Everything good with that photographer?"

"Better than good. This normal thing isn't half bad."

"Don't get too used to it, my friend. Reality is only a few days away. Meanwhile, it might be a good idea if you could give me her number too. I kept trying to reach you but you haven't been paying attention to your phone. Just in case I need some emergency back-up."

Adrian leaned over toward Emma. "Would you mind if I shared your number with Darcy? He's nervous having no alternative contact information for me."

"By all means. In fact, why don't we give him Caroline's number too. Since they're both in D.C., that might be helpful to him. Caro always knows where to find me." She showed him her friend's contact number.

"Perfect. I'll pass these on."

"You remember the one who was with Emma at the event?"

Adrian typed in his text to Darcy.

"The redhead?"

"I knew you'd remember. So here's her contact information as well. Maybe you could reach out to her if you can't get hold of us at all. If you get my drift."

"I do have a little time on my hands…"

"I'm sure you'll figure out a way to fill it then. Now if you'll let me return to my life of anonymity."

"Don't do anything I wouldn't do, sir."

"Heaven help us all if I did."

Chapter Eight

CAROLINE'S phone jarred her awake shortly after she'd drifted off to sleep. After being up far too late the previous night with her new bartender buddy, she needed to catch some decent shut-eye. She fumbled in the dark for her cell phone, knocking over a glass of water in the process.

"Dammit," she muttered as she turned on the phone.

"Well, hello to you too," an oddly familiar, accented voice responded. "How are you this fine day?"

Who in the world could that be, sounding like a particularly posh version of Hugh Grant?

"The better question might be who is waking me from my beauty sleep at this ungodly hour?"

"Touché. I know we only met fleetingly, but you didn't strike me as the type to retire for the night at the *ungodly* hour of four in the afternoon. If it's any consolation, I can't imagine you even need beauty sleep."

Caroline gave herself a mental dope-slap, being that it was barely approaching dinnertime. "Okay, then. Um," she muttered in a sleep-graveled voice. "Would you mind telling me who you are?"

"Right. That might be helpful. Name's Darcy. Squires-Thornton, that is."

"So do they call you Darcy, or Squires-whatever-you-just-said?"

"Darcy, thanks."

"And you're calling me because—"

"Of course. You don't know that, now do you?" he said. "Calling about my mate. And your mate. Want to find out what you know. Check on her, see if she's legit. That sort of thing."

"My mate? I haven't the slightest idea what you're talking about but I'm reallllllllly tired, so if you can cut to the chase so I can get back to my pillow…"

"You're the one who works with this Emma woman, right? The photographer? Adrian passed on your phone number, said I could reach out to you if need be. So I'm reaching out to you."

"Who the hell is Adrian? And can you stop speaking in code?"

"You met him at the reception. His Royal Highness Crown Prince Adrian. Seems he's on a spontaneous holiday with your friend."

"Ahhhh," Emma said, drawing out the sound. "That Adrian. Of course. I should've known that already."

"Because?"

"Because how many Adrians do I know? Precisely none. Well, if you don't count him, which I don't, because I don't even know him."

"Now that we're clear on who's who," Darcy said. "What say you fill me in on the details. For starters, what's her story? Why would she agree to pick up my good friend on the spur of the moment like that? Where are they? Do you think one of us needs to go wherever they are to check on them?"

"Excuse me?" Caroline said. "Are you suggesting my friend is somehow not trustworthy?"

"I don't know what your friend is. I just want to make sure she's legitimate."

"Legitimate? How do I know your buddy's on the up and up? I mean he's the one who kidnapped my friend!"

"Kidnapped? Hardly," Darcy said.

"I think that's debatable," she said. "He came up to her, covered her mouth, then told her to be quiet. That sounds to me like he accosted her to me."

Darcy was silent for a moment. "Well, all right. I'll concede that doesn't sound great. Truth is, he's harmless as a puppy dog. And to be fair, he was trying to get away quickly."

"What, is he a bank robber or something?"

"Ha-ha. No. But he had a brief window of opportunity to

slip out. It's not the easiest thing in the world to go incognito when you're so recognizable."

"Yeah I have that problem all the time," she said, deadpan. "But seriously, Emma is on the up and up. Wouldn't hurt a flea. She rescues stray cats and volunteers at soup kitchens. Adrian picked a good one to skip town with."

"Well, that's reassuring at least," he said. "You don't suppose there's a need for one of us to go down there and check on them?"

"To the beach? In December?" she said loudly. "Who goes to the beach at this time of year, unless you're hiding out? Thanks, I'll pass. No sunbathing? No way. Although, on second thought, my skin can't take the sun these days, so maybe winter at the beach isn't such a bad idea after all. A little getaway, some relaxation, read a few books…"

"Ah, yes, you're the redhead, can't take those damaging rays," Darcy said.

"Then you remember me?"

"How could I not? Gorgeous, very vivacious."

"Gorgeous? Vivacious? Why, I'll take that as a compliment, thank you."

"It was intended as one. So, what do you say the two of us meet up, maybe compare notes, just so we're all on the same page with this situation?"

"I'm not sure I have to be on any page with this," Caroline said. "This is between our friends. Why's it our business?"

"Well it's certainly my business. I'm responsible for Adrian's welfare. I'm his right-hand man. I knew he needed to get away, but the more I think about it, the more I'd like to ensure he's perfectly safe. Not that I have any reason to believe he's not, but you must understand, I have the queen breathing down my neck and if anything were to go awry…"

"God, I hate it when the queen breathes down my neck," Caroline said.

"I'll pretend you're not completely provincial," Darcy said.

"Provincial? If that's not an elitist comment—"

"Elitist? How about your reverse snobbery?"

Caroline took this as a cue to stand up. "I'm not a snob! And sorry if I can't relate to your rarified world of semi-precious chess pieces you have to maneuver around."

"Chess pieces? They aren't any such thing. Besides, I hate chess!"

"Seems to me they are, if old mommy-o is manipulating Adrian into marrying some twit he's not interested in. Checkmate!"

Darcy sighed. "Fine, you got me there. So she is manipulating things a bit. That's why Adrian's escaped for a while, to figure out how best to stop her before this becomes madness. And I'm left to cover up everything like the good boy that I am."

"Awww, poor widdle royal courtier. It *must* be rough," Caroline said in mock baby talk.

"You certainly do have a distinctive wit about you," Darcy said, grumbling. "Look, enough of this word jockeying. I need to know: if I have to go down there to check on them, will you agree to help me do so?"

Caroline hesitated for a moment, stuck between being annoyed he was trying to railroad her and thinking a road trip with the cute friend of the prince might be just what she needed to knock out those winter doldrums that always kick in around this time of year. "Wellllllll.... I suppose I could help out. But what's in it for me?"

"You're a tough nut to crack, you know that? I don't suppose being a kind host to a foreign guest is enough these days?"

"I tell you what, I help you with this and you invite me to some swanky royal soirée. In your own country. I won't even make you fly me there. I'll get there on my own. But you get me the invite, maybe even find a place I can crash, and we can seal the deal."

"The things I do out of loyalty," he muttered, sighing. "All right, fine. I'll ensure that you've got an invitation to something. Sometime. Somewhere."

"Yippee! I've always wanted to attend a fancy royal ball. Like Cinderella. Minus the wicked stepmother. Ooooh, this will be divine. Imagine how jealous Emma will be when she finds out!" Caroline danced around her apartment, high-fiving the air.

"Let's not go there," Darcy said. "For all we know she's already lined up her own invitation by now, if she's anywhere near as mercenary as her friend."

"I'll ignore that comment," Caroline said. "I'm too jazzed about my big debut on the international social scene to allow a snide remark to drag me down. So, what do you need me to do?"

"First things first, we'll have a meeting of the minds," Darcy said. "How soon can you be ready?"

"You mean tonight?"

"Of course I mean tonight," he said. "When and where?"

"You don't waste any time," she said, sighing. "I suppose, if you insist. I'm going to have to dive in the shower though. And straighten my hair. Slap on some make-up. The usual. Meet at seven, Mi Piace, in Adams-Morgan."

"Just to be sure I know who I'm looking for," Darcy said, jotting down the address. "After all, we met only briefly, and the light was dim. What will you have on?"

"All you need to know is I'm the one with the red hair. And maybe something slinky."

With that, she hung up the phone, leaving Darcy to wonder what he'd just gotten himself into.

Chapter Nine

"**YOU** are an exceptional cook," Adrian said as he pushed his plate away and rubbed his full belly. "I haven't had a meal that good in forever."

"I have a hard time imagining my cooking skills are on par with what you're used to," Emma replied. "I mean granted I make a mean slice-and-bake cookie, but still."

"I'll have to take your word on that until I get to try one myself for dessert."

"Your wish is my command," she said, grabbing two bowls from the kitchen cabinet and pulling the ice cream from the freezer. She scooped ice cream and then topped them off with two cookies each. "Voila. Manna from heaven."

She tipped her bowl against his in a toast.

Adrian took a bite, and his eyes rolled back in his head. "Good God, that's amazing," he said, digging into his second bite.

"Aww, it's nothing. Just me and that little doughboy," she said, pointing at the slice and bake package on the counter.

"I'll take your word for it."

"So I was thinking," Emma said. "What say we get in the car and drive around checking out Christmas lights? You haven't lived till you've seen how Americans can go obscenely overboard on holiday decorations."

They embarked along the beach road, checking out illuminated decorations on some of the larger homes first.

"Check this one out," Emma said, pointing to a beachfront

Something in the Heir

McMansion covered in so many multi-colored lights it was hard to see the cedar shakes that were holding the complicated network of light strands together. "Those homeowners clearly have too much time on their hands." She snapped a few pictures from her phone to text to Caroline for laughs.

They didn't have to drive much further along till they came to a yard filled with animated holiday characters, from Santa to baby Jesus, looking as if they were all attending the same Christmas party.

"I sometimes wonder who is rolling in their grave when this stuff gets all muddled together," she said. "I mean really, the Virgin Mary and Frosty the Snowman, united forever, here?"

Adrian laughed. "Can't say that I've ever seen that exact holiday combination before. We do things a little more subtly back home."

"Oh really?" she said. "How exactly do you celebrate Christmas?"

"It's very traditional and not at all commercialized," he said. "People dress in their regional costumes, and often go door-to-door caroling, and there is dancing in the town squares. Decorations are usually made with traditional materials: pine, fruit, that sort of thing. We use Christmas lights, but mostly small white ones, like fairy lights, and lots of candles.

"We put candles on our trees instead of electric lights. And we do have a lot of bells. Most everyone hangs a bell on their door for Christmas, to call in the good spirits of the season. And there are small Christmas markets in every town and village. But unlike the ones in larger European countries, in which they sell products more likely made in China, all of our products are handmade in Monaforte."

"Sounds lovely," Emma said. "Old-fashioned. I like that. We have gotten a bit away from traditional in America. I mean not that it's wrong to be so 'in your face' with holiday cheer, but I like it to be a little more understated. That said I am the first to get in line to drive around looking at this stuff. I mean it is so over the top, it's downright hilarious. It's sort of my holiday entertainment."

They drove by a house with about a dozen giant blow-up characters, everything from Homer Simpson with a Santa hat onto a seven-foot-tall Rudolph with glowing nose. The figures swayed in the night air, what with large fans beneath forcing air up them for support.

"By dawn these things look like dead soldiers," she said. "I guess the people go to work and don't want to run the air pumps all day, so all of the characters are slumped on the ground like the Wicked Witch of the West once she's melted."

Adrian nodded. "Even I get that cultural reference," he said. "I'm almost surprised they don't have an inflatable witch, now that you mention her. I see there's even an Easter bunny over there with a Santa hat on, so why not throw in some *Wizard of Oz* characters, maybe Voldemort from *Harry Potter* while they're at it?"

Emma just shook her head in disbelief.

"So tell me more about your family holiday traditions," Emma said, curious to learn something of his country's culture.

"Keep in mind that mine is a small country," he said. "So people know each other. Even as royals, we mingle with fellow countrymen much more so than in other countries with royalty. We open the palace to visitors during the holidays so that people can enjoy the festive decorations. Chef makes a massive gingerbread house, so large that children can wander through it. It takes up much of a ballroom, and kids under a certain age can go and explore it. It's like an edible play fort.

"Finally on the day after Christmas, which is a special holiday known as Santa Christus Day in Monaforte, invited guests get to eat the gingerbread house down to the ground. Only crumbs are left, and rest assured our dogs take care of them."

"Really? A massive pig-out with the gingerbread house? That sounds like my kind of holiday. Though I might like it better if it were chocolate chip instead of gingerbread. But I can't be picky with these things. I'll take what I can get."

"You'd like to get your hands on that house?"

"Are you kidding me? I'd be in line at midnight, the first one," she said. "I'd probably run to the back of the house and work my way forward. After all, everyone else would be busily gnawing away at the front and I'd have all that back end to myself."

Adrian leaned back in his seat and stared at her in the dark. "You seem to have given this some thought."

"Not really," Emma said. "It's the same strategy as at an amusement park. When they open, I begin backwards and ride the roller coasters at the far end, because most people start out toward the front, and then they're stuck in long lines immediately, whereas I can then ride and ride and ride for a while before people work their way to the back. I figure the same thing for gorging on your cookie mansion. So tell me, is there lots of candy with it?"

Adrian nodded his head vigorously. "So much candy. Once when I was a boy, I had a stomach ache for two days afterward, I ate so many marshmallows and so much chocolate."

"Yummm...chocolate and marshmallows. What perfection. Throw it in a mug and heat it up with a candy cane and I'm golden."

"I take it you have a sweet tooth?"

"Sweet tooth? You don't know the half of it. I have a sweet mouth. Or sweet face. Maybe sweet body. I can't get enough of the stuff."

"Sweet face, indeed," Adrian whispered.

"Did you just say something insulting?" Emma asked as they pulled up to the next home, which was blasting Christmas carols in beat to a throbbing light show projected against the wall of the house.

"Hardly," he said.

"C'mon! What'd you say?" She chucked him in the arm like she would a brother who was teasing her.

"Nothing!"

"Of course you said something. What was it?"

Adrian sighed loudly. "If you must know, I said you have a sweet face, okay? I agreed with you. And if you want, I'll throw in that you have a sweet body as well. Are you happy now?"

Emma squinted her eyes at him. "Are you teasing me?"

Adrian shook his head, bemused and irritated all at once. "Do I look like I'm teasing you?" He reached out his hand toward her chin and with just the tips of his fingers tilted her face toward his. "You have a beautiful face, Emma. One I'm growing to like quite a bit, thank you." He leaned forward and gave her the tiniest kiss on her forehead.

Emma blinked at him, not knowing how to respond to his sweet gesture. On the one hand, was this a sort of "just friends" thing, with a perfectly platonic peck on the forehead? Or was he testing her, reaching out to see if she reciprocated his feelings. *Did she?* The prince who packs? That stunning shirtless chest? The golden-boy smile? How could she not?

Suddenly Emma could no longer deny that she had it bad, which wasn't good. She couldn't crush on Adrian. She was charged with keeping him under the radar for a few days, nothing more. After that she'd never see the guy again. Well, maybe she'd see his ten-page wedding spread in *People* after he succumbed to his mother's pressure and married Serena. Serena—the name stirred the acid in her stomach. What a complete rhymes-with-witch. Why did she get all the luck of being entitled to become the officially sanctioned Mrs. Prince Adrian? Which made Emma realize she knew little to nothing about Adrian, including his last name. Clearly she would not be a candidate to marry him — she didn't even know his surname.

Adrian had fixed his eyes on Emma's, which was making her squirm. Suddenly she remembered she needed to respond to his compliment. She was so busy being a complete doofus about this situation she was going to be rude on top of it.

"Oh, God, thank you," she said. "I mean, oh, God, I forgot to say thank you. Not 'Oh, God, thank you.' I don't want you to think I'm like praying to God or anything for what you just did. Nor do I want you to think I was so exceedingly thankful to you because I never get compliments. Oh, God, not that I get a ton of compliments. I mean, I don't, but I'm not a total loser. I'm just not on anybody's radar, I guess—"

"Emma?" Adrian brushed some hair away from her eyes, still staring at her, not letting his eyes leave hers.

"You probably think I'm a certifiable lunatic." She babbled on. "Poor Emma, can't even accept a compliment, she's so unaccustomed to anyone paying her one."

Adrian raked his fingers gently through her hair. "I was thinking nothing of the sort. I think you're rather charming, in a nutty sort of way. And I think it's refreshing that you don't soak in flattery like a thirsty houseplant demanding water. There's something to be said for someone being completely unaffected by attention."

Emma snorted. Lovely sound, that. "It's not that I'm unaffected," she said. "It's more that I'm just uncomfortable with people singling me out for things. Maybe it's a side effect of being on the back end of a camera: I'm used to not being noticed. I hide behind my equipment, I suppose. So if someone puts me front and center, I honestly don't know what to do."

Adrian affectionately tweaked the tip of her nose. "It's what's most charming about you, Emma. You're totally you. No pretense, no ego. I've been with women who shamelessly fish around for the second compliment the very minute they get the first one."

"Yep, that's me, good old Emma, estranged from even the possibility of a compliment. It bounces off of me with the power of my flattery-rejection force field. I deflect it like a superhero dispels bullets."

Adrian kept staring at her, compounding her discomfort tenfold. "You are an interesting bird," he said. "I don't think I've ever met anyone quite like you. So different from the women who show up on my doorstep."

"Women show up on your doorstep?" Emma said, smiling.

"Don't you have palace guards to take them away to the dungeon? Maybe a spare guillotine lying around so you can lop off their—"

Adrian shook his head and then took her face between his hands and pulled her toward him. "I'm not quite sure what is possessing me to do this," he said, leaning in even closer. "Part of me thinks I must be mad, but the other part of me thinks I must be mad about you."

With that he settled his warm lips on hers, pressing softly against hers as he pulled her closer to him. Emma let out a quiet groan, wrestling with whether to join in the fun or resist. It was sheer folly to think this could go anywhere at all, but he was right here, and those blue eyes, the dimples when he smiled, so charming, so *Prince* Charming, so—

"Wait! What am I doing?" she said with a start, halfway pushing away from him. "I can't kiss you! You're a prince. I'm a commoner. An American one at that. This has no future whatsoever, and I can't engage in going-nowhere-fast activities like this that are totally counterproductive and so completely out of character—"

Adrian pulled her closer again, this time his tongue reaching out and grazing the tip of her lips. "Shhhh," he implored her. "Maybe you shouldn't think so much, and instead, let's just *be*, okay? It's just me, and you and these giant air-filled Christmas decorations enjoying a quiet—with the exception of the confounded air pumps and blasting holiday tunes—moment. Let's not spoil it with thoughts about now or later, shall we?"

At that Emma let out a sigh and released the tension in her body that held her tight like a bow ready to launch an arrow far off into the ocean. And with it she melted just a little bit into his grip, opening her mouth to him as he tilted his head just enough to fit perfectly to her lips. Outside she could hear the dulcet strains of a rapper chanting, "Give up the dough on Christmas, yo," oddly juxtaposed with the huge house blasting the song. But Emma barely heard the noise through the sounds inside the car of his breathing and her gasping and a few moans and a groan or two and the sounds of their tongues dancing in unison as they explored one another for the first time.

Adrian's hands slipped from her face and worked their way down her body and *oh, right there, yes, oh, yes,* Emma's mind was chanting silently to him as he tried to lean across the gear shift of her car in an attempt to gain some leverage and access and all those good things one wants when one is trying to get to know someone just a little bit better while enjoying the local color. Emma's hands glanced across a few of Adrian's spare parts, and she realized the rumors about what he was packing just might well be true. *Don't get your hopes up, girl. He's a look-don't-touch guy for you.* But damn, she'd be thinking about that package for the next umpteen years if she had any say over it.

Just as Adrian was gaining a toehold against the gearshift and his hands had started landing on Emma's most prime real estate, they heard a loud rap on the window. Emma gasped and jumped at the unexpected interruption. They both looked up, startled, only to realize the windows were completely steamed up and they couldn't even tell who the damned killjoy was who'd stopped their most important forward momentum at such an inconvenient time.

"Oh, my God, I feel like it's eleventh grade all over again with Randy Michener back behind Dogwood Park," Emma groaned.

"Should I know what you mean by that?" Adrian asked, wiping his lips with his shirtsleeve.

"Hell, no," she said. "Bad boyfriend number three, I believe he was. It was early days, still, well before I realized that all males were evil incarnate. Sadly, I was hot to trot for Randy but Randy was looking for just one thing from me and I wasn't putting out. At least not as far as he'd expected. We were making out in the back seat of his father's mid-life crisis Mustang and darned if the windows weren't steamed up just like this, and then we heard someone pounding on the window and—"

There was another knock, this time even harder. Emma sat

up fast, straightened out her mussed-up clothing and flattened her tangled hair, then wiped a sight line across the driver's side window, only to see a nosy cop staring in at them.

"Oh, man, it's Randy Michener, redux," she moaned. "What is it with me and The Man?"

"'The Man?'" Adrian asked as he tried to make himself look less obviously in the throes of hot and bothered teeny-bopper make-out session behavior, hoping the dark would adequately hide the bulge in his brand new surfer-boy pants.

"The cops. PoPo. Men in blue," she said, as if that made more sense. "Though I guess for you, men in uniform are usually at your beck and call, so they never would threaten your moves, even if you were underage in the back seat of a car with some girl with her shirt half off and your hand up her skirt."

"Believe me, I was working on that," he practically sobbed back at her, dismayed at this completely unfair *make-out-us interruptus*.

"Excuse me while I get this. And how about you act completely innocent so they don't run an identity check on you. And don't say a word. That accent will arouse more suspicion than we need to deal with."

"As if we need any more arousal around her than we already have," he said. Emma just rolled her eyes at him while she wiped lipstick smudges away from her mouth with the back of her hand.

She pushed her window button to make it go down. "Officer? Can I help you?"

He peered in with suspicion, no doubt assuming it was a couple of fourteen-year-olds, surprised at their comparatively stately age. "Some neighbors noticed you loitering and saw the car rocking and called us to check up on what was going on. I think they were worried there was some sort of struggle happening inside."

Emma blushed, grateful no one could see her crimson-stained cheeks in the dark. The car was *rocking*? Unbelievable.

Something in the Heir

Seems she couldn't even discreetly make a fool of herself, and instead had to act like an oversexed, hormonally charged beer wench or something. "Sorry, sir. I'm afraid we got a little carried away. 'Tis the season and all that." She shrugged her shoulders and held her hands palm-side up in a *what're ya gonna do* gesture, trying to make light of the situation so he'd leave her the hell alone in her shame.

The cop paused for a minute, aiming a blinding flashlight into the far recesses of her vehicle, peering more closely, ensuring nothing untoward was going on inside her car. Well, nothing more untoward than they all knew had been happening in there, but at least it was between two consenting adults.

"I'd suggest you move along, ma'am, maybe get a room," the cop said, nodding toward Adrian as well.

"Absolutely, officer," she said, mortified, quickly pulling on her seatbelt and getting ready to peel out of there as soon as he stepped one foot away from them, silently muttering *get a room* under her breath, appalled at herself.

The cop tipped his hat toward her. "Have a good evening," he said, dusting his hands off like he'd completed his work there. Emma tried hard not to cringe and instead probably looked like she had bad gas.

As soon as he was a safe enough distance from her car, Emma took off like a bat out of hell.

Chapter Ten

"**THAT'LL** teach me for behaving like a, like a, a, a—"

"An insatiably adorable and surprisingly sexy rescuer of wayward royalty?" Adrian asked, filling in the blanks.

Emma's jaw dropped open for a split second. "I was going to say more like a dog in heat," she said. "But your version sounds far more upstanding, thanks."

"My pleasure," he said, emphasizing the word.

She rolled her eyes at the innuendo.

"No, really. My *great* pleasure."

Emma groaned, yet again. "Adrian, that was a foolish mistake on my part. We can't do that. I'm in charge of keeping you out of the public eye for a few days. That's it. In no way am I supposed to be your, your girl-toy while we do so."

"Girl-toy?"

"It's the opposite of boy-toy. Sorry, it's the only terminology I could come up with on such short notice. Pardon me, but I'm a little under the gun here."

"You really would have been under the gun, if I'd have had a few more minutes to get us situated," Adrian said.

"Was that a sexual reference?"

"Do you want it to be one?"

"Your gun?" she asked. "As in that's what you're packing?"

"Think of it however you want, Emma."

Emma turned down a side street that ran perpendicular to the beach road, happy to get away from the prying eyes of uninvited cops.

"Speaking of packing," she said. "I read that article."

It was Adrian's turn to roll his eyes. "Oh, that one? The 'royal secret,' exposed, as it were?"

Emma nodded. "So, uh, it's true, then? Inquiring minds want to know."

Something in the Heir

"I knew I'd rue the day I let some team of simpering designers dress me for that charity event at Fashion Week in Milan," he said. "All these minions happily slapping outfits on me and undressing me with equal fervor. At least in Monaforte when someone helps me to get my dress colors on, they're not measuring the girth in my crotch.

"Here I was doing this to help out my father's favorite charity in Italy. Little did I know they would put word out to gossip rags about *it*." Adrian took a swig of a water bottle next to him in the cup holder.

"It?" Emma asked, grateful he hadn't given it a name. Nothing like a guy who names his penis Schwartz or Johnson or Big Boy, or whatever else they liked to tag it with. But weird that she was sitting there chitchatting about the princely penis with the guy. "Um, forgive me if I'm wrong, but isn't that something most men would be happy to have broadcast to the world? I mean, after all, the bigger the package, the bigger the pleasure, right?"

With that Adrian choked on his water, splattering some of it onto the windshield. Emma reached over to pat his back to help clear his airway.

"You okay?" she said, grinning.

"I have to say, I've never had such a frank conversation with a woman about my — how would you say this graciously? My endowment? — before," he said. "It's almost a bit embarrassing."

"Almost," she said. "But you're a guy. So if you've got it, flaunt it."

Adrian reached over for Emma's hand, which was resting on the stick shift. She squirmed in her seat, realizing she was only making matters worse with her suggestive talk but unable to stop herself.

"So how about we pick up where we left off?" Adrian asked with a hopefulness of one who always gets what he wants, when he wants it. "After all, you even admitted it: the bigger the package…"

"It's a lovely idea in theory," Emma said. "But honestly, I've promised myself I will not get in any more go-nowhere relationships. I simply can't dabble in men; it's just not good for my psyche."

"Your psyche? What does your psyche have to do with this? Can't you just take pleasure in the moment? Don't worry about what will happen in ten years. For the here and now we were having a lovely time and I'm quite convinced it was about to get much lovelier, had we not been so rudely cut off by that killjoy."

"I suspect that killjoy was simply a manifestation of my conscience, reminding me of my vow of quasi-chastity, made under duress after about the thousandth encounter with the wrong man. I need to stop engaging with men who aren't good for me. Not that you're not a good man. But you're not my man. Nor will you ever be my man. And by extension you're not a good man for me. Does that make any sense to you?"

Adrian knit his brows. "I want to understand what you're saying but honestly, I think it's nonsense. We like each other, we enjoy one another's company. We are clearly attracted to each other. So what is the harm in following through on that to see where it leads?"

"Where it leads? You're here hiding out from your mother, who is telling you how your entire future is to unfold, and it does not involve a lowly photographer from across the pond, I can assure you that. Your mother would want to see me on your arm about as much as she'd welcome news that you were gay. Which I'm sure you're not. Not that there's anything wrong with that."

"No, no, of course not," he said. "But I wish you'd reconsider. Can't think of a better way in which to pass the next several days together. Think of it: you and me, alone together, nothing but the sound of water lapping along the shores, and our hearts beating as one." He waggled his eyebrows trying to milk his pathetic plea to her as much as possible.

"I hope you're not trying to pass yourself off as a poet."

He squinted at her. "Didn't work?"

She shook her head. "Nope. I think we should get back to the house and call it a night, before we happen upon more compellingly romantic holiday decorations that'll make me feel the need to rip my clothes off."

"Are you trying to torment me?"

"It seems to come with the territory with me. Sorry. Let's go back to the house and have a taffy pull or maybe we can practice our knitting or something equally unsexy so that temptation doesn't take hold again. Deal?" She reached out her hand to shake his.

"That is so not my deal, but I'll respect your wishes if that's what you'd prefer." He shook her hand, trying to hold on a little longer just because it felt so perfect.

Emma helped Adrian get settled into her parents' bedroom and retreated to her own room as soon as possible, locking her door just in case she failed in self-control (which was guaranteed, if Adrian chose to show up unannounced, in, say, an hour). She drifted off to sleep, thinking this royal rescue stuff she'd gotten herself into was apparently harder work than she could have imagined.

Unable to fall asleep, Adrian sent a quick email on his phone to Darcy.

"It's the damndest thing," he wrote. "For the life of me I can't remember a time in which a woman completely shunned my advances. It's making me crazy! Not to mention horny. It's made me realize that I rather like a woman who buckles at even the most fleeting of attention I pay them. Sure, it's a little pathetic, but it's so damned easy that way.

"I say that, but then again this challenge from Emma is a bit intriguing. The more unlikely she is to reciprocate my advances, the more determined I seem to be to press on. What the hell is the matter with me? Am I that daft? Or just desperately horny?"

Adrian could only laugh when he read Darcy's minimalist response a few seconds later.

"Horny."

Adrian sighed. It was going to be a long night.

Chapter Eleven

"**BOB**! You frisky devil, you!" Emma's mother Ellen squealed when her husband squeezed her ample behind as she mounted the steps to their beach house.

"I still got it, don't I sweetheart?"

"You've got something, that's for sure," she said with a laugh, opening the front door and then lugging her overnight bag and toiletry kit across the living room to the master bedroom down the hall. Her husband followed closely behind with his own duffle, and grabbed her just as she was about to enter their bedroom.

"Across the threshold, my dear," he said, bowing, and with a gallant swoop, lifted his bride up and over his shoulder to gales of laughter from her as she pounded on his backside to let her down. Her bottle-blonde graying hair dangled upside down from her roots toward the floor, and her face turned red from being the wrong direction.

"You're going to throw your back out again! And you know how long it takes to get an appointment with Dr. Farrington!" She flailed her arms and legs, an aging damsel in faux distress.

Bob crossed the doorway with her, not even bothering to flick on the overhead light, and instead dropped her onto the queen-sized bed, whereupon Ellen squealed even louder.

"Ouch!" she said. "What the devil is the lumpy thing under this quilt? It feels as if there's a body beneath me!"

"There will be in two seconds if I have any say—" her husband said with a growl, only to be interrupted by a near-naked Adrian sitting up abruptly, jarred from a deep sleep and face-to-face with two raucous strangers who seemed about to have much better luck in the sack than he'd had.

The woman let out a scream that certainly would have woken the man up had he not already been frightened awake upon having a two-hundred-pound woman hefted atop him like a sack of concrete in the middle of the night. Adrian yelled, which then caused Ellen to scream louder. Bob fumbled for the nearest potential weapon, which unfortunately happened to be the lamp on the nightstand, and he had to choose between shining some light on the situation or clocking the stranger in his bed with the thing. Only he couldn't figure a way to get a good grip on it without the lampshade getting in the way.

"Robert!" Ellen shouted, invoking his birth name, something she reserved for rare occasions, like, say, if she was furious with him for having finished off the pie she'd been saving for her dessert. "Do something! There's a strange man in our bed and he's naked!"

Adrian, groggy but finally grasping what was going on, fumbled around for some more sheet to pull up over him as he wrested his way out of the bed, as if modesty was the most important thing at the moment—a hazard of the job when you were royalty, especially after your brother's been caught starkers in the tabloids. Besides, with an enraged man and shrieking woman at arm's length, flapping those family jewels at this moment would be a particular mistake, likely even jeopardizing their very existence.

But thank goodness he did cover up enough, or Ellen would've fainted clear away at the sight of this evidently well-endowed — if *People* magazine was to be believed — unclad crazy man standing over top of her.

"Robert! Call the police!" Ellen shouted, even though at that point she was perfectly capable of reaching the phone on the nightstand just as easily as he was.

In the distance, in the middle of her REM sleep cycle,

Something in the Heir

Emma heard what sounded like some sort of fracas and at first thought it was a really fun party she was attending in her dream. She was with Adrian and that little friend of his, who was making out with Caroline in a corner. Typical, that hussy. Emma was holding Adrian's hand and somewhere someone was introducing the royal couple and all of a sudden she realized that it was she! Well, it was they! Well, they were the royal couple that were being announced while Caroline sucked face with that Darcy fellow back behind the bar, where her hottie bartender was shaking cocktails just like he did the other night, oblivious that Caroline had gone to greener — and more sexily accented — pastures.

But the screaming was getting louder and louder and even though Emma was so excited that she was Her Royal Highness Mrs. Adrian Whatever-his-last-name-was, somewhere in the back of her sleep-fogged brain she recognized that squealing screaming sound—her mother. Surely her mother wasn't objecting to her being married to a prince. Hell, Ellen wouldn't object to Emma being married to a toad, for that matter. As long as the creature put a ring on it. But then Emma morphed out of the reverie of her dream and realized there was a whole lot of screaming going on.

Flummoxed by the sounds, she raced out of bed and down the stairs and back to her parents' bedroom, flicking on the overhead light to find a kerfuffle on a grand scale unfolding before her very tired eyes. As she assessed the situation she saw her mother on her back kicking her legs in the air like a toddler having a tantrum, her granny pants exposed, and her father — what was left of his hair askew atop his head like a nutty professor — fumbling around in search of what? A weapon? And Adrian standing there so damned close to his natural state that Emma's mouth dried up at the thought. She raced over to separate her parents from Adrian before any injury ensued, and found herself wrapping her body around Adrian to prevent her father from striking him with the hand mirror he'd just picked up off the dresser. Talk about seven years' bad luck!

"Daddy! Stop!" Emma shouted as Adrian slung one arm around her while still holding up the sheet against his crotch and inching ever more backward away from her father's reach. Emma couldn't help but notice how warm Adrian's body felt pressed up against hers, but she banished that thought immediately in order to prevent bodily harm from coming to him, not to mention emotional harm to her. *Adrian is off-off-off limits, down doggie,* she mentally repeated over and over.

"It's me, Daddy, Emma, your daughter," she shouted at her father above her mother's operatic yelping.

"Baby doll?" her father called out. "Sugar?"

"Yes, Daddy, it's okay. This is my friend, Adrian. He's not an intruder and he's not going to threaten Mom's virtue, trust me." She winked at Adrian. "Mom, you can calm down now. Everything is fine."

Her mother's noises settled down to a quiet whimper finally as her father regained his composure and smoothed his hair back into its normal slicked-back position. Adrian, though, held tight to Emma as he gazed with mistrust upon these two demented gray-hairs who'd accosted him. Her father was wearing a pair of very bright green pants with erect-standing English Pointers embroidered all over the things. His crisp knit golf shirt was red, white and blue plaid; his matching skills were notoriously ghastly. Adrian hesitated to look too closely at her mother, whose girdle was exposed from her kicking around in her floral print dress while flat on her back on the bed. He gave her a minute to straighten up before glancing at her again.

In the meantime, Emma noticed that Adrian was holding up the sheet only over the front part of him, and she could see in the nearby mirror that his back half was all hers to reach for if she just moved her hands a few inches downward, which she simply couldn't resist. It was a moral dilemma whether to look at the mirror, at him, or at her parents, who had no idea what was going on. Finally she had to suck it up and talk to her folks, keeping her hand firmly planted on that gorgeous butt of his nonetheless, hoping no one would notice in the dim light.

"Mom, Dad, or I should say, Ellen, Bob, I'd like you to meet my friend Adrian," Emma said, finally letting go of Adrian. Only Adrian realized there was no way in hell he was releasing her in this state, what with having had this hot girl pressed up against his sensitive male parts, one with whom he'd already experienced an unrequited make-out session already tonight. Just the mere touch of her body to his, coupled with a flashback to earlier in the evening, was enough to expose Adrian's true intentions toward their daughter to Bob and Ellen, a fact he would prefer to keep to himself, particularly under the circumstances.

He reached around Emma to shake their hands, holding the sheet around his crotch just so. All the while trying hard not to stare at Emma in her tiny pink camisole top with her luscious exposed belly — the one that was just in the most perfect contact with his own but a few minutes ago — and how much he'd love to be exploring that with his tongue instead of naked-meeting the woman's parents. All he knew was if his mother learned about this she'd kill him. That was, after frog-marching him down the aisle with that wretched Serena.

Normally Adrian wasn't naturally inclined to shake hands, being that most people bowed or curtsied in his presence. But he knew protocol was differed in the States, and he knew he had some making up to do in the parent department with Emma's folks. It was bad enough he was an uninvited guest, but to be one stark naked in their bed, well, he supposed it could be worse. At least he wasn't in it with their daughter in a mutual state of disrobing. Must look on the bright side…

"So very pleased to make your acquaintance," Adrian said, "albeit I'd prefer to have done so in a more conventional manner."

Bob eyed him with a modicum of suspicion even though Emma had already vetted the man. Nevertheless he stuck his own hand out, taking care to not get too close to Adrian in so doing, just in case he'd grab something else by accident. He'd lose his lifetime membership to the Manly Man Club for that type of transgression.

"To what do we owe this, er, surprise?"

"He's my friend, Daddy," Emma said. "Adrian and I were working together."

"Oh, a photographer?"

"Not exactly," she said, locking eyes with Adrian while trying to discern how much truth she could reveal to her father. "I worked with him recently and we got to be friends."

Her father looked from his daughter to Adrian and back again, sizing up the situation. The two of them wore game faces, not revealing anything more than one could while barely covered in the middle of the night. The fact that they had been in separate bedrooms on separate floors of the house attested to the veracity of the relationship.

"Not exactly the warmest of hospitality, dropping in on you like we did!" Ellen said, giggling. "Can't say I've ever had that happen to me before! I'm just grateful you weren't a dead body!"

"Since when have you ever found a body in your bed, Mom?" Emma asked, her eyes wide open, wondering what the heck had gotten into her vivid imagination.

"You missed the beginning of this whole fiasco, honey," she said. "Your father was being a joker and dropped me on the bed with a thud, right on top of your sleeping young man here."

Your young man. Leave it to her mother to slap on the possessive to the relationship. Wishful thinking, much?

"I suppose in hindsight it's all very funny," her mother continued. If they only knew Bob plunked her mother down on top of a very naked European prince. Her mother would probably pee her pants in horror at that one. But thank goodness this way Emma could be spared the indignity of maternal matchmaking with an entirely fruitless relationship. Because she'd not put it past her mother to try to pair her up with Adrian. Not that she wouldn't even without Emma's unwitting assistance. But throw in the royalty aspect and her mother would need a drool cloth to stop the slavering. Nevertheless, this forced Emma to think quickly to keep her mother from trying to pair the two up. It was what she did best. She winked at Adrian, indicating he needed to play along with her ruse.

"Adrian just got over a relationship with a colleague of his," Emma said.

"Oh, my, heartbroken over a girl?" her mother asked. She had a little bit of a ditzy old lady squawk to her voice, which sometimes made Emma cringe just a bit, especially when she was turning on the nosey.

"Actually..." Emma said. "His name is Darcy." She looked from her mother to her father and back again, then glanced at Adrian, who looked ready to flay her, something his ancestors probably did quite readily during the Inquisition. They probably first flayed then fricasseed their enemies over an open pit. While wearing suits of armor. And firing things from catapults. This was the extent of Emma's recall of European history of yore, so it was good she wasn't sharing her ignorance with Adrian, who was at that very moment stewing over being wrongfully outed from a closet in which he hadn't been hiding.

"Oh, so you're—" her mother started to say, then turned to her daughter. "Why is it the best-looking ones are always gay?"

Emma threw a surreptitious glance at Adrian. If her mother only knew. "I know, it's so unfair," Emma said with a pout.

"Excuse me, but—" Adrian started to say before Emma reached around and squeezed his behind to silence him. She clearly had the perfect touch to get her way, as he closed his mouth right up.

"Even right down to that delightful accent," her mother added. "Where'd you say you're from again?"

Emma piped in before Adrian could get a chance. "He's uh, he's British. Studying here for a while."

"Interesting," Ellen said. "What are you studying?"

"Royalty!" Emma shouted out before giving either of them a chance to come up with something better.

"Why would an Englishman, who is steeped in royalty in

England, come to America to study that?" her father chimed in.

Emma felt like she ought to be wearing tap shoes, dancing around this mine-infused conversation as she was. "It's just that—"

"While there is clearly an American fascination with our royalty," Adrian said, picking up Emma's slack, "there's an equal fascination on why Americans are so obsessed with it. After all, you Yanks went out of your way to get rid of the royals, didn't you?" He gave her mother a sly wink, which she appreciated, keeping her on the inside and all.

"You mean like with Emma and me waking up in the middle of the night to watch the royal wedding of Kate and William?" Ellen smiled broadly, but Emma turned ten shades of red. Nothing like being called out as a shameless royal-sniffer by your mother in front of a prince to make you feel like a complete schmuck.

"Waking up in the middle of the night?" Bob cackled. "You don't know the half of it! They had their friends there too, fixed bangers and mash and had English Breakfast tea if I'm not mistaken. Although the bangers and mash were well worth the early wake-up call, mind you."

Oh Lordie, just shoot me now.

"Bangers and mash, eh?" Adrian asked Emma, one eyebrow cocked skyward. "What, no Pimm's Cup?"

"And those ridiculous hats they wore," her father continued, as Emma mentally melted into a puddle of embarrassment. "Feathers shooting everywhere. Practically poked my eye out. Couldn't believe they could find such monstrosities in the States. We have pictures if you don't believe—"

Adrian's grin grew wider the more details were revealed of Emma's secret fixation.

"Daddy, let's stop blathering about nonsense," she interjected. "It's late, we're tired. And I'm sure Adrian would rather conduct a lengthy conversation tomorrow, when he's more conventionally dressed. Can't we please just get back to sleep?"

Her mother covered her mouth in surprise. "I forgot! We woke you needlessly! We're so sorry about that!"

"I won't even ask what brought you here at such a late hour," Emma said. "Just let me find my bed already!"

"Why don't we let your gentleman friend sleep here and we'll take the fold-out sofa in Emma's room," her father offered.

"No, I couldn't deprive you of your bed, sir," Adrian said. If he had an ulterior motive in mind, it would be conveniently cloaked in his newfound gay status. "Please, allow me. No need in having the two of you give up your own bedroom."

Emma's mother looked at Adrian, then Emma, then Adrian again. To her great dismay, there would be no matchmaking with this one, so she knew Emma's honor would be well-protected even with this man sleeping in her room. "If you insist," she said with a tired sigh. "After all, I could use a good night's sleep and was looking forward to sleeping late in the morning."

"By all means, madam," Adrian said with a bow-like flourish, laying it on thick, considering he was still for all intents and purposes virtually naked. Not to mention he wasn't one to have to bow to anyone in his lifetime.

Emma gritted her teeth and fixed a hard look at Adrian. How in the world was she going to sleep a wink with him in the bed right near her? Naked, no less? Curses, he was too darned clever for his own good. But she could resist his charms. It might take some fortifications, but she could do it.

"Well...if you insist," Emma's mom said. "Can I help you make the bed at least?"

Emma interrupted. "No worries, Mom, I'll deal with that. You just get yourselves to sleep."

With that she grabbed the tail end of the sheet that had been dragging on the floor near Adrian, and twisted it around him three times, successfully covering up anything about him that might be even remotely tempting. And then she started wondering if she could dig up a snowsuit for him to sleep in for the next few days.

Chapter Twelve

"**WELL**, this is a fine mess you've gotten us into." Emma sighed as she plunked herself down on her bed.

Adrian was too busy gaping at the explosion of pink enveloping him from all corners of the room to reply immediately. Large, pink pipe cleaner flowers, fluffy fuchsia stuffed animals (including a monkey, hippo and platypus), a fuzzy pink telephone even, all competed to distract him from the rest of the world. It was as if the bright color had vomited all over the room in an act of cheery vengeance.

"Let me guess," he said drily. "You like the color pink?"

"Ya think? Truthfully, when I was a girl my grandmother decided I liked the color pink and so it became my de facto color. I'm relatively neutral for it, when it gets right down to it. But what could I do? I didn't want to make my grammy feel badly so I just let her do it. And now that she's gone—" Emma's voice faltered. "It would be like getting rid of a piece of her to change it at all."

Adrian had been preparing to repudiate the characterization she'd wrongfully lumped on him, but now that she seemed so sad about her grandmother, how could he even go there? Instead he got up and went over to her and reached out to pull her into a warm hug. Until she pushed him away with both hands.

He squinted his eyes at her. "What was that all about?"

Her eyes tracked him from his ankles to his chest and back again. "Do you really need to ask that? The only thing between you and me is a flimsy bit of eight hundred thread-count cotton. Not gonna happen. I promised myself: no more men." She shook her head vigorously.

Adrian grimaced, his lips pursed together in frustration. What was with this woman and her ridiculous resolution? Just because there were some bad apples out there didn't mean he was going to follow suit. Although if he were to be honest with himself, if he thought his mother was outraged by his failure to fall into line over Serena, she'd be downright apoplectic to consider him having any sort of relationship with a commoner from across the drink. There was unreasonable and then there was unreasonable. So maybe Emma wasn't so off-base after all. While it would be easy to answer those throbbing impulses (and one look down would indicate that adjective wasn't much of an exaggeration), a moment's pleasure could lead to a lifetime of Emma hating his guts, and he wasn't interested in making enemies with her now that they'd become friends. He'd just have to befriend a cold shower.

"Look, Emma, I can't exactly hide my feelings toward you.' He looked downward with a sheepish grin. "That happens when you're only wearing bedclothes. And by that I literally mean the clothes for the bed. But I respect you too much to work my wiles on you. And believe me, my wiles are pretty workable. I suspect we both know we'd have a hard time making a go of it, regardless. Just too many complications."

Emma snorted. "I'll say."

"Believe me, I have enough I'm trying to figure out right now. It would be unfair to both of us for me to throw 'us' into the mix. I'm still trying to figure out how I'm going to kill my mother's current plan for my life destruction."

They both laughed at his exaggeration, even though they knew it would destroy the life he'd choose if his mother forced him into a marriage with Serena.

"Friends?" Adrian asked her, his outstretched hand a gesture of solidarity.

"Friends," she said, shaking his hand. "Now, let's get you set up in this bed so that we can catch some shut-eye."

Although she knew shut-eye was far less likely to occur now. She'd be sleeping with one eye open the whole time, worried she'd have to fend off his advances once his own resolve dissolved.

Chapter Thirteen

DARCY traced his footsteps repeatedly in front of the hostess station at the intimate Italian bistro Caroline had directed him to. He feared he would soon wear a pathway into the tile floor if the woman didn't get a move on. Clearly she was avoiding public exposure, sending him here, as quiet and secluded as the restaurant seemed. He could barely tell another patron was even dining at the place.

He was about to abandon his cause when he saw the door open and he thought perhaps he heard a choir of angels break into a harmonious song of praise. Either that or he'd lost his head momentarily. Which was more than likely the case, because before him stood a much sexier version of the redhead he sort of half-noticed at the reception. She must have cleaned up well or something, because he sure didn't remember her *that* well. But this woman in front of him, well, she was smokin' hot, with her flame-red hair licking a trail past her shoulders and smoldering green eyes that had captured and held his gaze.

He wiped his sweaty palms on his pant legs and quickly extended his hand toward her.

"Darcy," he said with a sly grin. "I think we've met."

"Ah, yes," Caroline said. "Darcy with the hyphenated name. How do you do, yet again?"

"I do just fine, now that you've arrived," he said, that adorable accent of his nearly causing Caroline to betray her exterior coolness. Soon enough he'd know it was just a ruse and she'd be all over him like a down comforter on a freshly made bed. But until then, she could play it cool.

"I've made your day then?" Normally she'd be thrilled if she'd made a handsome man's day, but for some reason she really wanted to pluck his last nerve, just for fun.

Darcy nodded. "Well, I can't quite proceed with the plan

without you, can I?"

"In that case perhaps you should cut to the chase."

He shook his head. No way was he going to get in and out that fast with this one. He wanted to take his good old time, savor the moment. "What say we enjoy a nice meal together, break some bread, share some fine wine while we talk this through?"

"You had me at fine wine," she said with a wink. No point in him knowing she'd have even stuck around for a cheap bowl of pasta.

"So," Darcy began, raising his glass after they placed their orders and their drinks had arrived. "Here's to a long and fruitful partnership."

"I think I'd best be a bit wary of your intentions, Mr. Darcy Hyphenated," Caroline said. "I wasn't operating under the assumption anything long or fruitful was before us. I thought it was merely going to be a quickie relationship." She arched her brow suggestively.

He laughed. "It may well be a quickie, given our time constraints. But perhaps we can extend the pleasure a bit longer, if the need calls for it."

"And what, might I ask, is this need, exactly?"

"My need is pure and simple: safeguard the prince, at all costs."

"Oooh, you remind me of Kevin Costner in *The Bodyguard*, getting all manly and protective like that." She licked her lips suggestively.

"Laugh all you want but it's the truth. Adrian is like a brother to me, and I'm his right-hand man. Which means I will do what I need to ensure that he is safe and happy."

"Wow, I wish I had someone hanging around whose sole

job it was to make me happy." Caroline took a sip of her wine. "So then, who's in charge of making you happy?"

Darcy sat up taller for a second while he pondered that question. "Come to think of it, I don't believe there is someone out there who's taken on that project. Except maybe my mum."

"And yet you'll drop everything to protect this Adrian guy?"

"'This Adrian guy' is the heir apparent to an entire nation! Of course I'd protect him. Our country needs him!"

"Okay, okay, don't get so defensive!" She held up her hands in surrender. "I was just trying to get a reaction out of you anyway!"

"Mission accomplished," he muttered under his breath. "Let's dispense with formalities and cut to the chase. Enough of this chitchat. I think we need to go down there, wherever they are, to check up on them. Him. Whatever."

"And do what? Say 'we don't trust you children to handle your own affairs, so let the grown-ups take over?'" she said. "They're adults, Darcy. I think they can handle themselves!"

"You would think that," he said. "But you don't realize, Adrian has never been on his own before. He's gullible."

"Gullible? Are you implying he's gullible to the manipulations of my untrustworthy friend? That's absolutely ridiculous! She was a Girl Scout, for goodness' sake. She's no doubt taken him under her wing to save him. She's probably working on her rescue badge, as we speak. Gullible my ass!"

Darcy held his own hands up in mock surrender. "Fine, then. Don't go getting your knickers in a twist, sweetheart. Let's try a different tack. Maybe they're both in over their heads. Maybe they need some outside guidance."

"A) I'll disregard the pejorative sweetheart comment, and B) honestly, I couldn't disagree more. He needed to get away — you said so yourself! — and quite frankly, Emma could use the diversion," she said. "She's a great gal, but she's sorta lonely. She really could use some, uh, entertainment. A male diversion. A boy-toy."

Something in the Heir

"What the bloody hell do you mean, a boy-toy?"

"You know, a little fun distraction. A little tête-à-tête if you will."

"Are you mad, woman? This is the future king of Monaforte you're talking about!"

"Do you mean to suggest by the way you phrased that that your boy doesn't get a little on the side every now and again?"

"Well, yes, but," he stammered. "Er, that's, well, that's different!"

"Different because it's on his terms, not hers?"

"Perhaps," he said. "And different because he's vulnerable to gold-digging women."

"Oh, puh-lease," she said, pounding the palm of her hand on the table. "Don't even go there. Emma is a self-sufficient woman. She doesn't need some wealthy pretty-boy Euro-trash princeling to sweep her off her feet. That is so not my friend."

"Euro-trash? *Euro-trash?*" Darcy's eyes practically bugged out of his head. "Are you aware that you just insulted a man whose lineage dates back to medieval Europe? Euro-trash, indeed. As if!"

"Well, I can promise you that Emma's doesn't even date back to the *Mayflower*. Might not even pre-date the Tournament of Roses, I don't know. I'm sure she's not of pure lineage. But that doesn't mean she's not good enough for your homeboy. She's a great catch!"

"First of all, I hope that your home*girl* is not currently sinking her claws into Adrian. And second of all, it would be entirely a moot point anyway, because the whole reason Adrian's flown the coop is due to the fact that his mother is breathing down his neck to accede to an arranged marriage."

Caroline grabbed the wine and filled both glasses as the waitress placed their entrees before them. They waited for the waitress to grate Parmigiano onto their pasta before continuing.

"Arranged marriage? They sure do hearken back to the Middle Ages in that family, don't they? Is that how it's done when you're royal? Someone else tells you who you're going to be stuck with for the rest of your life? And then what do you do — you just have discreet affairs on each other because neither of you wanted to be wed in the first place, it's just a marriage of convenience, like you had to merge two empires together and, oh well, tough luck?! It's all very Henry the Eighth to me."

Darcy set his fork down to clap his hands. "I'm impressed. You were able to speak non-stop for several minutes while inhaling pasta, seemingly without taking a breath."

"Years of experience," she said. "But back to this marriage thing. If you're all about taking care of your bro, then why aren't you putting an end to this delusional ploy of his mother's? Can't you stop it? It's so old school to force a marriage. Didn't she get the memo, it's the new millennium?"

"Yes, well, the queen is decidedly 'old school,' in that case. But it's not because it's a merger of any sort of world powers. Rather it's her dearest friend's daughter. And she is of a certain lineage, which I don't doubt appeals to the queen's sense of propriety."

"Chick sounds like a control freak to me," Caroline said with a half laugh, taking a swig of her wine.

"She's not, normally. Really, she's a lovely woman. She's just got her head set on this, and I suppose her friend's daughter is keen to marry Adrian as well. After all, he'll be king someday, and who wouldn't want to become a princess?"

Caroline nearly spluttered her wine. "I'm sorry, but where I come from, these are truly foreign concepts. Something straight out of a Disney movie. 'Who wouldn't want to be a princess' is right up there with 'Who wants to be a millionaire?.' But now that I say it like that, I guess either of them wouldn't be so bad, would they?"

"My point precisely!" Darcy said, banging his fist on the table a little too loudly. Good thing no one seemed to patronize the restaurant, empty as it appeared to be. "Who's to say Emma isn't going to get all swoony and weak at the knees, fantasizing about a lifetime with a prince who sweeps her off her feet?"

Something in the Heir

Caroline shook her head vigorously. "Oh, no, no, no. See, you don't know Emma. That would be a deal-breaker for her. For one thing, she is so over men. The last thing she'd be after is a relationship with someone who is so off-limits it's not even worth starting anything. It's bad enough starting out one in which you might hold hope for a future, only to have it implode on you — and trust me, she's been through that ringer plenty. But it's a whole other thing to enter into something with a guy like your friend, who's either only after one thing with a woman, or who's ultimately stuck with her because his mother says so."

"Fine, so let's say you're right about this in theory. But you have these two young adults, both reasonably good-looking. Both with time on their hands. One in active defiance of his elders, the other just doesn't give a whit one way or another," he said, launching into his theoretical nonsense. "So what exactly do you think they're up to? How would they fill the time?"

"Knowing Emma, I'd say they're either watching classic television shows on cable, or she's teaching Adrian how to quilt. In between whipping up a few decent cocktails. She's good with a shaker, but not as good as me."

Darcy sighed. "I don't know. The longer he's gone, the more leery I'm getting with Adrian being out of my realm like this, and I simply can't fathom that this won't descend into hanky panky."

Caroline burst out laughing. "Hanky-panky! Are you for real? Just say it, say the real thing. Say 'I'm worried they're going to fornicate!'"

"Fornicate? Who uses words like that?"

She slapped her knee. "I do crack myself up sometimes. I assumed that's the sort of word you'd use if you had to go all technical on it. I have enough faith that my friend is doing no such thing that I'm willing to prove it."

"Prove it? Do you have some sort of sex-cam set up on her person? Or have you already set a private eye on her with listening devices and cameras?"

"I don't need anything so high-tech, honey," she said. "I

know my girl, and I know she's got too much restraint for a fly-by-night hook-up, even if your boy is such a 'royal' catch."

"Then let's put your money where your mouth is," Darcy said. "Take me down there so I can see for myself. As it is, it's going to get harder and harder for me to defend this escape plan of Adrian's, so at least if I know everything is fine it'll be easier to be on board with it."

"It's a deal," she said. "You'll see. That Adrian guy would be lucky to end up with Emma. But Emma's sworn off men, so there's nothing to worry about it. Of that I am most certain. Shake on it?"

"Shake indeed. And let's get an early start in the morning. The sooner the better."

Darcy had just returned to the hotel when his — make that Adrian's — text alert dinged. He pulled out the phone and read the imploring message from the queen.

"Adrian, my mother's instincts are telling me you're very much not sick. I do not know what you are up to, but I expect you to return my phone calls. You might be an adult, but I am still your mother."

Darcy sighed. He really didn't want to pull out the big guns, but maybe Caroline was right. Maybe he did need to intervene on his friend's behalf. Besides, Darcy was rather enjoying his little engagements with the queen. Never could he address her so candidly as he could while pretending to be her son. It was a fun little challenge, circumventing a lifetime of protocol. Maybe he could be considered for an Academy Award when this was all done.

"Contrary to popular opinion, I have far more on my plate than to be at your perpetual beck and call, mother dearest."

Something in the Heir

"Mother dearest? Since when do you disrespect me?"

"I wasn't disrespecting you, just driving home the point. I'm a grown man now. Please respect that I am my own person."

"Of course I respect that," she responded. "But you need to understand that as the ruling monarch, I must run a tight ship. I need to know everything that is happening, where and with whom. It's my job to be on top of every microscopic detail."

"Actually, Mother, that's why you have staff. They're there to do those things. It's why you have Lady Sarah at your disposal. There are people you pay good money to take care of the minute details of your life on your behalf."

"But it's not the same, Adrian. You're my firstborn son. You're my heir."

"Look, Mother, of course I'm your heir. But I'm also your son. And I just need some space," Darcy typed into Adrian's phone. "Please, I beg of you, just give me a few days to clear my head a bit."

He waited a few minutes until her reply dinged through.

"And then you'll agree to Serena without any more argument?" the queen asked.

"I won't make any promises about anything right now, Mother. I've already told you that."

"But what about this childish nonsense, wanting to get away from me so much that you'll not communicate with me? You're a grown man. Act like one!"

"Firstly, I am communicating with you. Just not in the manner in which you demand of me. Secondly, most grown men have the opportunity to make their own decisions. You make it abundantly clear that I certainly don't," Darcy typed. This was getting easier by the text message. He'd practically say the same thing to his own mother. Well, maybe not precisely. But if he could give a voice to his friend when his friend most needed it, what was the harm?

"Why, I just cannot believe you are behaving so scurrilously. This is not the son I raised!"

"It's late. I'm going to sleep now. Good night, Mother. I

love you."

"This isn't the last of this conversation, Adrian."

Chapter Fourteen

ADRIAN woke the way most men did in the morning. At attention. As if it wasn't bad enough practically on public display last night in front of her parents, he now had to have a command performance, alone with look-don't-touch Emma, in her psychedelic pink bedroom? To compound matters, he still had nothing but that darned sheet as a barricade.

He tried for a few minutes to wait patiently until he heard Emma stir, to no avail. He didn't dare get up and wander into the hallway in search of a bathroom, in order to avoid coming face to, well, you know, with her parents. That would be a bad plan, under their current guise of Adrian batting for the home team. Though in truth it would be a bad plan even if they were they not feigning this ridiculous story Emma hatched on the spot last night. God, what in the world had he gotten himself into? Maybe his mother was right. Maybe he should just go back home and succumb to her irrational wishes.

But no, actually. That would be the stupidest thing he could do. And for what it was worth, while this current situation was certainly a bit of a sticky wicket, it was actually rather challenging. And interesting. Even fun, if he were to admit it. All sorts of intrigue, minus the danger of anyone getting hurt, or stuck in a bad marriage. All good. Well, if only he could take care of this immediate inconvenience.

For thirty minutes Emma waited in the dark beneath the relatively chaste safety of her grandma's quilt, not sure of the appropriate protocol when sharing a bedroom in such close proximity to a European prince on whom she had a royal (excuse the pun) pain-in-the-ass crush while her curious parents slept within shouting distance, under the mistaken impression they let loose a royals-obsessed gay grad student into their presumably heretofore pristine daughter's bedroom. Knowing all the while if it was purely up to Adrian's libido, removing his (and of course her) common sense from the equation, the two of them would have been going at it like rabbits the whole night long and at the moment be sweat-drenched and only finally drifting off to a very satiated sleep. As it was she was thoroughly exhausted, considering it wasn't exactly easy to sleep practically next to a very gorgeous, very eligible, very receptive and very naked man as she had while fighting natural instincts. Ooohhh, what was a girl with too much common sense and bad romantic history with a long succession of losers to do?

She had to pee so badly, but didn't dare get up for fear of waking him. Though on second thought, perhaps slipping out while he was asleep made more sense. Talk about awkward, being there when he did finally get up. And then she heard it.

"Pssssst."

"Is someone there?" she asked, not knowing how to respond to his whispered contact.

"Pssssst," he repeated. "Are you awake?"

"Yeah. You?" Nothing like asking the obvious.

"You could say that," he said, looking down at what was without a doubt quite wide awake and ready to take the world (or at least Emma) by storm.

Unfortunately for Adrian, Emma chose then to click on her bedroom lamp. Bathing him in more than enough light to betray that morning wood, better known in his neck of the woods (heh heh) as morning glory. Glory indeed. Would be far more glorious to be able to put the damned thing to use.

Emma glanced over at Adrian, then immediately looked away, awkwardly and transparently pretending she hadn't looked in the first place.

Something in the Heir

"I sort of need your help," Adrian said. "I haven't got any clothes here, and I left my washing-up things in your parents' room. I'm not quite clear on what to do with myself right this moment."

Lord she could think of a thousand things but she wasn't going there. For that matter he could think of an equally vast number of diversions that would make them both far happier. Instead they each remained perfectly still in their respective beds. Until Emma took the hint and got up, revealing her cute little pink boy shorts pajama bottoms had wedged up her perfectly rounded behind while she slept, leaving Adrian to groan in misery.

"I'll just excuse myself to the restroom and retrieve your things, then you can take a turn," she said, blushing.

"Take your time," he said, not at all meaning that.

While she was gone he stood up, wrapped the sheet around himself like Tarzan, and wandered her room, noticing all sorts of details he hadn't seen before: a picture of her playing tennis with her mother; a photograph of her standing next to a plump, gray-haired woman with the sweetest blue eyes and a crown that said "World's Best Grandma"; a picture of her parents and grandmother flanking a very young Emma dressed like a bride, with white dress and veil on.

"My first communion," she said, surprising Adrian by barging in on him mid-snoop. "Mother refused to submit to my demands for a tiara. Instead I had to settle for the veil."

"You look adorable," Adrian said. "Clearly you'll make some man a beautiful bride."

Emma shook her head hard. "Uh-uh. No way. Not gonna happen," she said, balking. "My life is fine just the way it is, thank you."

"But weren't you just saying you were in a funk? Or was that some other photographer I've kidnapped in order to facilitate my sudden flight from responsibility who told me that?"

"So glad you have an elephant's memory," she said. "I tell you something, assuming you'll forget it in an hour, and instead you throw it back at me when I least expect it."

"I'm not throwing anything at you! I simply said you would be a beautiful bride. And you would be."

"Except I'm not going to be a bride. But thanks for the compliment."

"So if not a bride, then what?"

Emma lifted an eyebrow. "Must I have a man to make my life complete? Maybe I'll take some time off to go work in a refugee camp in Hungary. Would that make me a more worthy human being?"

"There is no worthy or unworthy here, Emma," he said. "It's only about what you want. What's right for you. And only you can decide that, which of course you know full well, based upon the overheated reaction I am getting by merely referring to the concept of being a bride to you."

"Overheated?"

"Perhaps that's too harsh a word. Defensive, maybe?"

If she was being completely honest with herself, upon further consideration, perhaps he should have said "undersexed," which could possibly explain the overheated reaction of which she was sort of guilty.

"Oh all right. Maybe I'm being a bit prickly. But I get frustrated with people always asking me 'When are you going to get married?' or 'What are you going to do with your life?' The fact is I *am* doing something with my life! I have a job, I own a home. I'm already living a life. It's just not fitting into the cookie cutter mold that society seems to want to impose upon me."

Adrian turned to face Emma, and, placing his hands on either side of her face, pulled her closer to his.

"Emma, *you* know what's best for you. No one else. Don't let people's opinion undermine what you want and need," he said, feeling the pull of her hazel eyes, the golden flecks in them practically sparkling. And then he leaned forward just a little bit more and pressed his lips to hers. Just enough for Emma to be forever grateful she'd just brushed her teeth, while not giving a care he hadn't. And hoping that he didn't have to excuse himself to the bathroom too quickly, especially since she'd forgotten his stash as promised. So instead of worrying about all of that, she just yielded to the moment and the impulse and the really amazing feeling that marooned her whenever she was in such intimate contact with him.

Adrian snuggled in closer to Emma, his hands guiding her lower back so that there was no mistaking they were warming up to one another. Yet again. Make that grinding up against one another. Yet again. Before they knew it, Adrian had Emma up against the bedroom door as she hushed their silent gasps against the potential of parental interception, which could come at any minute, while her one leg tried to jimmy up Adrian's body as if she were climbing a fire station pole. Make that a stripper pole. Emma pulled him closer by grabbing onto his lovely behind, just beneath his bunched-up Tarzan-style sheet pajamas, which elicited a giggle.

"You're laughing at me at a time like this?" he asked, rubbing his nose to hers.

"I'm not laughing at you, it's more of a laughing with you," she said. "This sheet is sort in the way."

"We can do something about that," he said, trying to reach down with one hand to loosen it up in the hopes it would drop of its own volition.

"Here, let me," she said, trying to untangle it, made all the harder because she was pressed into it. And him. And it. Oh, God.

"Yoo hoo! Emma?" she heard from just down the hall. "Emma Leigh! Did I hear you up?"

With that sounding alarm, Emma practically pushed Adrian onto the ground, nearly taking his sheet with him. Which on the one hand would have been a good thing – had her mother not been just feet away from her bedroom door.

She had to think fast. "Mother! Shhh! He's still sleeping!" Emma's mother would feel awful if she woke their houseguest yet again, so she knew that would keep her away.

116

"In that case, I'll leave you to sleep longer. Let me know when you're ready for breakfast!"

Not again. Thwarted just in the nick of time, dammit. Emma stared at Adrian, whose ever-so-earnest deep blue eyes implored her to pick back up where they were so rudely interrupted. Those eyes, those very, very, blue eyes.

"Did you know your eyes turn to sapphire when you're, um, horny?" she asked him, which caused him to burst out laughing. She had to put her pointer finger to her lips to warn him to quiet down to keep her folks at bay.

"What is this American word you're saying?" he said with a crooked smile, deliberately putting her on the spot.

"You know! Hot and bothered. Hot-to-trot. Amorous." She always knew how to deflect an awkward situation, just by making light of it. Which might be why she hadn't been getting past the awkward roll-in-the-hay phase lately. That and her determination to avoid any sticky emotions and even stickier hurt feelings.

Adrian got up and pulled Emma back toward him, as they tumbled against her bed. "It's true. You make me hot," he said. "I wouldn't say you bother me, but I will be bothered if I can't do anything about how hot you've made me."

"But my mother's right down the hall," she said, her voice pleading. "She can't know anything. She thinks you're gay! How would it look if all of a sudden she caught us like this?"

"I'm willing to take a chance on that," he said, chuckling. Which must have meant he was desperate, putting his reputation on the line with his gracious hosts. Even though he didn't actually have any particular reputation while posing as the faux student Emma had purported him to be. In which case, there wasn't much image to destroy, was there?

"Oh, no, no, no," Emma said, opting to be the party pooper. "My mother's timing was impeccable, just as I was losing self-control. I have to remember I'm not swimming in this pool anymore!"

"Oh but swimming is so much fun. So many strokes to

learn," Adrian said. "You don't want to stay out of the water because you're too scared to splash around a bit, now, do you?"

"It's not that I'm scared. It's just that I'm, oh, I don't know what I am. Maybe I just don't know how to swim."

Adrian drew her chin toward his face with his hand. "I know what you are. An intelligent, beautiful, fun, warm, generous woman to whom I am impossibly attracted."

Gulp.

Impossibly attracted? That sounded like exactly how she'd describe her feelings.

"I want you, Emma," he said, running his tongue along her lips, moving toward her ear, nibbling on the lobe, following the shape with his tongue, breathing so closely to her it could only arouse her already overly stimulated feelings even more.

Emma groaned. "I'm not being clear-headed," she said. "Despite my better judgment, I'd love nothing more than to see where this could go. But the sensible part of me knows it can't go anywhere, so I can't set myself up for hurt. I'm sorry, Adrian. Really I am. Because under other circumstances…"

Adrian inched one hand beneath her tank top, which was already riding up, and the other reached down to just where those bottoms had disappeared between those adorable cheeks. And he thought he was going to die, first because he couldn't believe how amazing his hands felt precisely where they were at that moment, but then also because he remembered he still hadn't made it to the bathroom from the night before. But he was willing to sacrifice for the cause, if the cause was willing to yield to the sacrifice. His upper hand reached around, finally at its destination, and he weighed her soft breast in his palm, his fingertips toying with her hardened nipple. She gasped.

"You are so not playing fair," she said in between shortened breaths.

"All's fair in love and war," he whispered as he made his way down her neck with small kisses and tiny nips. As he maneuvered his hands on either end he insinuated his knee between her legs, allowing her free reign for her to press down on him and relieve her need.

"You've got your technique down to a science," she said as she moaned as quietly as possible.

He knew he didn't want to chalk that up to many years of experience. Talk about a buzz-kill line.

"You inspire my creativity," he said instead, giving a little mental pat on the back for that one.

"Isn't creativity what killed the cat?"

"I think that's curiosity."

"I could argue that you're being awfully curious right now," she said, letting out a tiny groan as his fingers finally reached their destination, at the warm, moist juncture of her gorgeous, toned legs.

"Ah, but isn't curiosity the mother of invention?"

"That's necessity," she said.

"And it seems to me that necessity means need, and right about now I need you and you need me, so what a perfect pairing!" He slid his fingers between her slick folds and she could have about killed herself for being such a sucker but oh, wow, that was so perfect. "God, Emma, you're so wet for me." His breathing was getting harder, neck and neck with hers.

"You're turning me into a shameless hussy," she said, moaning yet again as her head fell back in sheer pleasure. Between Adrian's mouth and hands she figured she had all of about thirty seconds before she went over the top.

"I would argue you're anything but shameless," he said. "You're practically glowing you're so perfect. No shame in enjoying a little pleasure. No shame at all."

Emma's instincts were telling her to grab a hold of that sheet and rip it off and mount the man, *stat*, but then again her instincts clearly left a bit to be desired. Plus, he was taking care of her just fine, so maybe she could let him finish his business and she'd worry about the rest if she could just—

"What was that?" she asked, her ears perking up, sure she heard someone outside the door.

Adrian, meanwhile, had begun inching down her body, landing small kisses and licking a trail right to where his hands had been masterfully working their magic.

"Did you hear that?" she asked again.

But Adrian ignored her, shimmying those boy shorts off in one swift move, spreading wide her legs, and when his tongue finally, *finally* found that perfect spot, she nearly screamed out loud, which would surely have been the worst day of her life, sending her parents rushing in, fearing as they would for her safety, only to find their on-second-thought-maybe-he's-not-so-gay houseguest with his head buried between their daughter's most willing legs. Instead she pulled a pillow over her head and bit down on part of the pillowcase while she pressed Adrian's head closer still, telling him in no uncertain terms that what she said and what she meant might have conflicting intentions, but to just do what he was doing and the rest they'd worry about later.

For a few minutes Emma just let herself yield to the pleasure of this man's mouth stroking her just in the right places. For a moment or two she didn't think about the fact that he was royalty or damn near betrothed to some other woman (well, not willingly, at least). Instead he was just a red-blooded man with a toolbox full of useful skills and, hey, she sure could use a handyman every once in a while, right? Emma thrust her hips toward Adrian as she grew closer and finally she reached climax, trying so hard not to scream into the pillow and instead focusing her energy on clutching on Adrian's head, willing his mouth to remain till he'd wrung every last bit from her.

As she lay there panting, she realized she was mentally wrestling with whether international protocol required that she reciprocate the honors, which of course meant she was still on board with this plan that she purportedly was opposed to. Meantime, Adrian scooted back up toward her and took her mouth in his, pressing his very expectant self up against her. What was a girl to do under the circumstances but reach her hand down to see for herself the truth about what Adrian was packing? After all, it was only good manners, right?

Except then the doorbell rang, and a minute later Emma's mother was banging on her door and oh, my God, what now? She said there were visitors, Caroline and some man?

Adrian, meanwhile, was shaking his head no, back and forth, back and forth, groaning and muttering something about being so close, but yet so far.

Chapter Fifteen

"**WHAT** about the words 'I want to be alone' did you not understand?" Adrian whispered through gritted teeth to his friend. "I was this close." He held up his hand, and you couldn't fit a tiny sugar ant in the narrow space between his thumb and pointer finger. "But no, you have to go trying to land her friend by persuading her to take a little road trip to rain on my parade."

"I'm telling you, mate, I didn't know I was going to be barging in on anything," Darcy pleaded. "You know I'm not that kind of guy. After all, I'm your wingman!"

"Yes, well, use those wings and fly off somewhere far, far away." He flicked his fingers at him. "It's bad enough I'm dealing with the parents." He nodded toward Emma's folks, who were chattering with Caroline for a minute at least.

"They seem like friendly folks," Darcy said.

"They think I'm gay," Adrian said.

"Gay? What the——?"

"Don't ask," his friend said. "In the confusion of their late-night arrival and interrupting me from a sound sleep, somehow Emma thought it would be a brilliant idea to suggest I was a gay graduate student with an obsession with royalty. Oh, and they think some chap named Darcy is my ex-lover. So welcome to the club."

"You've gone and changed my sexual preference without even checking with me?" Darcy said, eyes wide open, jaw dropped. "How am I going to work my wiles with the lovely Caroline then?"

"Gee, sorry. Looks like you'll need to get a room," Adrian said. "Go ahead and charge it to the palace. It's the very least my mother can do at this point, pay for us sinners with her vast cash reserves. Considering neither of us would be here were it not for her."

"Speaking of your mother," Darcy began.

"Is she all right?" Adrian asked, worried.

"Oh, she's as right as can be. Maybe even as right as humanly possible, in her mind at least," he said. "But I took the liberty of strongly expressing your opinion on your behalf. I hope you don't mind."

Adrian winced. If this could get any murkier. But he couldn't even be bothered with such nonsense at this point: he was busy trying to devise a situation in which he could get Emma alone and willing all over again. And worried he'd need an act of nature to get to that point. Which he was willing to work toward, if need be.

They gathered from the shift in the direction of the nearby conversation that their attention was being enlisted.

"So this is your Darcy?" Emma's mother asked with more than a hint of curiosity, lifting up his arm and inspecting him as if it was the sleeve of a sweater hanging on the sale rack at *Macy's*.

Adrian nodded. "Indeed, my good pal Darcy."

"But I thought you two had broken it off?" she said.

Caroline cocked her head and squinted her eyes, and Emma elbowed her softly in the ribs in the hopes she'd keep her mouth shut.

"Oh, right," Adrian said. "We did, but we've been friends for too long to let any hard feelings get in the way."

"Absolutely," Darcy said. "If Adrian wants to run around with other men and flaunt his eligibility, that's his business." He shot his friend a sly wink.

Luckily Emma's father broke into the conversation, dressed in the infamous Statue of David apron, spatula in hand, to announce breakfast. Thank goodness. Perhaps with everyone being busy tasked with chewing food they'd not flap their lips needlessly.

Something in the Heir

As they walked through the small house to get to the kitchen, Darcy was struck with the odd labels all over the walls.

"What's with the words everywhere?" he asked Emma. "You teaching someone the English language?"

Emma laughed. "That's my father's little quirk," she said. "One of many. He has this labeling machine. It's like a gun-shaped thing and you punch in words and they print out on a sticky label. Dad likes to be sure we know which light switch lights up which light fixture. Same with the fans. You'll notice he also has little informational bits about where the keys can be found for the sliding glass doors and such. Just in case you can't seem to find them yourself."

"Don't think I'm not picking up on your sarcasm, young lady," her father said, swatting her with his spatula. "You're lucky I'm in a generous mood. Now eat your sausage."

Emma looked at Adrian and nearly burst out laughing. If only she'd gotten that far earlier in the morning. Poor Adrian could only be reminded of the state in which she left him, scrambling as they were to throw on some sort of clothes and race to the bathroom to wash up with their friends lingering in the doorway.

"Ah, is it bangers and mash, then, Mr. Davison?" Adrian said. "Replicating your daughter's little royal wedding brunch, are we?" He winked broadly at Emma, who frowned back.

Darcy was confused, what with the danger of an actual potential royal wedding on the horizon, one that his friend was desperate to avoid.

"Royal wedding?" he asked.

"Emma! You told him about us?" Caroline said. "How could you, under the circumstances?"

Emma had pulled Caroline aside en route to the dining room table just to brief her, and so she kicked her beneath the table as a reminder.

"Circumstances?" Ellen asked in her squawk of a voice.

"Caroline just meant we never told any guys about that,"

124

Emma said. "But Adrian and Darcy aren't exactly 'guys,' are they? I mean not in that sense. I mean of course they're guys. Just not *guys*!"

"Precisely," Caroline added. "Telling these two would be like confiding in your hairdresser. And of course I'd tell my hairdresser about our party."

"Tell him? He was there!" Emma said.

"Wait a minute," Darcy said. "Let me get this straight. You had a royal wedding party. In the middle of the night. Complete with bangers and mash. And hairdressers."

"And those huge hats, with feathers like weapons," Bob chimed in.

Shoot me now, Emma thought. *Put me out of my misery.*

"Were they working hairdressers, or just guests?" Adrian asked.

Emma blushed. "It was just for fun. They offered to do our hair. We had lots of food and we stayed up drinking all night. It wasn't as weird as it sounds."

"And every time the announcers said certain words, we all had to chug our mimosas. Curse that Pippa girl," Caroline said.

The guys looked at each other knowingly. The last thing they'd want to do with that Pippa girl was curse her.

"You Americans sure do know how to have fun," Darcy said with a tepid laugh. Emma frowned.

The cheeky bastard. We can't all gallivant off at royal balls and off-shore Mediterranean yachts for our jollies. Emma knew she couldn't say that aloud, not with her parents nearby. She had to remember to smack him one for that later on.

"Well, this is an unexpected surprise, having all these houseguests here," Ellen said, holding up her glass of orange juice to toast everyone. "Welcome to our home!"

"Not to worry, Mrs. Davison," Adrian said. "You don't need to worry about hosting Darcy and Caroline. They'll be fine staying at a nearby hotel."

"I wouldn't dream of it! And please, we're Ellen and Bob,"

she said, beaming.

"No, really, ma'am," Darcy said. "We wouldn't dream of imposing on you. In fact, Caroline and I have already checked into a hotel room, haven't we?"

Her eyes grew large, wondering what his plan was with that. "Uh, er, yes, lovely. Seashells everywhere, very cute room. Nautical theme."

"That's no huge surprise, being that we're at the beach," Emma said. "I'd be worried if you told me it had an alpine ski theme." She couldn't help but throw that one out there. It was how she and Caroline were with each other. The smart-assier the better.

"Touché." She said, then mouthed *I'll remember that* to her friend, with a nod.

"Thank you so much for your hospitality, Ellen, but I think you've got your hands full with my friend Adrian," Darcy said. "Having him here can be like hosting royalty."

Adrian nearly spat out his scrambled eggs on that one. As it was Emma choked enough that her mother felt the need to whack her on the back to dislodge any potential asphyxiation hazards.

"You all right, dear?" her mother said, worried.

"Yes, thanks Mom, I'm fine. Must've gone down the wrong pipe."

"Funny you said that, what with him studying royalty for his graduate degree and all," her mother said to Darcy.

Emma needed to steer the conversation in a safer direction. "Hey! You guys want to rent bikes and ride along the beach road?"

"Sorry, your father and I are tuckered out," her mother said. Which was fine, since she hadn't meant to invite her folks. Because the last person she wanted joining them was her mother. Or her father. The whole idea was to escape their prying eyes. Shame she and Adrian couldn't get that hotel room. Though they probably could. But the truth was that would be a bad, bad plan. Once again, she had already girded her loins, those ever-so-satiated loins, so to speak, to resist his temptations.

"That would be lovely," Adrian said.

"Can I ride a bike in heels?" Caroline asked. The woman was never in anything less than three-inch heels.

"We'll find a way," Emma said. "Darcy? You game?"

'Indeed," he said. "I'd love nothing better. In the meantime, why don't Adrian and I clear the dishes after this lovely meal?"

Oh, how he enjoyed watching Adrian play amongst the rabble. This would be too fun.

Once at the kitchen sink they were able to speak sotto voce.

"So you take the scrub brush here," Darcy said, holding the brush in his hand. "And you rub the bristles against the dirty plate, like this." He rinsed the food away.

"You've got me in stitches with your hilarity," Adrian said. "You're practically ready for your own stand-up routine. For your information I've already helped to cook a meal. Before you know it I'll be ready to live on my own."

"Rue the day," Darcy said.

"You never know, my friend," he said. "If push comes to shove."

"Speaking of shove," Darcy said. "I gave your mum a little bit of push-back. Just softening her up for you."

"Oh, God," Adrian said with a groan. "Is she sending out Interpol in search of me?"

"Not yet, but I do think she's suspicious of what's going on."

"Please tell me you didn't say anything hurtful."

"Nothing hurtful. Honest, maybe, but not hurtful."

"Honest?" As in 'I'm being truthful, Mother,' or as in 'Yes that dress makes you look fat' honest?"

"The former, absolutely," Darcy said. "I wouldn't call your mother fat!'

"Of course not. You also would never get me into hot water with my dear mother. So spill."

"Well, I might have suggested you needed to cut the apron strings. Or she did. I can't remember who had to do that."

Something in the Heir

"Perfect. I'm sure that went over well."

"Then I said even though she's never had to wear an apron since she doesn't cook."

"I'm sure she warmed up to that one."

"And I said something about needing to be a man."

"She tuned that one out, no doubt."

"The rest was just chitchat."

Adrian arched a brow. "Chitchat?"

"Just sort of closing out the conversation."

"Did you cut her off?"

"Not exactly. More like I said I had to go. Without letting her demand anything more of you."

"Great," Adrian said. "So the next person who shows up on the doorstep is going to be the royal entourage, with my mother at the helm, bearing the standard for the great nation of Monaforte. I'll keep my eyes open for that."

Chapter Sixteen

"I'M glad to see they taught you how to ride a bike," Emma said to Adrian as she pedaled alongside him.

"You laugh, but I begged my governess to teach me," he said. "She bucked it to her husband, who came in every day for three weeks until I mastered it myself."

"You had a *governess*?" she said, incredulous. "I thought they were only in the *Sound of Music* or *Mary Poppins.*"

"You're a strange bird sometimes," he said to her, laughing. "Pardon me for following the protocol of my nation as expected of the heir to the throne."

"What other heir-y things can you tell me about? Do you get special briefings from the prime minister? Full of top-secret information? Do you have a hotline, complete with a button that could launch missiles against the enemy? Do you *have* an enemy? Do you have a wardrobe full of crisply-pressed uniforms with brass buttons and epaulets and swords and crops for riding your dappled steed? Oh, wait, what about a suit of armor? I would love to see your suit of armor. And then could I see the crown jewels?"

"Ahem," he said, clearing his throat exaggeratedly. "I was thwarted in that attempt just this morning, lest you forget."

Emma felt her face turn hot. "Yeah, about that," she said. "While that was certainly a lovely little diversion—"

"Diversion? I beg to differ," he said. "It was far more than a diversion. At least to me it was."

"What I mean by that is that you know you're kicking a dead horse with this. Or barking up the wrong tree. Or—"

"I prefer to think of it as answering the call of the wild," he said with a wide grin. "Emma, I happen to like you. I find you most attractive. And charming and sweet and adorable and sexy. And fun to be around. And you are a wonderful tour guide, make a mean omelet, and your parents are terribly quaint."

"That's so sweet Adrian, but—"

"But I'm not good enough for you?"

Emma laughed. "How about you're too good for the likes of me? You know and I know that even if we fell madly and deeply in love, you and I can't ever have a future together. So why go there? We'll only get hurt. Or at least I know I will. And I don't think I have the stamina to go through rejection again. I think I spent three months in a dark room sobbing after that last break-up. It took so much out of me, and I promised myself I'd not get caught up in that again. Life's too short to waste on heartbreak."

Adrian sighed. "Let's not talk about this now. Let's just enjoy this day."

And it was a lovely day: unseasonably warm, the sun beating down to make it feel like late September rather than early December.

"Agreed?" he asked with a slight pout.

"Fine, agreed."

"Hey look!" Darcy shouted out. "No hands!"

"Darcy! Watch out!" Caroline yelled, a split second before he careened into a mailbox, his bike jackknifing as his head slammed into the metal box.

Caroline was there in a split second, tending to him, pulling tissues from her pocket to press against the gash on his forehead.

"Oh, poor baby. Does it hurt?" she asked. "Wait, don't answer that. That's a really stupid question. Of course it hurts. Are you all right?"

Poor baby? Emma mouthed to Adrian.

"I need some TLC, stat," Darcy joked as he pulled her closer to him. His friends couldn't help but notice the proximity of the two.

"In that case you've come to the wrong place," Emma said. "We used to called Caroline Nurse Ratched when she was a kid. If someone fell or got hurt on the playground she'd tell them to buck up and get a move on."

"That is so not true!"

Emma just looked at her with a deadpan face, suppressing a grin.

"Okay, so maybe it's a little bit true. But not because I'm cold and heartless."

"I didn't say you were cold and heartless, I just said you were Nurse Ratched."

"But she was cold and heartless!"

"Yes, but we knew better with you. Which made it all the more fun to tease you, since it made you so crazy. And for what it was worth, when my beloved pet bunny Hoofer died, you were a hundred percent sympathetic to me. You didn't yawn once while I cried, nor did you tell me to stop bawling my eyes out."

Caroline turned away from her friend to deliberately shun her. "So, Darcy, let's take a look at your noggin." She removed the tissue and peered at the gash. "Looks pretty angry. What do you guys think — maybe some stitches in there?"

"Lord, no. Anything but that," he said.

"I don't know. Looks pretty deep. Plus how dirty is that thing? Rusty metal? You probably need a tetanus shot." Darcy's face grew white.

Adrian started to laugh. "For as heartless as your friend was during childhood, Darcy was fearful. At least when it came to medical procedures. Needles and Darcy don't go hand in hand."

"Oh, please," Darcy said. "I'm not afraid of a little stick."

"Good, then," Emma said. "Because we're going to get that looked at and sewn right up. You're not going to come down with a bad case of trichinosis on my dime."

"I think that's tetanus, and it would be on your watch," Adrian corrected.

"I guess your governess taught you that?" Emma said, cracking a broad smile. "You do know I'm just giving you a hard time, right?"

"Yes, I do. Though I seem to recall a few days ago you told me you'd stop with that mockery, if I'm not mistaken."

"D'oh. You are so right about that. Let me apologize yet again."

"Not to worry," he said, helping Emma back onto her bike. "I'll find a way for you to make it up to me."

"Says you."

"Says me. Now let's get this patient fixed up."

Two hours later they were on their way back from the emergency clinic, Darcy with six stitches holding together his sliced forehead. He sat in the backseat with Caroline, who was being awfully empathetic for her usual non-doting self.

"If you want, I can kiss it and make it better," she said in treacly baby talk.

Emma glanced over at Adrian when they were at a stoplight and pretend-stuck her finger in her throat. *They've kissed?* She mouthed to him, her eyes wide open in surprise. He just shrugged. Clearly someone was moving fast there. Or at least it seemed to be from the outside looking in.

"Awww, that's sweet of you," Darcy said.

"Not sure that's the cleanest of options," Emma said. She shifted her rearview mirror in a futile attempt to spy on what they were up to in the back seat. The best she could tell — aside from her friend grimacing and sticking her tongue out at her — was that Caroline's hand was happily perched atop Darcy's thigh. Which in the scheme of things wasn't surprising, because Caroline was nothing if not a flirt. But from the texts she'd gotten from her, Emma was under the impression Caroline was set on playing hard to get with Darcy. Seemed that hard to get became Easy Ellie when bloodshed was involved.

"Now that we've eliminated bike riding from the schedule, our entertainment options are a bit limited what with it being off-season, but I think there's one putt-putt golf we can go to, if you're game," Emma said.

"Putt-putt golf?"

"Hardly Saint Andrews in Scotland, I'm afraid, but it's a fun diversion," she said. "Then we can take a walk on the beach, before it gets too cold."

She turned into the parking lot of Blackbeard's Treasure Hunt and pulled into the very first space.

"Looks like we won't have to wait in line at least," Caroline said, noting there were exactly no other cars in the lot.

A pimply-faced teenage boy with dark hair combed directly over his eyes so as to obscure himself from the world took their money while they all selected putters and golf balls.

"Guys against the girls? Or should we pit couple against couple?" Darcy asked.

"Most decidedly couples," Adrian said. "We're going to kick your bony—."

"Now, now, no need to get sassy," Emma said. "Even though we are so totally gonna kick your asses." She smiled at Adrian. "Didn't think it was particularly regal for you to be saying such things, but I, as a card-carrying member of the masses, am entitled to charming colloquialisms like that." Adrian gave her a little shove in protest of her mockery.

Adrian proved to be masterful at his short game, putting away shot after shot with barely a backward glance. Emma, it turned out, wasn't so bad either. "Dad made me take golf lessons when I was little." She scrunched her nose. "I didn't have the patience to keep up with it, but it works for putt-putt."

Darcy's putting skills were pretty good as well, but Caroline whacked the ball this way and that, rarely making it into the hole without a good eight attempts, and most of her balls ended up going over walls and into water traps. Four times she had to hunt for the thing. It was lucky the place was empty or she'd likely have downed a couple of victims with her wayward whiffs.

"It's a good thing you're beautiful," Darcy said to her. "Because if you had to rely on your golf skills to get by, you'd be a goner."

"Thanks a lot," she said, laughing. "I never claimed I was any good at this game!"

"Put her in a fifty-yard dash and she'd leave you in the dust," Emma said, coming to her defense. "Plus she makes a mean photographic assistant."

"Yeah, flirting with her subjects," Darcy said.

"I was not flirting with my subjects!"

"You mean to tell me that look you gave me that night at the reception, sizing me up, that wasn't flirting? I felt like human flesh on the auction block.."

"You weren't meant to see that! That was for my eyes only. Well, sort of." She winked at him and swatted him on the butt.

"You American girls," Adrian said, shaking his head jokingly.

"You mean we American girls whose mommies don't force us into marriage with someone?" Caroline said in a taunting singsong voice.

"Ouch!" Emma said. "She got you there."

"Indeed," he said. "Let's ignore that comment. I'm trying to forget about that."

"And you're succeeding quite well, mate," Darcy leaned over and whispered to him. "From the look of things."

"Most certainly," he whispered back. "But for a bad case of blue balls, I'm good to go."

Darcy burst out laughing.

"What?" the girls both asked, looking mistrustful of the guys.

"Nothing, nothing at all," Adrian said. "It's your shot, Emma."

Chapter Seventeen

THE foursome finished off the day at one of the few waterfront restaurants still open in the off-season.

They decided to splurge on a bottle of champagne with dessert.

Once the flutes were all filled, they raised their glasses.

"I promise you the last thing I expected when I agreed to that Library of Congress photo shoot was to take on a royal stowaway," Emma said. "But I can honestly say I'm so very glad you kidnapped me and forced me into royal subjugation." She laughed as she spoke.

Adrian leaned over and whispered into her ear, "That might have happened had I had five more minutes this morning, love. But give me time."

"Yes. Give him time, Em," Darcy, clearly a master eavesdropper, said. "He loves to subjugate his, er, subjects."

Emma blushed.

"That was not meant for your ears, my friend," Adrian said.

"Just trying to up your chances, mate."

Adrian squinted at him. "Thanks. I think I can handle this on my own."

"Uh, hello! We are sitting right here and can hear everything you're saying, you know," Caroline said. "Honestly. Men." She shook her head in dismay.

Adrian reached over to reassure Emma, who was seated next to him, and clasped her hand, twining his fingers with hers. It was so unexpected but felt so right, Emma decided she didn't want to be a naysayer right at that moment, so she held on tight.

"So what say you to a moonlight stroll on the beach after dessert?" Emma asked.

"Sounds perfect," Darcy said, glancing over at Caroline with swooning eye like a desperate puppy.

Something in the Heir

After Adrian paid the check with Darcy's credit card, they drove to a secluded section of beach that Emma knew well.

"This is a place I used to walk along with my grandmother," she said. "It's far enough away from the houses that it doesn't attract the tourist crowd. I love how it makes you feel like it's your very own island or something."

She decided not to make any jokes about Adrian probably actually owning his very own island, and instead they began to walk. At first they walked four astride, but soon the couples split off, with Darcy wrapping his arm around Caroline to ward off the December cold, and Adrian then doing the same.

"Don't think this means you're getting anywhere with me, buddy," Emma said.

"Not to worry, I know I'm up against an impenetrable army of man-fear," he said.

"When you put it like that, it sounds sort of silly."

"Gee, you think?"

"Remember back when we'd all go skinny dipping in the ocean?" Caroline said. Big mouth.

"And you and that Teddy—"

"So, how'd the stock market close today?" Emma said, trying to change the subject.

"Nice try. We want more information! Caroline's got dirt on Emma," Darcy said, singing that last part. "Come on, spill."

"Nothing to spill," Emma said. "Yet another in a long list of losers."

"Oh, come on, Ems," Caroline said. "We had fun, even if he was a jerk. I mean it's not your fault he was two-timing you!"

"Thanks, Caro. Feel free to toss in a few more ingredients in the 'Emma's-a-loser' soup."

Adrian stopped and pulled her closer. "You are not a loser, Emma. Teddy is the loser. Or was the loser. I don't know if he's lived to be a better man. If anything, you were the winner for not having been stuck with the likes of him."

"Oh yeah?"

"Absolutely. It's all a matter of perspective. When someone

136

imposes something bad on you, that isn't a reflection on you —it only looks badly on them. I don't doubt that it hurt your feelings but to let it change your mind about every man out there seems nuts."

"Nuts, eh?"

"Indeed. In fact, I think you should make up for it by skinny-dipping with me."

"Skinny dipping? Are you mad? In case you didn't get the memo, it's Christmas time! That water would kill you in about two seconds."

"Um, hate to disagree with you, Ems, but what about the Polar Bear Swim?"

Caroline and that big, fat, oversharing mouth of hers.

"First a guy named Teddy. Then a polar bear swim?" Darcy asked. "You got something for ursines?"

"No, I have no bear fixation. But yeah. Emma and I did a polar bear swim when we were in college. We came down here over New Year's, and on New Year's Day we joined about fifty other brave souls and took the plunge."

"You took the plunge and you didn't die, then?" Adrian asked, chuckling. "And it's even colder in January."

"As a matter of fact it was quite refreshing. Especially considering the hungover state we were in."

"Hungover, were you?" Adrian continued. "In that case, I'd say it's practically expected of you as a host to show your guests a good time. If you can do it half-drunk in the dead of winter, with a bunch of strangers, then surely you can with your good friends. On the count of three."

Adrian began to peel off his clothes, with Darcy hot on his heels.

Caroline soon joined in, wincing at her friend's lacerating glare.

"When in Rome?" She shrugged, then turned to Darcy. "By the way, don't get that forehead wet.".

Before she knew it Emma was surrounded by three naked

people, who were encircling her and taunting her to not be a weenie. And while Emma wasn't one to succumb to peer pressure, she had to admit the circumstances were a little unusual. It's not every day you had a future king and his right-hand man both naked as the day they were born, demanding that you strip your own clothes off for the cause.

"Oh, all right. Fine," she said as if someone was persuading her to eat Brussels sprouts against her will. "But when we did it last time, at least we had bathing suits on to keep us warm."

"No worries, darling," Adrian said. "You'll have me to keep you warm."

"He clearly hasn't considered he's going to be awfully busy keeping a certain part of his own self warm," Caroline said.

Emma started to laugh and Adrian helped lift off her sweater and unzip and pull down her jeans. 'Now we're talking.' He gave her a thumbs-up, and she couldn't help but feel she was swimming against the tide. In very frigid water.

The four of them held hands along the shoreline and counted to ten, and ran as one to the ocean.

"Bloody hell, it's *freezing*," Darcy shouted, gasping as he hit the water.

The girls just screamed and squealed. Adrian was the only one to dive underneath a wave, and came up shouting.

"If only the queen could see you now," Darcy said, laughing.

"On so many levels it would not be good," his friend said. "But that's what's so perfect about this. I'm me. Doing my thing. Without rules, without a palace, without bodyguards. I'm free!"

And it was then that Emma really understood how much fun it might not be to be owned by the state, or a family, or whoever it was who might impose their unacceptable standards on you. And to truly appreciate that she had the freedom to live as she pleased, even if she made stupid mistakes, like skinny-dipping in the Atlantic Ocean in December.

"Uh, guys, I don't know about you, but things are starting to turn numb on me," she said.

Adrian came up to her and pressed his ice-cold flesh to hers.

"Then let's warm you up." He rubbed her body with his arms and pressed himself against her so they were sandwiched as one. And then he leaned forward and kissed her, hard, pulling her mouth toward him and kissing her as if it was the most important thing he could do in the world.

And at that very moment, Emma knew she only wanted to be a part of whatever this thing was. Even if it couldn't ever go anywhere, at least she had the chance to live it while she could. It no longer made sense to live now for what might happen later. How stupid was that? She had a hot (well, cold) naked man in front of her at this very minute who wanted only her. Who was she to decide that was a bad idea?

When they came up for air, the two of them looked to their right, to see that Darcy and Caroline had made it to the wet, hard-packed sand along the shoreline and were rolling around in the sand like a couple of very happy canines.

"So much for Caroline playing hard to get," Emma said as the freezing waves crashed against them. "I don't know about you, but I need to warm up. You're doing as fine a job as possible under the circumstances, but I think body heat plus some warm clothes, maybe a fireplace, and absolutely no ocean water involved, is in order."

"Only as long as you promise I get to sleep in the pink palace tonight," Adrian said.

"Well you're not sharing my folks' bedroom," she said, grabbing his hand. "Come on, let's warm up!"

They wedged their cold, wet bodies into their clothes, even though clothes never seemed to want to go on over wet skin. Caroline moaned and complained that she was perfectly fine warming up the way she had been just minutes earlier, despite a near-Siberian wind chill factor.

"Yeah, well you two can warm up at the Loggerhead Inn," Emma said. "I presume you'll be able to get some extra blankets, being that you're the only guests."

"Heh. We won't need blankets to keep us warm," Darcy

said, giving Caroline *that* look. The one that would have made Emma roll her eyes, except she had the very thing on her mind, with one slightly bedraggled but nonetheless quite handsome prince.

"I just thought of something," she said to Adrian. "I can call you the Prince of Tides, now that we took our ice plunge into the Atlantic. Get it? Tides? Ocean?"

They all roundly booed her bad joke, and Adrian simply urged her to get a move on, heat blasting, as they dropped their friends off at the hotel.

Except that as Darcy and Caroline were about to get out of the car and their friends speed away in anticipation, Darcy's text dinged. Make that Adrian's text dinged, in Darcy's pocket.

Darcy and Adrian groaned in unison.

"Please, no," Adrian said as Darcy pulled out his phone and looked at the message.

"Oh, boy. You're going to love this one," he said to his friend and began to read:

"Adrian, it's me, Serena. We need to talk. It's sort of urgent. Name the place and I'll be there. I can't wait a minute more."

Chapter Eighteen

THEY were faced with an awkward dilemma, starting with what the bloody hell would Adrian say to her? She was no doubt going to tell him how desperately she wanted to marry him, and that he might as well yield to it because it was all but signed, sealed and delivered. Another problem was that he was supposed to be incommunicado. But if she spoke with him, then couldn't she find out where he was? And how awful would that be?

After a few minutes' debate, Adrian and Darcy decided it best for them to text a reply, telling Serena he could talk with her when he got back home. Whenever that was. Though with Christmas approaching, it was going to have to be sooner rather than later. Which made Adrian sad to realize that would be the end of his ever-so-enjoyable little escape from reality.

A few minutes after sending the message, she replied.

"Adrian, we have to talk now. It's urgent, it really cannot wait. Please, tell me where you are and I can meet you."

Adrian told her that was simply impossible, and that he'd let her know as soon as he returned. At that point, he turned off his phone, slipped it in his pocket, and they bade goodnight to their friends.

They beelined to the glowing fireplace the minute they returned to the beach house. Emma's mother was engrossed in some documentary about Prince Edward and Wallis Simpson on *BBC America*, undoubtedly only further reinforcing that Adrian must think her and her mother to be some strange Euro-groupies intent on delving into a world in which they entirely didn't belong.

"Do you mind my asking what you're watching, ma'am?" Adrian asked, making small talk.

"Oh, it's a scandalous story about Wallis Simpson. Do you know about her? Of course you must, being a British royal scholar and all. Why, that woman dug her claws into that man and ruined him," she said, wringing her hands at it.

Adrian chuckled at the academic commendations being bestowed upon him erroneously. "I'm sure I have heard of her somewhere along the way." His mother constantly warned him to avoid those types of foreigners who were after a quick entrée into royal society, not to mention bank vaults. If he'd heard it once he'd heard it a thousand times how badly he needed to marry one of his own. What that never explained was what if you didn't love one of 'your own'? Then what?

Adrian and Emma stood face to face by the fireplace rubbing each other's arms, trying to warm up. Only then did her father look up briefly from his book—yet another World War II story, a subject she thought he'd probably read until there was no more information to glean. But it was his obsession. That and tacky wide-wale corduroy pants. Tonight he donned bright green ones with embroidered red Santas on them. She figured if there was any question about whether Adrian would stick around with her family, this would send him packing right back to his small Mediterranean principality, stat.

"Where's Adrian's little fellow?" Ellen asked.

Only her mother would refer to a man's former "boyfriend" like that.

"They're staying at a motel not far away," her daughter said. "They insisted on not putting us out." She couldn't imagine juggling all the lies if everyone was under the roof the entire time.

"And here I was looking forward to a little slumber party!" she said. She looked at them and frowned. "You know you two look a little wet."

Well. No one thought about having to explain away that one.

"Um, yeah," Emma said. "We got caught in a small rain shower."

"Rain shower?" he mother said. "I thought it was crystal clear out when I looked up at the sky earlier!"

"Indeed," Adrian chimed in. "Strange sort of weather system. Just rolled in off the ocean and that was that. Maybe you needed to be right on the water's edge to get it?"

"Yes, a microclimate," Emma said.

"Microclimate? What were you doing on the water at this time of year?"

"We took a walk along the shoreline," Emma said. We were just having fun, enjoying the ocean."

"A few more degrees and you could've gotten some snow instead," her father said, not lifting his eyes from the page.

"You don't say," Adrian said. "That might explain why I felt like an icicle out there."

Emma shook her head. "I could give you a few reasons why you felt like an icicle."

"Oh really? Do tell," he said, challenging her. Only then did she realize she had to zip her mouth shut.

"Heh. Just joking." She stifled a yawn, stretching her arms out. "Think I'm going to call it a night."

"That's fine. Your young man friend can join me on the sofa to finish watching the show," her mother said, turning to Adrian and patting the seat next to her. "I think you'll find this royal scandal most fascinating."

Clearly Ellen had found one of her tribe once she learned he was gay *and* loved royals. Only thing better to her would have been if he could sort of un-gay himself so that he could woo her daughter. But some things weren't meant to be.

Adrian looked at Emma wide-eyed, imploring for an escape clause. No way could he be assured of keeping up the ruse without Emma to run interference.

"I think Adrian's still suffering from some jetlag, Mom," Emma said. "I'll just tuck him into bed and he'll sleep like a baby

I'm sure."

"If you insist," Ellen said. "But please feel free to join me if you can't get to sleep!"

"Most definitely," Adrian said, thinking he'd never dream of running the risk of being alone with her and chance spilling the truth.

"Good Lord, this is getting complicated," Emma said as she shut the door and slumped against it, warding off any more unwanted attention.

"You're not kidding. I think it's more private being a public figure than it is being a stowaway. At least around you!"

"How was I to know this place would become Times Square?"

Adrian walked toward Emma and pulled her up against him, his mouth just inches from hers.

"If it takes living in a circus in order to do this, I'll sacrifice for the cause," he said, leaning forward and ever so gently grabbing her lower lip with his teeth, before settling his mouth on hers for a kiss. He could feel Emma loosen up and finally just yield to his efforts. *So this is what it would be like if she stopped thinking and just went with it.*

"I'm so glad I finally got you all to myself," he whispered between kisses.

"I'm afraid this is as far as it's going to go, however," Emma said, pushing him away yet again. "We can't risk detection. My parents can hear everything."

"Are you kidding? Your father seemed thoroughly oblivious to the presence of other humans, engrossed as he was in that compendium he was reading. And your mother is glued to that television program. She's practically in Buckingham Palace, or Windsor Castle, or wherever it is those two were trysting," he said, a slight whiff of desperation to his voice. "Speaking of trysting, you promised me the pink palace tonight!"

"I know, I know. I'm really sorry, but I've had a change of heart," Emma said.

"Again?"

"A woman's prerogative to change her mind," she reminded him. "Believe me, it's not what I'd choose. But it's all just too complicated. It's making me exhausted trying to figure it all out. And now you've got that Serena girl putting the full-court press on you.

"Tell you what: I'll make a deal. After you clear up all this engagement stuff and you've convinced your mother that you would like nothing better than to have a little trans-Atlantic fling with the likes of me, and she provides her unequivocal stamp of approval — and it needs to be a royal stamp, maybe even an official royal decree, for authenticity's sake — then talk to me about continuing this, this, whatever it is this is." She held her hands out to try to encompass her confusion over it all.

Adrian pinched the bridge of his nose as if staving off a migraine. In all his years he'd never met such a steadfast rejecter of his advances. It was like she was some bizarre force of nature, a hurricane pressed up against his own gale-force winds of momentum to the contrary.

"It's a good thing I'm an honorable man," he said. "But I can't be held accountable for anything that might transpire while I'm sound asleep. I might develop a sudden sleepwalking habit, for instance. And with your bed right there..."

"I'll risk it," she said, handing him his T-shirt and shorts. "Now, off to bed with you."

Emma was the one who was unable to sleep, however, and

found herself before dawn curled up on the sofa, working on her grandmother's quilt.

"Hey," Adrian said, rubbing the sleep from his eyes as he entered the living room thirty minutes later. "You so anxious to work on that thing before the wedding you're never going to allow yourself to have that you got up in the middle of the night?"

He sat down next to her.

"Ha. Ha. You've got me in stitches. Get it?"

Adrian leaned forward and inspected her handiwork as she slid the tiny needle through the layers of fabric and batting.

"I don't know how you can even see what you're doing there," he said as she dipped the needle up then down five times before drawing it through.

"Trust me, at this hour I can't see it so well," Emma said. "I couldn't sleep, so I decided to commune with my grandma. It's what I do when I need to think. It soothes me."

"You needed soothing? I could've taken care of that, you know." He patted her knee.

She reached over and scratched his head. "I know you could. But it's not quite the same." She took a deep breath and released a long sigh. "As long as I could remember, I would sit next to my grandma as she worked away on those tiny stitches, for hours at a time. It was a testament to her commitment, that's for sure. Of course she was alone, so she had a lot of time on her hands."

"Your grandfather wasn't around?"

She shrugged. "He died when I was a baby so I never knew him. I guess my grandma sort of latched onto me as a coping device back then."

Adrian waved his hands. "I'd hardly call you a coping device. I'm sure she adored you."

Emma nodded. "Of course she did. I didn't mean it like that. I guess I was a really good distraction for her in her loneliness."

"What about you? Were you lonely?"

"Me?"

146

"You didn't have brothers or sisters, so perhaps it was a bit lonely for an only child?"

"Heck, I don't know. I guess that's why I found comfort in my grandma —she was always there for me. My parents always seemed to be so paired up with each other. But me and Grandma, we were a team."

Adrian glanced over at here. "You miss her a lot?"

"Like mad, sometimes. She was my calming influence. She's the one I'd talk to — oh, never mind."

"What?"

"When I'd have boy troubles. My grandmother always reminded me it was them, not me. When I got another puncture in my self-esteem, she was there to plug up the hole."

"So you watched your grandmother being alone all those years and it didn't make you yearn to have someone yourself?"

Emma set down her needle for a second. "Huh. I hadn't thought about it that way. Now that you mention it, my grandmother was all about wanting me to settle down at some point with the man of my dreams."

"Wise woman, your grandmother."

"Yeah but it's all an illusion. Don't you see that? That's why I'm just not interested in the pursuit anymore. For what? To get my hopes up, only to have my heart crushed yet again as some man steamrolls over it?"

"They don't all end that way, you know."

"For me they do."

"Maybe you're just frontloading your statistics so it appears skewed. Perhaps you've rid yourself of all the bad luck and from here on out it will be only good. Did you ever think of it that way?"

Emma just stared off in the distance. If that were the case, then she'd end up with Adrian. And she knew that wasn't going to happen. Not in this lifetime, anyhow.

"Can I interest you in a cup of tea?" Emma asked. "I'll put the television on quietly so you can keep busy while you're wide awake at the wrong hour."

She stood up, revealing that she was draped in a cheap-looking, too-long, zebra print straitjacket of sorts. Adrian just sort of stared at it for a minute, furrowing his brow.

"You think this is strange?" she said, her arms spreading across her coverall.

Adrian chuckled. "I'm sorry, I don't think I've ever seen whatever it is you're wearing before. It's just, I guess I'd say it's, um, interesting."

Emma spread her arms and gave a twirl. "You don't like my zebra Snuggie?"

"Snuggie?"

"Yeah," she said. "It's a super tacky trend from a few years back. To be truthful, I never cared for the things, but my grandma bought me this for Christmas one year, so it's something I've held onto as part of my collection of all-things-grandma. Usually no one sees me actually wearing the thing."

"Consider yourself fortunate."

She popped him jokingly on the head. "You're just jealous you don't have a matching one."

"Keep reminding yourself of that while I happily go on about my life not looking like a zebra about to be hauled off to a mental institution."

Emma stuck out her tongue at him as she disappeared into the kitchen to make him tea.

A few minutes later she handed him his cup of tea and then scrolled through channels until she found Nick at Night, which was hosting a *Beverly Hillbillies* marathon.

"What kismet! This is perfect. For you, good sir, no better taste of Americana than this, for your viewing pleasure." She rubbed her hands together with glee. "It's is the stuff of my childhood; it'll give you great insight into who I am. And not necessarily in a good way."

They sat quietly, the television turned very low, for a few hours, she working on her quilting project, he engrossed in Jed and Elly May, Jethro Bodine and Granny Clampett.

When Ellen awoke a while later, she suggested they invite Darcy and Caroline for breakfast. Adrian tried to contact Darcy, only to realize he must have turned the phone off the night before, so Emma texted Caroline, telling him Adrian wanted Darcy to switch the phone on for emergency purposes.

A short while later there was a knock at the door.

Since Emma was helping in the kitchen, Adrian answered it.

"Well, well, well, it sure took the two of you a long enough—" Adrian said as he started to look up, only to gasp at what stood before him. "Serena?"

"Adrian! It's about time I tracked you down!" she said, wrapping her arms around him in a tight squeeze. As she loosened her hold and her hand dragged down his arm to grab his hand, Adrian glanced down to notice a gleaming rock on the third finger of her left hand. *My God, it's even worse than I thought! She is so desperate to be engaged to me she got the ball rolling with an engagement ring of her own choosing?*

"Serena?" he stammered. "What might I ask are you doing here?"

"I could likely ask the same of you," she said, smiling in a devious way as she tapped him on the tip of his nose with her well-manicured pointer finger. "Not exactly your usual sort of hangout."

He pulled her out onto the front porch. "How the hell did you find me here?"

"Let's just say I have a close friend in the national intelligence service," she said. "I told you it was urgent and we needed to talk but you kept dismissing me."

"Because I didn't want to be disturbed!" he hissed.

"Calm down. Now, now, no need to get snippy," she said, looking around at the modest house, assessing his new digs.

"This part of your world domination tour?" she asked, arching her eyebrow.

"What is it you so desperately need from me, Serena?"

Just then Bob opened the door wearing one of those

nightshirts you see the dad in *'Twas the Night Before Christmas* wearing. Could things get any stranger?

"Son!" he said to Adrian. "Well, er, is son okay to say? I'm not sure about your type, if you prefer something a little less, uh, masculine?"

Serena's eyes bugged open and she nodded in query to Adrian.

"By all means, son is perfectly fine," he said. "Though I suppose it would be inappropriate to call you Dad?" He winked and forced a laugh, trying to deflect the entire conversation.

"Who's the little lady here?" Bob asked. "More company for breakfast I see?"

"Why breakfast would be lovely," Serena said, reaching out her hand to introduce herself. "I'm absolutely famished. I've been flying all night!"

Adrian glared at Serena. Geez, if Emma thought things had been complicated before, now they were in quicksand up to their thighs.

"Are you another friend of Adrian's?" he asked. "Though I'm sure you're not that kind of 'friend.'" He made air quotes around the last word.

Serena squinted at him, first wondering who this strange man in a dress addressing the future king of Monaforte so casually was, and secondly what in the world he meant.

"Serena is an old friend from back home," Adrian said. "We've known one another since childhood." He nudged her to just play along.

"Well, come on in and sit down, then!" Bob said as he ushered them both inside, his cheery voice booming in the early morning quiet.

"Adrian, would you ask Darcy and Caroline what they'd like to drink?" Emma shouted from the kitchen.

"I would, but they're not here. I can ask *Serena* what she'd like, however," he said, putting heavy emphasis on her name.

"Serena?" Emma said. "Good one! Are you trying to torment me or something?"

"I don't believe I've ever known anyone to consider me a torturess before," Serena said as she stood in the doorway of the kitchen, her arms crossed authoritatively.

Emma's ears perked up at the posh, accented voice of a woman a few feet behind her, and she spun around and took in all five feet nine inches of lithe, blonde and loathsome Lady Serena Montague. Thoroughly unwrinkled and very nearly perfect in an expensive-looking red silk poplin dress that made her look like a huge ribbon tying up an early Christmas gift for Adrian. The contrast to Emma's schleppy get-up was downright mortifying.

Emma dried her wet hands and tried to fluff her hair, realizing too late she still hadn't even brushed her teeth. And at least she could've looked cute in her adorable pajamas but instead had on that wretched Snuggie. It would hardly be a toss-up as to who showed better at this little smackdown.

"I'm sorry. Please forgive the way that came out," Emma said, stammering. "I've heard so much about you."

"Which led you to feel tormented upon my arrival?"

Adrian interrupted. "It's a long story. It really has very little to do with you, Serena, and much to do with my mother."

Serena nodded her head. "Indeed, which is what brings me here."

"Hup two," Ellen piped in before Serena could continue. "Let's everyone wash our hands and get seated. I wonder where the others are? Their food is going to get cold."

"Hup two? You're a drill sergeant now?" Emma muttered, withering just a bit more in embarrassment.

They all took turns washing their hands like good little children after further introductions were completed, and finally sat down to a most awkward breakfast.

"Dear, would you start passing the scrambled eggs," her mother said. "I'll send the pancakes the other way. That way no one has to wait."

Her mother had made pancakes in the shape of rudimentary

animals, just like when Emma was a girl.

"Mrs. Davison, your breakfast-making skills are fantastic," Adrian said before tucking into his plate of food. He was desperate to steer the conversation clear of anything potentially life-altering. Like everything.

"Take this dog, for instance," he continued, holding up a pancake. "I can't say I've ever seen someone craft animals into breakfast food before. Or should I call these vittles?"

He was clearly coming down from Granny Clampett overload. Emma chose to ignore that comment.

"Oh that's not a dog," her mother said. "It's a kangaroo!"

Emma rolled her eyes. "Just go with it," she whispered to them.

Before Emma could think of an appropriate reply, they heard a loud rap on the door. Adrian couldn't jump out of his chair fast enough to answer it. Which led Serena to wonder into what universe she'd been transported, with His Royal Highness being reduced to servant boy.

"Sheesh, mate, no phone," Darcy said, shaking his head as he walked into the living room. "I sure hope you've got it on you somewhere."

Adrian pushed the two of them back out onto the porch as he tried to explain about their unexpected visitor.

"Serena? What's that slag doing here?" Darcy asked upon hearing the news of their special visitor. "She's hunting you down, is she? Gonna drag you back by your hair, right down the aisle. She's a veritable cavewoman."

He started whistling "Here Comes the Bride" and Adrian was ready to clock him one.

"I don't know why she's here or how she even found me, but I do know she's got an engagement ring on! She's trying to rope me into this so badly she bought her own ring!"

"Oh, God. And you had the phone. Which meant it was traceable. How could we have let that happen. Though never did I think she'd be the one hunting you down. I thought your mother would be front in line for that honor."

Adrian just shook his head in dismay.

Darcy and Caroline made their way to the dining room table, and feigned surprise at the uninvited guest.

"So, uh, Serena, is it?" Caroline said. "What brings you to our neck of the woods?"

Emma kicked her under the table, not wanting to bring that up around her parents.

"Adrian and I have some things to discuss," she said cryptically.

'Really?" Caroline said. "Do tell!"

Emma kicked her again since clearly the first time didn't hurt enough.

Serena cleared her throat, reaching for her orange juice glass with that rock glinting in the morning light. "I'm afraid it's a conversation I must having in confidence with Adrian. I'm sure you'll understand."

Adrian gulped, dreading this.

"So while you're in town, you'll have to be sure to hit some of the local highlights," Caroline said. "Bumper boats are always fun. Maybe that strip club on Highway 58 as you're leaving town."

Emma's mother choked on her pancake. "Caroline!"

"Joking, Mother," Emma said. "Caroline always loves to be the comedian. You know that!"

"Perhaps you could take a stroll on the beach," her mother said. Which caused Adrian to choke a bit, what with his experience on the beach the night before.

Darcy cough-spoke, just to get a laugh, "Skinny dip." Which caused Adrian to kick him under the table.

"Thanks, but I won't be staying long," Serena said. "I need to get back immediately."

"All night is a long time to fly just to have a conversation," Bob said.

Adrian squirmed in his seat, his eyes fixed on his plate of pancakes. He kicked Darcy again to encourage him to redirect the conversation.

"Oh yeah, I'm sure I could show Serena the town," he said. "After all, Adrian's quite busy."

Adrian hoped that would fix that and he could get on with his business of being an escapee from The Firm.

"I'm sure Adrian can take a few minutes to discuss the future of the Firm and his role in it," Serena said. "I think he'd like a say in that, wouldn't you, Adrian?"

The Firm. An insider's term referring to the royal family. *She's acting like she's in already.*

"Firm?" Ellen asked. "You work for a law firm back home too?"

Emma intervened. "It's complicated, Mom," she said. "They have some mutual family and friend things that Serena was jokingly calling a firm. That's all."

Serena looked around the table, convinced that she was surrounded by a bunch of lunatics, certain that the sooner she got out of there the better.

"So what do you do back home?" Ellen asked her new houseguest.

"Oh, me?" Serena hemmed and hawed. "Well, I'm engaged to be married."

Adrian turned white as a ghost and Darcy kicked him so hard beneath the table he yelped in pain.

"Everything all right?" Ellen asked.

"Fine, fine," Adrian said. "But if I could perhaps excuse myself for a moment?"

He got up and nodded his head, pushing his chair in as he wandered down the hall to Emma's room.

"I'll be right back," Serena said to the group sitting around the table, rushing away, leaving her pancakes untouched.

Serena didn't even bother to knock, but rather pushed her way into the pink palace, and stood with her jaw wide open, staring at the room.

"My, my, my, how the mighty have fallen," she said. "I didn't exactly expect to find you sleeping on a park bench, but this? Though honestly, this isn't a whole lot better! What gives? I

154

find you at this squalid little house with these, these, these *people*, and you're wearing surfer clothes in the dead of winter, no sign whatsoever of your royal status, no staff but for Darcy, who hardly counts as staff. What has gone wrong with you?"

"This home is not in the least bit squalid," he said. "It's homey. And they have been generous to allow me to take a little break from the demands of my life and for that I will be eternally grateful to them. So I will thank you to put away that attitude and be gracious."

Serena eyed him suspiciously, squinting. "Aha! I knew if I said something rude like that it would get you to talk. So you're taking a break from the demands of your life, eh?"

Busted. Adrian snapped his finger and shook his head, mad at himself that he fell for such a rookie maneuver. "I needed a little time off."

"What's the matter — your mom got your tongue?"

"What?"

"Maybe a little problem with your mother demanding, let's say, a bit too much of you?"

It was Adrian's turn to squint at Serena. "What are you getting at?"

She held out her hand. "Does this ring a bell maybe?"

"I'm not quite sure what you mean."

"This foolish idea of your mother's, trying to get us to get married!" she blurted out.

Adrian stared at her. "You mean you don't want to be married to me?"

Serena cackled.

"I don't think that's the kindest of responses," Adrian said.

"I didn't mean it like that," she said. "It's just that I already have someone in my life with whom I'm in love. I know the man I want to marry, and I'm sorry, Adrian, but it's not you."

"But what about all of that stupid behavior of yours," he said. "All that time, you were forcing yourself on me?"

"What?" she said. "I never forced myself on you!"

"And those parties, you were drunk as a boiled owl and falling all over yourself. And me, for that matter."

"Oh, please," she said. "I wasn't truly drunk! I was faking it. I tried my hardest to make your mother not want me in the family. Like I said, I have a man in my life. I just want to be able to live my own life and choose who I can marry."

Adrian started nodding his head in agreement. "Yes! Precisely! Me too!" he said. "I got so tired of my mother forcing you on me I had to get away to try to figure out how to get out of this obligation. But I see it never actually was an obligation."

"Oh trust me, if it was left up to your mother and mine, we'd have been married off already."

"So this ring?" Adrian asked, lifting her hand to inspect it more closely. "You didn't do this to force an engagement to me?"

"To you? You have got to be kidding me." Serena laughed out loud, shaking her head in amazement. "Adrian, you must think even worse of me than I had assumed you did. No, I'm not that brazen — or stupid — that I'd force an engagement on a man against his wishes."

Adrian stared at Serena, realizing maybe she hadn't been the monster he'd thought she was.

"So, uh, who's the lucky fellow?"

Serena held her hand out and splayed her fingers, admiring her twinkling engagement ring. "Roberto Fournier. You met him last year on the day after Christmas, eating the gingerbread house at the palace. You may recall he and I were eating a candy cane at the same time from different ends."

"Huh," Adrian said, scratching his head. "I guess that should have been my clue, eh?"

"Yeah, well, I guess the two of us worked so hard to avoid each other that we never paid much attention to our lives at all."

"I'm happy for you, Serena," he said. "You look truly at peace."

She smiled. "More so than ever, now that I know we're on the same page with this thing and can do something about it. My mother was giving me fits over this whole thing. After all, she's never one to refuse your mother."

Adrian sat down on Emma's pink quilt. "Well, if this isn't the most unexpected of things. So what do we do now?"

"It's why I was so desperate to talk to you, yet you kept refusing to speak," she said. "I figured we'd have strength in numbers if neither of us wanted the other, well, then, what could they do?"

Adrian raised an eyebrow. "An arranged marriage?"

"Surely our mothers aren't that cruel."

"I don't know. I wouldn't put it past mine. She sure does dig in when she doesn't get her way."

She reached out and hugged him, trying to cinch the deal.

"So come back home with me. We'll face them together and put an end to all of this nonsense," she said. "After all, I have a wedding to plan. And, uh, nothing personal, but not with you!"

Chapter Nineteen

ADRIAN heard a knock on the door and before he could untangle himself from Serena, Emma was there, staring in disbelief at them both, her face betraying her emotions.

"Well, you two sure didn't waste any time," she said. "Snap my fingers and voila, you're on my bed going at it."

Adrian blanched. "Emma, you've got it all wrong," he said, releasing his hold on Serena. "To the contrary, no one's going at anything."

"It's okay. It's fine," she said, pressing down her Snuggie only to realize how stupid she looked and instead pulling it off. The static it left behind caused her short pajamas to cling to her in a most revealing manner, which didn't help matters for Adrian. "Really it's perfect. You two were meant for each other. I'll just let the both of you straighten up and get decent before you come back out to the living room."

Before Adrian had a chance to defend himself and tell her he wasn't *not* decent, he heard a phone ring. The phone. The one he'd remembered to turn back on only thirty minutes ago.

"Adrian here," he said.

"Ade—" his brother said, his voice sounding distraught. "It's me, Zander. It's Mum. I don't know what is going on, but she's had some sort of attack."

"She was attacked?" Adrian said, the shock of what his brother was saying washing over him.

"No, no. No one attacked her," he said. "But she's had some sort of thing. I don't know if it's her heart or what. She was in her sitting room and she was going on about how upset she was with you disappearing and she was yelling at me again about my swimming pool episode and all of a sudden she grabbed her heart and—"

"Is she all right?"

Jenny Gardiner

"I think you need to get to her immediately," Zander said. "There's no telling what is going on. Father's with her upstairs. She's resting now, I've called for the doctor. But I think it's time for you to come home."

"Right," he said. "Of course. I'll get Darcy to arrange everything. We'll leave immediately."

They hung up the phone and Adrian sat there for a few moments, dazed.

"Something's wrong with your mother?" Serena asked.

"You know how she can get," he said, which only served to enhance Emma's frown even more, what with all these family secrets those two shared. "She gets so worked up about things, but this time Zander said she reached for her heart, then she passed out."

"Oh, your poor mother," Emma said. "You must go to her immediately. I'll help you get your things together."

"And it's all my fault," Adrian said. "If I hadn't been selfish, if I just listened to her, this never would have happened."

Emma crossed her arms across her pajama-clad body and frowned. How much of this was her responsibility? She had a part in this. She'd encouraged Adrian to defy his mother. She didn't know enough about his family and background to have made those decisions. She was operating from a lot of presumptions based on the life she knew, not the life that only Adrian (and maybe Serena) could understand.

Perhaps it was for the best that Adrian and Serena marry. After all, that old adage, mother knows best, was often right. No doubt his mother knew what was right for The Firm. And that decidedly would never include the likes of Emma.

It was easier this way. No long goodbyes. No wishing for what couldn't be. He had his family; he had The Firm. Duty called. And never would she be part of that duty.

Something in the Heir

"Sorry to have to leave you just as we were getting to know each other," Darcy said, sighing, his arms around Caroline, his forehead pressed up to hers.

"Remember, you owe me a ball," Caroline said.

Emma's parents looked confused, considering all they knew was that Darcy was Adrian's former lover. And now here he was in an intimate posture with Caroline and she was telling him about some ball debt.

"Well I'll be darned," her father said, watching Darcy with Caroline. "I guess it works both ways."

Emma rolled her eyes. "Dad, it's not like that. I'll explain later."

Conveniently Serena's driver was waiting for her to whisk her back to her jet, which was at an airport about an hour and a half away. Darcy only had to place a discreet call to the embassy, which had a helicopter on the ground at the Beaufort airport before they knew it. His Royal Highness would be on his way home to Monaforte before he digested his animal pancakes.

Emma had thrown on a sweatshirt and a pair of ratty jeans, but still had a pair of fluffy slippers on her feet as she stood outside, despite the winter cold. A few snowflakes had started to fall while they milled about in the front yard, saying their goodbyes.

Adrian pulled Emma aside, away from everyone's view. "Listen, Emma," he said. "I'm so sorry this has to end so suddenly. You know I really do have feelings for you. And I'm sorry we couldn't explore this any further. I guess my life is too complicated."

Emma shook her head. "It's okay. I knew this day would come. Maybe not quite so abruptly… But I understand. It's your mother. Of course you have to be there for her." She stood rocking on her heels with her hands in her pockets, her shoulders slumped. "I don't want to bother you at all so maybe you can just ask Darcy to let Caroline know how she's doing and then Caroline can update me?"

Of course they'd never have any more communication than that. What were they going to become, pen pals?

"Maybe I can tell you all by myself, rather than playing any more silly telephone games."

Emma frowned. "It's okay. I don't think it's worth it. It would just drag things out longer. Probably just as well to leave you to your life and me to mine."

Adrian pulled her toward him and wrapped his arms tightly around her. "Em," he said. "I don't want to do that."

"I know you think that. But once you get back to your world, to your life, this will just be some long-forgotten thing."

He scruffed her already messy hair. "As if I could forget you that easily."

He leaned forward and kissed her. At first she refused to go along, but she knew resistance was futile, and she knew she'd never feel the same way about kissing another man again, so she might as well enjoy it while she could.

"Have a great life, Adrian," Emma whispered, fighting the tears pooling in the corners of her eyes.

Adrian dabbed at her eyes with his sleeve.

"We'll be in touch, soon."

"No, really," she said. "It'll only make it harder for me. Best to just let it go. Or if you feel strongly about staying in touch, you can always keep me on your Christmas card list."

Serena came around the corner and called to Adrian. "They're waiting for us. We need to go."

As they walked toward the waiting car, Adrian leaned in and gave Emma one last kiss, leaving their audience — not the least of which was her parents — to wonder what was up with the two of them.

Emma cupped her hand and waved a tiny goodbye as the snow began to fall more heavily. As soon as Adrian got in the car, she ran back into the house and took to her room for the rest of the day.

Something in the Heir

"Knock knock!" Caroline walked into her friend's bedroom as dusk was settling in. December could be so bleak, getting dark as early as it did.

"Thought I'd give you a little time to pout in peace before I came to pull you out of your purple funk," she said, plunking herself down next to Emma, who was lying on her stomach, face down in her pillow. "Although with this room I should call it a pink funk. Let's go, girl. Up and at 'em!" She tugged to no avail on her friend's arm, only hearing a low grunt in response.

She then reached down and tucked a hank of Emma's hair behind her ear. "Hey. Psst. You there?"

"No one's home. Go away." Emma's muffled voice could barely be heard through the pillow.

"C'mon, Ems," her friend said. "Talk to me."

"Don't wanna talk. Wanna sulk."

"You're doing a fine job of that I can see."

They sat in silence for a few minutes.

"Your mom is making spaghetti for you," she said with a little sing-song to her voice. "She knows how to lure you out: woo your stomach."

"Not hungry."

"Geez, for someone who wasn't going to fall for any man, particularly one so decidedly unavailable, you sure did a good job of not holding up your end of that bargain to yourself."

Emma rolled over. "Urgh! I didn't fall for him!" She pounded her fist against the pillow.

"Oh, really? So that's why you're sprawled out like a cadaver on your bed all day, unwilling to speak to anyone and acting like a lovelorn tween? If you didn't fall for the guy, you sure as hell at least tripped a bit."

"Oh, hush up," she grumbled. "I'm not a lovelorn anything and I haven't tripped or stumbled or anything of the sort. I think I've just got a touch of allergies."

Caroline smiled. "It's December, you nut! What are you allergic to, Christmastime?"

"All right. Fine," Emma said. "Maybe I'm just a little sad."

Caroline sat up taller on the bed. "Good! We're making progress. Acknowledging your feelings is the first step. Now tell me what makes you sad."

"Winter."

Caroline nodded her head. "Yup. Winter can be sort of gloomy. But it's Christmas! We've got a bunch of parties you're going to shoot coming up, so that should be fun."

Emma sighed. "I'm so bored with that stuff. So we get to go to some stodgy old doyenne of society's sprawling mansion for a fancy schmancy party with a bunch of old codgers we don't know who try to pinch your butt because they think they're still frat boys. Big deal."

"But they pay really well!"

"I guess that's not such a bad thing, considering I've got a mortgage to meet. And since that's about all I'll ever meet at this point, I'm guaranteed be alone for the rest of my life anyhow. Alone with my bills." She started crying and Caroline tried to get her to stop bawling and talk but instead Emma just choked and gasped in between tears.

"Do you suppose I should bring your mother in here to help you? Would that make you feel better?"

"Noooooo," Emma cried. "She's not that kind of mother. She's more like a better wife than comforting mom. Which doesn't mean she's a bad mother, but she's not the mother who comes in and helps when I'm crying."

"So I should leave her to her spaghetti sauce then?"

"Definitely," Emma said as she nodded her head and wiped her tears. "And I'll just wallow a little longer if it's all the same to you."

"Hey," Caroline said, grabbing Emma's chin with her pointer finger and looking her right in the eyes. "You know things will work out, right?"

Emma nodded slowly. "Yeah. Maybe not how I'd choose in my alternate universe. But whatever will be will be."

"Precisely."

"Besides, he was never mine, anyhow."

"It's no secret that he liked you, you know," her friend said. "But his life is complicated. He's not like normal people, who can just pick and choose who they're with."

"But he acted so darned normal, I could almost forget he wasn't!" Emma said. "That's the problem. If he was some hoity-toity, snooty royal thing, then it would be easy to just ignore it. But he was just like you and me, only famous."

"And richer than God."

"But sweet."

"With an amazing wardrobe, I bet."

"But I liked his surfer clothes."

"He must have too," Caroline said. "After all, he took them home with him. And I can't think he'll have much use for board shorts in Monaforte."

"Except when he summers on the Mediterranean," Emma said, tears threatening to resume.

"Where he'll have no choice but to remember that wonderful vacation he had with none other than Emma Davison."

"Lucky me."

"Exactly right, young lady," she said. "You're incredibly lucky! So a dumb boy left you. Big deal. You are your own boss, lady. You're queen of your world! You don't need a useless prince!"

"But what if I want a useless prince?"

"I'll buy you his latest CD." She poked her friend in the ribs. "Now c'mon. There's a pot of spaghetti with your name on it. And   I'm   hungry."

Chapter Twenty

ADRIAN and Serena raced into the palace in search of Queen Ariana, and found his brother Zander kicking a soccer ball around the Great Hall.

"Dude," he said, nodding hello to Serena while holding up his hands in surrender. "Don't blame me. Blame that mother of yours."

Adrian looked confused. "What do you mean 'that mother of yours'? She's yours too."

"Yeah, well, once you see her you're probably going to disown her like I did after she made me lie to you."

Adrian blanched. "What do you mean?"

"Sorry, Ade," he said. "But she forced my hand. She's so ticked at me still about that whole Vegas thing. She's holding it over me like the Sword of Damocles."

"So she made you lie to me to get me to come home?"

Zander shrugged. "They don't call her the queen for nothing."

"Queen indeed," Adrian said, finally piecing the puzzle together. "Somehow she's confused her imperial entitlements with some mistaken belief she has carte blanche to mess with our lives. Excuse me, I need to find the great manipulator and set her straight once and for all."

He scaled the grand spiral staircase two steps at a time with Serena on his heels, and followed the Corridor of Elders down to her dressing room, where he found Lady Sarah placing one of the queen's many bejeweled crowns atop her well-coiffed head.

"Mother?" Adrian scowled and crossed his arms. "Near death, I see?"

"Adrian!" His mother stood up and reached out to give her son a two-cheek kiss. "And finally we see the whites of your missing-in-action eyes."

"What the hell are you all about?" He glared as he snapped at her. "I was summoned home immediately because you were in such poor health, and here you are glowing in Gucci and ready to please your masses?"

His mother fanned her face. "Yes, well, I was feeling a bit off, but I seem to have gotten over it. Sarah, is my driver ready?" she said, trying to give herself a quick escape plan.

But Adrian would have none of her toying with him and grabbed her wrist and pulled her close to him. "And this was more of your stupid game to get me to marry Serena? Because you truly believe she's so desperate to marry into the Firm? Well I've got news for you, Mother. She wants no more to do with me than I with her! Your plan backfired from both ends."

"Of course she wants to marry you, dear," his mother said. "You two have been fated to be betrothed since childhood."

Adrian rolled his eyes. "In your fantasy world, perhaps. But if you don't believe me, ask her yourself."

Serena appeared from around a large mother of pearl and mahogany screen.

"Serena, dear," his mother said. "So lovely to see you two together."

Serena glanced over at Adrian while her mother made herself look busy tidying up the queen's make-up in order to avoid the fallout of what she knew was about to be revealed.

"Yes, your majesty," Serena said, curtsying.

"Adrian is speaking some nonsense but I'm sure you can clear all of that up."

"Well, to be honest," she said, her voice trembling a bit. "The thing is, you see, I've become engaged to someone else."

"Engaged?" Ariana said. "Why, that's impossible, dear. Your mother and I had this all planned out."

"I'm afraid you forgot to clear your plan with the two principals, Mother," Adrian interjected. "It does you no good to orchestrate this mad scheme of yours when your unwitting victims had other things in mind."

Ariana stood, arms crossed, glancing back and forth

between Adrian and Serena.

"Why in the world would you become engaged to someone else?"

Serena, furrowing her brows, looked a bit confused by the question. "Because I'm in love with him, your majesty."

"Love? What's love got to do with it?" Her voice rose a notch or two in ire.

"It has everything to do with it, *Mother dear.*"

"Marriage is so much more than love. Why, look at your father and me—"

"Indeed," said a deep voice from nearby. "Look at your mother and me."

Crown Prince Enrico turned the corner to stand before his wife, shaking his head. "Lest you forget, my dearest Ariana, we, too, married for love."

"Yes but—"

"No yes buts, love," he said, placing his hands on her shoulders. "At the end of the day, we married for love. Which is how it should be, and will be for these two as well." He spread his arms out, motioning toward Adrian and Serena. "I only wish I'd gotten wind of your harebrained scheme before it went this far, Ariana. I know you meant well, but really, darling."

His wife wrinkled her forehead and pouted. "It wasn't harebrained in the least! These two were made for each other!"

Adrian and Serena looked at each other and began to laugh.

"Begging your pardon, your highness," Serena said. "But Adrian is just about the last person I'd want to marry."

Adrian lifted one eyebrow as he lowered the other. "I'm that bad, am I?"

"Heavens, no! I didn't mean that to be rude," she said. "It's not you at all. But I've no interest in living your kind of lifestyle, always being under a microscope. I value my privacy too much."

"Fair enough," he said. "Have we convinced you, mother?"

"I was only after your best interest, Adrian," she said, sighing. "I wanted to be sure you ended up with someone who valued our way of life and who is steeped in our traditions, someone willing to carry the torch."

"Adrian's choice for a partner is his and his alone," Enrico said. "Even if he selects someone you don't like, Ariana, it's his decision and you must live with it."

He reached out and grabbed her hand in his. "But I have a feeling that he'll select someone we both adore. He is our son, after all."

Adrian only wished that his father's all-encompassing acceptance would extend to someone beyond the borders of their humble state, but he suspected a crazy American photographer didn't exactly qualify.

Chapter Twenty-One

"IF I have to photograph one more bejeweled political patroness yukking it up on Santa's lap I'm going to slug somebody," Emma groused to Caroline.

"Seriously, did you see that old gal, the one whose face was so Botoxed she could barely open her mouth, let alone smile?"

"Yes! The one who looked like she was trapped in a wind tunnel, her face was so stretched back from all the surgical lifting?" Emma said. "Just because you've got gobs of money doesn't mean you have good sense. Does she really think she looks better trying to pretend she's an ingénue when she's a matron? Whatever happened to aging gracefully?"

"Meanwhile if they're so hot on Santa, they should realize he's old! He doesn't want some young thing!" Caroline said.

"I beg to differ with you. Did you see him pawing at that twenty-something woman in the really tight, really short red spandex cocktail dress with the Mrs. Claus fur trim on it? I'm not sure who was more trashed, Santa or her."

Caroline pointed a thumb toward the door in the far corner of the hotel ballroom. "Looks like a match made in heaven," she said as the not-so-saintly Saint Nick slipped out the back door with the young woman. "Maybe Santa wasn't as old as we thought?"

"Ugh," Emma said. "I'm kind of tiring of seeing everyone, even Santa Claus, finding their mate."

"I hear ya, girl. But if you'd lower your standards like me, maybe you'd find someone."

"But I did find someone," she said. "And I didn't even have to reduce my principles to do so."

"Shame he was unattainable." Caroline frowned. "But that friend of his. He was pretty hot." She shook her hand like she'd just burned her fingers.

Something in the Heir

Emma just stared at her, somber. "Have you met a man who you wouldn't consider hot, under the right circumstances?"

Caroline thought for a minute, scratching her chin in contemplation. "Yeah, that dude in the Santa suit. Not for one minute did I consider a holiday hook-up with him. But then again I hate white beards."

Emma smacked her in the ribs. "You are such a weirdo. Come on, let's get out of here. We can go have a drink somewhere. Preferably somewhere not so seasonably cheerful. I've got nothing to celebrate, thanks."

"Awwww, cheer up, grasshopper," her friend said. "Things will get better. Besides, I thought you didn't fall for Adrian."

Emma frowned as she thought about this. "I didn't exactly fall for him. But I didn't *not* fall for him, I suppose. I mean he was a really nice guy. And really cute. And the best kisser I think I ever met. And he had a custom-made tuxedo. When will I ever kiss a guy with his own tailor ever again? And did I say he was nice? And really normal too. He wasn't pretentious at all. You'd think someone of his stature would be such a Snooty McSnootster. But he was really quite lovely. And he had a great sense of humor. And we laughed a lot. We sort of 'got' each other."

"So when are you going to admit you fell for the guy?" Caroline asked, putting her arm around her friend's shoulder.

"What does it matter? He's there, and I'm here. He's who he is and I'm not. Well, it's okay that I'm not because if I was, then I'd be him and that would be weird. But I am who I am and I'm not for the likes of him."

"How do you know?"

"I know because I know! He has to be with some fancy, wealthy, skinny, upper-class Monaforter. Or is it Monafortian? Or is it Monafortable? What would you call someone from Monaforte? Monafortese? This is going to drive me nuts until I look it up."

She pulled out her phone and Googled the information. Only to find an image of Adrian, linked to a story about the holiday goings-on at the palace. She could feel those damned tears welling up in her eyes again, and she did her best to suppress the sniffle that she knew was just on the horizon once she started crying — yet again, dammit. She was so tired of boohooing in the quiet confines of her lonely split-level.

"I need to get a dog," she said. "Maybe I'll even get a male dog. That will be the extent of my involvement with anything with the XY chromosome. If male dogs even have that chromosome. I didn't pay attention to that in science class."

She mulled it over a bit more. "Yes, that is the perfect solution. I'll get a boy dog and I'll give him a good boyfriend name. John or Matt or Howard. Maybe for laughs I could even call him Adrian. Though if Adrian ever got wind of that he might be insulted. But then I can have the man of my dreams right under my feet, even if he is covered with fur and drools in his sleep. I could even have him sleep in my bed. That's it! So I'll be sleeping with Adrian for the rest of my life! But would I have to count that in dog years?"

"Why don't you just reach out to the man?" Caroline said, chiding her.

"Because I have my pride. And because if he'd wanted to reach out to me, he would have. And because he's him and I'm me and never the twain shall meet."

"I'm afraid that horse is long out of the barn, sweetie," her friend said. "The twain did meet, and while the twain maybe didn't exactly have a full-fledged booty call, it was moving in that direction enough to justify the twain meeting maybe one more time to see where things might go."

"Besides, he's probably planning his huge nuptials with Bettina!"

"You mean Serena?"

"Bettina, Serena. Whatever. Yeah."

"Maybe they won't get married, Emma. You never know."

"Please. No doubt they were going at it on that private jet all the way to Europe. You can only imagine what two young, virile adults could get up to for that six-hour flight with a gold bed in it."

"They had a gold bed on that plane?"

"I have no idea. It seems like the type of thing they'd have though."

"They weren't even alone, you ding-dong. My man was there too, lest we forget."

"Your man, eh?" Emma laughed. "You talk to him at all?"

"Maybe," Caroline said.

"What do you mean maybe? It's a yes or a no!"

"So maybe we haven't actually talked."

"If you haven't talked, then what?" But then Emma eyes got wider as she noticed her friend pretending to be particularly interested in a loose thread on her shirt. "Really? You're sexting with the guy? Are there pictures involved? Caroline, sweetie, have you no pride?"

"What? I didn't say that! You said that!"

"Your beet-red face says it all."

"I'm not blushing because I'm not embarrassed! So what if we've exchanged some racy messages. Maybe one or two pictures. All in good fun, right?"

"I truly do not understand how you can send pictures of your exposed body parts to this man halfway across the world from you. What if other people get hold of it?"

"You mean like some princely brothers maybe?" Caroline said with a sing-song teasing voice. "Maybe Adrian's got some doubly hot brother he can hook me up with."

Emma smacked her friend again. "I know you're not that much of a tramp that you'd ditch Darcy for one of Adrian's brothers."

"Ya never know," Caroline said. "I might just have a thing for crowns."

Emma laughed. "A thing for crowns? How does one acquire such an addiction?"

"Well when they try them on with their wedding gowns on *Say Yes to the Dress*, I always think I'd like to wear one."

Jenny Gardiner

"Those are tiaras, not crowns, stupid."

"Close enough. I could see wearing that for fun," she said. "Couldn't you?"

"I refuse to dignify that with a response."

"For all you know, Emma Davison, a tiara might be just around the corner waiting for you."

"More likely it will be a mugger, but one can hope."

"Chin up, darling," Ariana said to Adrian. "Must you look like someone just killed your puppy?" They were sitting in the royal box during intermission at the opera, not one of Adrian's favorite activities, but one he acceded to as patron of the Royal Opera Society.

"Of course, Mother. Duty calls. I realize that."

"What's gotten into you? Since you've returned you've not been yourself one bit!"

Adrian sighed. "It's complicated."

"I would have thought you'd have been relieved," she said. "What with your marriage called off and all..." She smiled at him and gently stroked his cheek with the back of her fingertips.

"Forgive me, Mother. Really. I can assure you I am more than thrilled to have that burden behind me," he said. "I suppose it's just that I've been thinking about someone I met, someone I grew to like quite a bit."

"And this someone is a woman, I'd imagine?"

Adrian laughed. "That's a safe bet, yes."

"So you're free now," she said. "What's holding you back?"

Adrian shook his head. "She's no one you'd embrace, Mother. You scared me enough with that passing out attack you had. I don't want to steer you to an official heart attack with this one."

173

"Nonsense, Adrian," she said. "I'm fine. Nothing you do will harm my heart. Besides, you're the future king of Monaforte, my dear. There's nothing you can't have."

"Mother, you said yourself that you want me to be with someone who is one of us. Someone with our culture, our background. Someone who can relate to our lifestyle. Emma is not that person."

"Emma, eh?" she said. "That's a pretty name. Tell me about this young lady."

"She's beautiful. And thoughtful. And smart. She never treated me as if I was special. She just acted like I was a normal man."

"How dare she!" his mother said, joking. "Doesn't she know you're to be on a pedestal at all times?"

Adrian shrugged. "She never got the royal memo. But I liked that about her. I liked that she kept me on my feet, she kept me wondering. And she kept me interested."

"Interested in what?"

"In her. In her likes and interests. In her mood and temperament. In her happiness. In everything about her."

"Sounds like a special young woman."

Her son just nodded, a faraway look in his eyes.

Later, as the royal entourage left the theater, the queen spotted Darcy. She locked arms in his and walked to the waiting car with him.

"You know I've still not forgiven you for playing that trick on me, pretending to be Adrian when my son ran off," she said. "So you owe me. And now I have a job for you. If you pay that back, I'll consider us even. Speak of it to no one, do you understand?"

Chapter Twenty-Two

EMMA sat alone in the living room of her house, unopened gifts intended for her parents parked beneath her sagging little Christmas tree. Her parents had long ago made plans to travel to Nashville to the Opryland Hotel for their Christmas extravaganza. Her mother was nothing if not addicted to Very Merry Christmases. Though she failed dismally in recognizing her daughter's lack thereof. It seemed nothing said Christmas quite like hoop skirts and a down-home twang, as far as her mother was concerned. But Emma had politely declined an offer to join them and swore to her folks that she would be fine, so what were they to do?

Emma had distracted herself all day long with a holiday filmfest, and had powered her way through several classics already, alternating cheerful with grim. Weird how that *Charlie Brown Christmas* seemed like a real downer if you weren't in a Christmas state of mind, what with the lame tree, the kids being mean to Charlie Brown and the subdued music. *A House Without a Christmas Tree* left her bawling, being that the girl's mother was dead and the dad had shut himself off emotionally. She'd already sat through *White Christmas* but had to turn it off when everyone ended up happily ever after. That was a foreign concept, thanks. Now she was engrossed in the more emotionally neutral *A Christmas Story*. Ralphie had just gotten his Red Ryder BB Gun. Clearly eye-damaging weaponry was much more her speed at the moment.

As Ralphie's family dined on Chinese duck following the demise of their turkey, Emma started thinking about her own lacking Christmas dinner, hoping she could find a Chinese restaurant open to satisfy her now-grumbling stomach.

She'd just pulled her phone out to see if Peking Gourmet was open when she received a text from Caroline.

Something in the Heir

"Pack your bags for a week. We've got last-minute plans. Bring something dressy. Remember your winter coat, and you'll need a scarf and gloves. I'll be at your place in fifteen minutes. Oh, and you might need your passport."

Huh?

She told Caroline: "Sorry, I'm about to run out to Peking Gourmet to get dinner. Nothing says lonely Christmas like Chinese food."

Her friend replied: "No worries. Duck can be arranged. Just be ready or you'll go in your pajamas. And trust me, you don't want to go in your pajamas."

Emma tried to ask for details but her friend didn't reply.

Without having a clue as to what to pack, she threw together a haphazard collection of clothes and shoes and toiletries and hoped for the best.

"I guess winter coat means I don't need sunscreen or a bathing suit," she mumbled. But the passport thing had her stymied. Maybe they were off for a rollicking week in Newfoundland. She always did like those dogs. Maybe they could seek out polar bears while they were there. But no, why would she need nice clothes for a polar bear trek? Unless it was a *Save the Polar Bears* cocktail party, in which case it might make more sense. She wouldn't put it past Caroline to do something impulsive like that. Besides, no doubt it was a super cheap flight to the barren Canadian north in the dead of winter.

"You really need to get a life if this is the extent of your vivid imagination," she said to herself.

Caroline arrived out of breath, pounding on the door.

"Hope you watered your houseplants. Let's go!" she shouted as Emma opened up the door.

She grabbed her friend's hand and pulled her toward the awaiting taxi. "You know how hard it is to get a cab on Christmas evening? Come on!" She practically shoved her into the backseat of the thing.

Emma squinted at her, trying to figure out what was going on. "You're not going to give me even a clue?"

Caroline shook her head. "You'll know soon enough."

After a twenty-minute drive, they arrived at Washington Dulles airport.

"You sure have my curiosity piqued," Emma said. "I mean I know you're a good friend and all, but it's not as if you'd spring for an entire vacation for me. Even for Christmas. Besides, weren't you going to be visiting your family in Baltimore today?"

"Honey, been there, done that. Blew out of there early. With what I've got planned for you, Bal'more can't hold a candle."

The taxi pulled into the parking lot of a private jet terminal, where a uniformed pilot and two flight attendants were waiting to take their luggage.

"What the—?" Emma said, dazed.

"I know, right? Just wait. It gets better."

They were led across a tarmac — no security line, no screaming kids, no scowling TSA agents, no water dumping, no inspections of mini-bottles of shampoo in small Ziploc bags, no shoe removal, no icky naked private part-revealing X-rays, no nothing that makes commercial air travel demeaning and dehumanizing — and mounted the steps to a gleaming white jet with no apparent identification on it.

"On the one hand I'd sure love for this to be taking us to, say, the Fiji Islands," Emma said. "But the winter coat thing throws that right off. I can't for the life of me imagine how you had the wherewithal to pull this off. And on the other hand, I could care less where this is taking us. Wherever it is, it beats marinating in winter doldrums, which was how I spent my day."

The flight attendant gave them a tour of the jet, with reclining white leather seats as soft as kid gloves that converted into beds. Beds! There was a large bar stocked with top-of-the-line liquor and an ice bucket with chilled champagne, and a gargantuan flat-screen HD screen with any and every movie available to watch. Emma planned on finishing up her Christmas movie binge under the improved circumstances. To top it off, dinner, they learned, was to be a catered affair, direct from Peking Gourmet.

"Can we stay on board this thing for the rest of our lives?" Caroline asked the flight attendant, who laughed politely as if she wasn't used to low-renters on board.

"Psst, Caro," Emma whispered. "Check it out: there's a shower. On a plane. A shower!"

"I think I've died and gone to heaven," her friend said.

The plane took off a mere ten minutes after boarding. It was as if there was no other plane at this enormous international airport that had needs. Only theirs. And as easy as that, the two women took off into the friendly skies with nary a care in the world, flutes filled with some lovely French champagne bubbling away in their grips. As the plane hugged the Eastern seaboard, the pilot made a custom fly-by over Manhattan, to Emma and Caroline's great delight.

Soon after that the flight attendant served them Hong Kong wonton soup, Peking duck and Szechuan beef proper. They ate till they were nearly ill, saving just enough room for the yule log cake that simply needed to be eaten by someone. It *was* Christmas, after all.

The girls began to nod off as *It's a Wonderful Life* drew to a close.

"This has been like the best slumber party ever," Emma said as she drifted off to sleep. "All that was missing was cotton candy and snow cones. But I don't even like cotton candy or snow cones, so who cares?"

"Don't forget the unicorns. The good news is the party's only just begun," Caroline said, just out of Emma's earshot.

They both awoke with time to shower and refresh themselves. And before they knew it, their plane was touching down in God only knew where. All Emma could tell was it was snowing. Fat chunks of snow gathered strength as the jet slowed down and finally stopped at yet another private terminal.

The pilot opened the cockpit door and greeted the women.

"Welcome, ladies. I understand I'm not to disclose where

you are, so my lips are sealed," he said.

There was a long, black limousine parked near the jet, and a driver with a black cap and crisp leather gloves and long black camelhair coat got out of the car and scurried to collect their bags. The girls were directed to the back of the limo, where fresh pastries awaited them with fresh-squeezed orange juice and yet more champagne.

"I don't know why but this good stuff doesn't give you headaches," Caroline said.

"I'm not one to drink at breakfast but considering I have no bloody idea where I am, what have I got to lose?" Emma said.

"You might just gain something," her friend said, leaving Emma with a quizzical look on her face.

"At this rate probably twenty pounds."

They drove for about twenty minutes past rolling countryside. Emma couldn't help but notice all of the adorable cozy farmhouses peppering the fields, with smoke whorling from chimneys, looking straight out of a Christmas card. The snow was falling heavier now, and a layer of white covered the roads and surrounding pastureland. The hillsides were dotted with black and white cows looking decidedly chilled as snow mounted atop their backs.

Soon the countryside yielded to more dense development, with beautiful old gothic buildings coming into view. Here and there were statues of Greek and Roman gods and war heroes, and for the life of her Emma couldn't figure out what the hell this was all about. And then the car came upon a mammoth building that looked like a castle, with spires and turrets and crenellations and all sorts of old battlements. No moat, that's for sure. But there were gorgeous gargoyles, a personal favorite since reading *The Hunchback of Notre Dame*. She wanted to be sure she wasn't going to have boiling oil poured on her head, were she to get closer. They drove alongside this large castle-like building, which was surrounded by a tall black wrought-iron fence with gold flourishes, the tops of which were garnished with gold fleurs–de-lis.

Emma stared out the window at this structure, so regal and palatial, and then the truth dawned on her.

She gasped. "Impossible," she said, turning to Caroline.

Caroline pretended to zip her lips shut and swallow the key.

"It can't be. Can it?"

Caroline shrugged her shoulders and turned to keep looking out the window. Even though it was daytime they could see fairy lights covering the building and even the gorgeous fence surrounding it. The limousine was ushered through two very tall gates, each bearing an enormous crest in gold leaf, in the shape of dueling griffins. The car pulled up the pebbled drive to the front of this palatial estate and came to a halt.

A few minutes later, two men standing guard in front of a grand marble staircase, wearing military attire that clearly required a whole lot of ironing, polishing and buffing, opened the door and greeted the women.

"Welcome to Monaforte, madame," one said to Emma, who became weak at the knees as he spoke the words she dared not ever expect to hear.

She stared at Caroline. "Monaforte?" she mouthed to her.

"Yeah, so maybe I told you Darcy made a deal for me to come to a big party here, right?" she said. "Well, I couldn't do that without my best friend, now could I?"

Emma deflated for a minute. So it wasn't for her that she was here. It was her friend, summoned here by Darcy. It had nothing to do with Adrian. *Oh well, it is what it is. Might as well make the best of things, enjoy this for what it is. After all, there weren't many Americans who get to party at a palace in Europe, right?*

Chapter Twenty-Three

EMMA and Caroline were escorted by a footman in a morning suit into the, well, what would it be called? Foyer? Lobby? Front hall? Giant bloody damned space designed for nothing but standing around feeling particularly small and inadequate?

Before them were two red-carpeted spiral staircases, one to the left and one to the right, the kind you would descend if only for dramatic effect on your wedding day with a fifty-foot embroidered and hand-beaded Belgian lace train held aloft by a team of virginal bridesmaids while small maidens led the way scattering rose petals for your Christian Louboutin-clad feet to tread upon. The railing — a gleaming gold, with an intricate pattern worked throughout — looked like it would be a real bitch to polish.

The footman, who Emma expected at any moment to launch into a lesson on proper grammar and pronunciation, beginning with *the rain in Spain falls mainly on the plains*, escorted them up the stairs and down a hallway he said was the Corridor of Elders, filled floor to ceiling with historic artwork, and opened a panel in the wall that was actually a door. A secret door!

A lovely woman with a somber, starched gray dress, a pressed white apron, and one of those poofy white maid's caps on her head greeted them and then asked them to wait while she disappeared into an inner sanctum. Emma and Caroline stood by nervously for a few minutes until a woman dressed in a stylish crimson satin suit jacket and skirt who looked a bit like Julie Andrews from the *Sound of Music*, her brown hair cropped short to her face, with soft blue eyes and a welcoming smile, greeted them. She extended her hands.

"Emma from America?" she said with just a hint of curiosity as she sized her up and down.

"Yes, ma'am. Emma Davison," Emma said a bit hesitantly,

sizing her up right back.

Caroline introduced herself as well.

"You can call me Ariana," the woman said in reply, nodding in acknowledgment at the nearby maid, who looked surprised at her informality.

And Emma's mouth went dry, and she went even weaker at the knees. "Ariana, as in *the queen*?" she said, gulping just a little bit.

"One and the same, I'm afraid."

"Nothing to be afraid of with that, ma'am. After all, who doesn't want to be queen? By that I mean queen of *peoples' hearts*. Or princess. Or whatever it was Diana was. Not that I'm looking to be queen, I mean," Emma said, mentally kicking herself the moment she launched into her jibberish. "I'm sorry. I'm a bit confused. How do you know who I am?"

"I understand you housed my little boy when he chose to run away from home," she said with a wink. "Further still I was told you took very good care of him, and for that I am eternally grateful."

If she only knew how much she actually failed to meet the man's needs— make that desires — this lady would be over the moon, might even owe her a steak dinner.

Emma nodded. "It was nothing, really."

"Why, it must have been something, as you seem to have left quite an impression on my son."

Which was news to Emma, especially considering she hadn't heard boo from him since he'd left. Even though she did tell him to not reach out to her, since it would only make it harder. Could it be possible he really did miss her?

"I just helped him to feel at home." Emma summoned up the image of Adrian in that Statue of David apron, which made her smile at the thought of how much fun they had together.

"I assume you're well aware of what Adrian was running from," his mother said. "It seems that in so running, he ran right into what he didn't know he wanted all along."

Emma squinted her eyes, trying to digest what she was

hearing. "And that would be?"

"You, my dear."

Emma felt her palms get all sweaty and she was sure she was hearing ringing in her ears. It almost felt as if her surroundings were swimming before her eyes. She took a handful of cleansing breaths, trying to get a grip.

"I'm still not exactly clear how I ended up on that completely sweet ride over the Atlantic," Emma said. "By the way, thanks for that. I will remember that for the rest of my life. I can't believe we didn't even have to go through security! I can't tell you how much better it is flying that way."

Caroline elbowed Emma in the ribs to shut her up. Ariana began to laugh.

"My dears, you are most welcome. I'm so glad you enjoyed your flight and hope that they took exquisite care of you."

"It was perfect," Caroline interjected before her friend could babble for even a second more.

"I should explain my intentions, why I summoned you on Christmas day, of all things," the queen said. "Please, come join me for a hot drink while I tell you what's in store for you."

A half hour later Emma and Caroline were ushered to their rooms — complete with large beds with goose down comforters that would swallow you whole, and pillows, and pillows that had pillows. The room was hung with seventeenth-century tapestries and decorated with antique silver so brightly polished you'd have thought it was new. There were two Labrador retrievers who followed close on their heels and if they hadn't felt at home till that point, that surely set the pace.

"Would it be weird if I asked if one of the dogs could sleep with me?" Emma asked.

"Uh, yeah," Caroline said. "Besides, with a bit of luck, you might have a much bigger dog to tussle with in that huge bed."

Emma blushed. "Stop it!"

"Stop nothing! You rubbed the magic lantern and here we are. You'd better enjoy that genie while it lasts."

"Come off it, Caro. You know I'm not here for Adrian, per se," Emma said. "The queen —can you even stand that I just said that, like we're buds or something —merely invited us here as a thank you for taking such good care of her son. Nothing more. He'll probably run for the hills when he sees me."

"Yeah, I see two hills he'll be heading straight for," Caroline said, pointing at Emma's chest with a laugh.

"You're a creeper."

"Am not."

"Are too."

"Okay, just calling it as I see it. The guy's hot for you, and I'll say that to infinity so you can't negate it. Just accept it and move on."

"Fine. Whatever. On a more immediate note, then, I can't believe they're providing clothes for us to wear. I feel like Cinderella or something."

"Yeah like that Dress Shack dress you packed wasn't fancy enough or something."

"It wasn't from the Dress Shack," Emma said. "I got that at Klothing Korner."

"My bad. Much higher-class establishment."

"Who knew you'd have to wear a ball gown to eat a gingerbread house?" Emma said. "Speaking of, I cannot believe we get to pig out at a party. Is this a great country or what?"

"Champagne, cookies and candy. I could be persuaded to stick around," her friend said. "Kidding! I know my carriage turns into a pumpkin at midnight. Yours, however…remains to be seen."

"Seriously, Caro. Things like this don't happen to girls like me. So don't start concocting crazy fantasies about this. I'm sure it'll just be two friends catching up and having fun eating till we throw up."

"You're such a romantic."

The next day, following a very late breakfast in their room, Emma was practically stitched into a sapphire blue velvet ball gown with a crisscrossing bodice, a sweetheart neckline and coordinating fitted shrug. Her hair had been blown-out and was pulled back in a high ponytail. A lady in waiting or some such thing had even put fake eyelashes on her. Emma was going to ask Caroline if they should expect ten lords a-leaping to show up soon, but she decided not to break the spell with her smart-aleck jokes. She felt as close to a princess as she would ever be. Caroline had chosen a burgundy satin v-neck gown cut on the bias that hugged her curves and flared out below the knee like a Spanish dancer.

"Damn, we sure do clean up nicely," Caroline said.

"We're almost like those women I photograph all the time."

"Just like 'em, if you ask me. Make that better."

They fist-bumped and slipped into their amazingly comfortable too-tall designer heels, all part of the fairy-tale wardrobe courtesy of the queen. Clearly she could get things done, if she could slap together outfits for the two of them, on a national holiday, no less.

"We're off to the ball, then," Emma said, gritting her teeth from nervousness.

"Correction," her friend said. "We're off to pig out."

"That I can relate to. Thanks for the reminder," she said as they followed their handler to the great ballroom.

Something in the Heir

"Cheers, mate," Darcy said, tipping his highball glass of scotch to clink with Adrian's. "Here's to the soon-to-be new year full of freedom."

Adrian offered a weak smile. "Yeah, to freedom." He gave his friend a nod as he took a slug of his drink.

"Just think about it. You could have been about to be dragged down the aisle with a ball and chain locked to your ankle. Saved by the bell."

"Indeed." Adrian frowned.

"Come on, man," Darcy said as he chucked him in the bicep. "This is the biggest party of the year. You'll have your choice of women tonight. Why not suffer through and make the best of a bad situation."

"Funny," Adrian said. "I know you're trying to amuse me, but I'm not in the mood, thanks."

"You're still mooning over that American girl?"

"Mooning sounds so pathetic," he said. "But yes, I miss her. Perhaps more than I even thought I would."

Darcy shook his head in concern. "You've fallen. And hard. Happens to the best of them, or so I hear. But I never thought you'd be so foolhardy. Since when have you been a one-woman man kind of guy?"

"I didn't say I was," Adrian said defensively. "I just rather miss Emma. We had a good time together. She was different than your usual fawning royal-sniffer type."

"Speaking of, to your left," Darcy said, kicking Adrian.

"Adrian!" Serena said, reaching out to give him a two-cheek kiss. "You're looking cheerful this evening. Newfound freedom becomes you."

"And likewise it seems love has left a glow about you," he said.

"Or is that indigestion?" Darcy said. They all laughed.

"Roberto and I are to be wed in the spring," she said. "I hope you two will be there. Maybe I can have you as bridesmaids." She winked at them.

Jenny Gardiner

"Count on it," Adrian said. "I look good in strapless evening wear."

And he could only be thrilled to be anything at Serena's wedding other than the groom.

Chapter Twenty-Four

EMMA and Caroline were tucked far away from Adrian's detection as the queen made the announcement to the gathered guests that it was time to deconstruct the gingerbread house. People scattered the minute the trumpets blew to announce it was fair game.

Adrian wasn't much in the mood for this. He thought about the evening he told Emma about the traditions of Santa Christus, once his favorite holiday. He laughed, remembering how certain she was of a strategy to eat as much of the house as possible, and he decided to follow suit and work his way up from the back.

By the time he got to the far side of the ballroom, there were a couple of ambitious participants making a crumbling mess of things. As he wound around to the farthest corner, he caught a glimpse of someone who looked so much like Emma he felt the need to race over to her, but she'd already turned the corner. Ah, well. He knew it was impossible the woman was Emma. First of all, she'd never be there, and second of all, she'd never be dressed up like that. After all, she tended toward yoga pants and sweatshirts.

Emma caught her breath when she looked out of the corner of her eye and finally saw Adrian, who looked lost in thought just around the corner. He was so handsome in his royal navy military tunic in a snappy scarlet color, gold braided cords on his shoulders, and a royal blue sash draped diagonally across his chest. He wore a forage cap with an eight-pointed star embroidered on it, and a gold waist belt with a sword sling, sans sword, thank goodness.

If she wanted to tease him, she'd tell him he looked a bit like Michael Jackson from back in his heyday. But teasing was the last thing on her mind. Because yowzaaaa, she never knew how much she loved a man in uniform until now.

She reached up above her and broke off a cookie shingle from the low-hanging roof of the house. The snap of the cookie drew Adrian's attention, and he looked up to see her.

She took a bite of her shingle. "Yum. Chocolate," she said, licking her lips. She extended a piece toward him. "Cookie for your thoughts, sailor."

Adrian stood there, holding his breath, staring at her, just taking her in. "Emma," he finally said. "I can't quite believe it's you standing before me. Are you actually there, or are you a figment of my very active imagination?"

Emma pinched her arm, her cheek, just to be sure. "I've been wondering the very thing about you," she said. "But I can assure you, I'm me, in all my glory."

"Glorious, indeed," he said as he rushed toward her and folded her into his embrace. He leaned forward and pressed his lips to hers. For a moment they had this small corner to themselves, and Adrian took advantage of it, deepening his kiss, his hands roaming over her body as discreetly as possible, considering they were at a relatively public event and he had to maintain the dignity of his stature. Emma was trying hard to find purchase amidst the layers of ceremonial garb Adrian was wearing, and finally was able to tuck her hand up under the tunic and get a solid grasp on his nicely solid behind.

When they came up for air, Adrian peppered her with questions.

"Did Darcy bring you here?" he asked as he held her hands tightly in his. "That would be ridiculous. He's not the sort of guy to bother with a sentimental plan like that."

Emma laughed. "Probably the last person you'd ever expect to have sought me out is actually responsible for my being here."

Something in the Heir

He wrinkled his forehead. "My mother?"

"Shocking, right?"

"Let me get this straight. My mother — as in *my* mother — orchestrated bringing you here today. For *me*?"

Emma nodded. "Seems she was grateful I took good care of you. Maybe she realized you might possibly enjoy my company, though I'm guessing it's more likely she somehow knew about my weakness for edible gingerbread houses." She pulled some peanut brittle garnish from a windowsill.

"But what? Why?"

"You'll have to ask her yourself. If you're lucky, maybe she's handing over the reins to you to run your own personal life."

"But that's so unlike her," he said. "She's always ruled things with an iron fist. Well, maybe an elegantly gloved fist. With a few diamonds involved. But she's called the shots."

"Yes, but you've taught me a lesson I needed to learn," he heard a voice nearby say.

The two turned to see Ariana walking toward them, a piece of gingerbread in her hand.

"Mother!"

Emma stood still, resisting the urge to bite her nails, she was so nervous about how she was supposed to act around the queen and how she was supposed to act with Adrian around the queen. This was all new territory for a girl from suburbia.

"You look lovely, dear," she said to Emma.

"Thank you so much, ma'am," she said. "Your highness. I mean your majesty, I mean—" She glanced at Adrian, her face bunched up in a scowl. He only laughed at her.

"I told you, remember? Ariana, please."

Adrian's eyes grew wide, and he stared at his mother like she'd just stepped out of a flying saucer. He could hardly recall when she'd ever told a complete stranger to address her by her name before. Usually it was on a hospital visit with little children dying of cancer.

"Thank you, Mother," Adrian said. "You've no idea how

happy this has made me."

Ariana looked at Emma and Adrian, hand in hand, and smiled, then affectionately stroked her fingers across her son's face. "I think I might have an inkling."

"So I take it to mean you're not going to throw a million roadblocks in my way?" he asked, pointing at Emma, a hopeful look in his eyes. Just then his father appeared.

"Your mother has sworn to me she will never meddle in your personal affairs again," Enrico said, wrapping his arm around Ariana.

"Can I get that in writing?" Adrian asked with a wink.

Soon Darcy and Caroline joined their friends as they ate their way through the gingerbread house till they could ingest no more.

"I hope my seams don't burst on this dress," Emma said, stifling a belch, always the lady.

"Fine by me if they do," Adrian said. "It'll make quick work of things for me later on."

"We can't do that! Here?" she whispered in his ear.

"Oh yes we can," he said. "Here, there and everywhere."

Later the two of them went outside to the fairy light and holly garland-festooned courtyard, where a steady snowfall had resulted in several inches of new accumulation.

"I cannot believe I ended my Christmas celebration — or lack thereof — in this fantasy world of yours."

"Soon to be a fantasy world of yours, as well, my dear," Adrian said.

"Ha-ha. Nice joke," she said. "I'll be heading home in a few days. But I'll have marvelous memories. Thanks for that, Adrian."

Adrian turned to her, flicking heavy snowflakes from her

hair. "It's no joke, Emma. I know we haven't been together very long. But believe me when I say I've known many, many women in my life. And I knew the instant you let me kidnap you that there was something very special about you."

"I knew you'd admit someday that you kidnapped me!"

"Emma, be serious, just for a moment."

Emma straightened her face, dismissing the smile that wanted to remain permanently etched on her face.

"Yes, sir. Serious, sir."

"Come here, you," he said, leaning over her. "I'm going to kiss that smirk right off that gorgeous face of yours."

He held her closely as his tongue explored her mouth. He planted light kisses on the tip of her nose, across her cheeks, and down her throat.

"Do you suppose you might find it in you to consider spending the rest of your life with the likes of me?"

"Me? Be a part of this?" She spread her arms out around her. She could barely believe her ears.

"Are you suggesting it might take some convincing?"

"Nah, I'm pretty easy," she said, laughing. "I'll need to finish that quilt my grandmother started. Plus I might require that gilded pumpkin carriage. A footman or two. And I will insist on your wearing your surfer clothes on our honeymoon. Especially when we do that shark tank dive. Agreed?"

"As long as you agree you'll never push me away ever again. Even though it was an interesting challenge trying to talk you into wanting me."

"Who? Me? I'd never be so crazy."

He grabbed her hand.

"Prove it to me," he said.

And she did.

Thank you so much for reading *Something in the Heir!* I hope you enjoyed it! If so, please help others find this book:

1. Help other people find this book by writing a review.

2. Sign up for my new releases email so you can find out about the next book as soon as it's available and get fun giveaways.
   http://eepurl.com/baaewn

3. Like my Facebook page.
   www.facebook.com/jennygardinerbooks

And I love to hear from readers! Let me know what you think about my books! You can write to me at jenny@jennygardiner.net, and visit me on the web at www.jennygardiner.net.

Get more stories from Monaforte, starting with book two of the IT'S REIGNING MEN series, HEIR TODAY, GONE TOMORROW. Turn the page for a sneak peek:

HEIR TODAY, GONE TOMORROW

Chapter One

"IT was a dark and story night," Caroline McKenzie typed into her keyboard. Only her *"m"* kept sticking, so instead of stormy, it apparently was story. Whatever that meant. That stuck key was pretty much a metaphor for how this embarrassing attempt at figuring out if maybe she could just drop everything in life and be a writer was going.

Ever since Caro's best friend, Emma Davison jumped ship for the small European principality of Monaforte and the gorgeous prince Adrian who'd lured her there, life had become a distinctly dull shade of gray (and no, not in a way that involved hot men and questionable bondage practices, thank you). Until then, Caro had worked as a photographic assistant for Emma while she was figuring out what she wanted to do with her life, and had enjoyed a perfectly fine time in her off hours flitting from one guy to another like a hummingbird, zipping from flower to flower drinking tasty nectar.

For her that nectar came in the form of mostly charming, usually handsome, and almost always entirely forgettable men. But now without that job, she really had to figure out what she wanted to do with her life, and maybe put a lid on that boy-crazy nonsense in lieu of figuring herself out. Considering she was fast approaching thirty with little grand achievement to show for it, it seemed time. At least according to her mother and sister (and father and grandmother anyone else she knew, come to think of it).

She closed out of her document, putting an end to her

fledgling writing career. She figured her time was better spent FaceTiming with Emma, who she'd been missing something fierce since she closed up her business, packed up her belongings, and departed for a life most people could only dream of. She opened up the app and dialed through to Emma.

"Caro! What a pleasant surprise!" Emma said.

"What up, bitch?" her friend said, sticking out her tongue and then putting her face so close to the screen Emma could see every pore on her nose.

"Awww, so glad to see you haven't changed on me," Emma said. "I'd bitch you back, but I'm trying to pay attention to decorum —"

"— now that you're going to be a real-life princess."

Emma laughed. "Honestly I still can't get used to that whole concept. *Me!* Of all people! Although I suppose if the media can dub Kim Kardashian American royalty— I mean, come on, now, seriously? — I guess anybody can be."

"Yeah, well, I'm still waiting on my chance," Caroline said, forcing her lower lip out in a pout.

"Still haven't heard anything from Darcy?"

Caroline and Darcy Squires-Thornton, Adrian's equerry and best friend, had seemed to hit it off, well, royally, when Emma and Adrian were getting to know each other — when Emma helped Adrian flee a forced marriage his mother was trying to impose upon him. Right up until the time Caro hastened Emma off by surprise to Monaforte to be reunited with Adrian. At which point Darcy weirded out and turned into a complete and total jerk.

"The guy's a complete and total jerk. I don't want to talk about it any more."

Only she did. Big time.

"Okay, let's change the subject then."

"Have you seen him?"

"I thought you said you didn't want to talk about him!"

"I don't," Caroline said, pulling strands of her hair outward and making long, thin braids with her gorgeous, bright, red hair.

"Maybe I should be a hairdresser?"

"Oh yeah, that would be perfect for you," Emma said. "You did such a good job frying my hair with a curling iron in college. I had hair sprouts growing out of my scalp for months. I'm still not sure if I've forgiven you for that."

Caroline sighed. "Too late. Now that you're a princess *to-be*, the slate's wiped clean. Guess it's back to the drawing board for moi. My writing career didn't pan out either."

"Caroline, you regularly got *C's* in English class. And didn't you drop that creative writing class your sophomore year?"

"Well, we had a really long paper due," she said, raising her voice in a whine. "Besides, that was the weekend of that super fun fraternity festival out at the lake. Priorities!"

Emma shook her head. Caroline always had been the good-time girl, nothing ever fazed her, so it bummed Emma out to see her seeming so down.

"Oh yeah, I remember. We had to hitch back to town and it was like ten degrees out and you kept sticking out your leg to try to attract cars and then that idiot Bruce Bishop stopped for us—"

"—but he'd been drinking all day long so we refused to ride with him. And he was so insulted, but he agreed to pull over on the side of the road and we all slept in his tiny two-seater car with the heat blasting, you and me squished together in that one seat, till about five in the morning, when the car ran out of gas and the heat died."

"And then we had to find a tow truck on a Sunday morning, and I think we had about a half a bar on our cell phones, so it took a thousand times trying to get enough of a signal to call someone."

"Ah, but I lived to tell about it. And then lived to watch my best friend grow up and have the kick-assiest life imaginable while I lingered back and became a has-been."

Emma tsk'd loudly, wagging her finger at her friend. "Hey, Car. That's not you talking. You're no has-been. You're an up-

and-coming. You just haven't gotten there yet. But in the meantime you're the most fun friend a girl — or guy — could have."

Caroline felt tears welling up, making her green eyes appear almost translucent. "If I'm so fun, then why did that jerkball bail on me, just when we were starting to have a great time? Was I that bad in bed?"

"Don't you mean in *beach*?" Emma said with a wink.

Caroline and Darcy sort of publicly went at it after skinny-dipping in twenty-degree weather at the beach in North Carolina where Adrian had holed up, and seemed to actually have some potential as a couple together. Back then, Emma was too busy blubbering about her own broken heart once Adrian returned to his real life to worry about Caroline. Besides, Caroline had a reputation as a love-'em-and-leave-'em type, which suited most guys just fine. I mean what's better than a girl who's full of life, loves to fool around a little, and then doesn't demand the guy put a ring on it?

"You never answered my question."

Emma arched her brow. "Which one was that?"

"Have you seen him?"

Emma shook her head. "Honestly, Caro, I've been so crazy busy since I moved here and Adrian has too that I haven't had a chance to think about much of anything except what is right in front of my face. I know a few weeks ago Adrian said something about Darcy's father being ill, so maybe he's been sticking close to his family lately. Plus you told me to not ask around, you said you'd feel stupid if he knew you were prowling."

"Yeah but that was before I didn't hear from him at all."

"How was I supposed to know you had a sudden change of heart?"

"You're my best friend. Of course you need to know that intuitively."

"Okay, then. I'll just double check in my crystal ball next time I have a chance to come up for air so I can second guess you from across the Atlantic Ocean."

Caroline rolled her eyes. "Rubbing salt in the wound that you're so far away. And that you're so busy you don't have time to deal with the likes of me."

"Oh, honey. I know you're upset with him and I totally understand that. But I hope you can understand that I'm just doing what I have to do to become part of this family."

"This *royal* family."

"Oh yeah, no forgetting that. I think I've seen more sabers in the past month than I'd seen in an entire Three Musketeers novel. And velvet. Wow, do we have a lot of velvet here. And ermine. The queen has a deep red velvet cape trimmed in ermine. If I weren't so sad about how many little ermine had to die to make that cape, I'd want to use it as a blanket at night. Even though I'm not sure what an ermine even is."

"A weasel."

"I don't think Darcy's a weasel, Car. I think he's just dealing with other things right now."

"I wasn't talking about Darcy, you dingbat! An ermine is a weasel."

"Huh. Wonder who decided it was particularly regal to wear a weasel. I could see something like a sable sounding more royal, but a weasel?"

"A sable's kind of weasely too, to tell you the truth."

"And you're an expert on royal fur trimmings because?"

"Remember that protest march phase I went through? Only I wasn't so wild when the group decided to throw red paint on fur-bearing women even if I did think their fur coats were better off on the original wearer?"

Emma nodded her head knowingly. "I was sort of glad you stopped that only because I wasn't up for having to bail you out of jail. Even though I total respect your conviction."

"Yes, conviction minus the conviction. To be honest, my parents threatened to take me out of the will if I got cuffed and put in jail. Considering I'm *still* paying off college loans, I didn't want to cut off my nose to spite my wallet. Or something like that. But enough about me. Let's hear more about palace life."

Emma walked over to sit in what looked like the world's most comfortable chair, something long and overstuffed but posh with what appeared to be hunt scenes involving leopards on the upholstery. It was right by a fire blazing in one of those mammoth fireplaces in which you could cook an entire ox on a spit. She put up her feet and leaned back, settling into the chair, which seemed to swallow her whole, it was so cushiony. A beautiful yellow Labrador was asleep beside her. It could've been a scene from a *Norman Rockwell: the Royal Years* painting.

"They call this a fainting chair. Do you love it?"

"I'd love it more if I was fainting in it, rather than sitting in my cold, barren apartment in Arlington."

"I hear ya. You know you have an open invitation to come over here any time."

"Thanks, Em. I know that. And believe, me, I'll take you up on it. As soon as I can drum up the funds."

"Once I'm feeling more settled, maybe I can figure out how I can enlist the royal jet to come for you. Surely I'll have some access to it."

"Don't force it yet. I don't want you getting kicked out before you're even in."

"I really do want to see you. And I'd love for you to be here to help me plan this wedding."

"Oh, my God. I still can't believe you are going to be married. You, of all people. The last of the holdouts."

"Tell me about it. If you'd have asked me two months ago if I'd even date someone, let alone marry them, I'd have cackled in your face."

"I think maybe you did that."

"Okay fine. You know what I mean. But really, Caroline, you're my maid of honor. There are going to be some times where it would be really nice to have you here."

"Like say a bachelorette party, being that you don't know a bleeding soul in the whole country? It will be the worlds smallest hen party."

"Oh you are so funny. Actually I really love Adrian's sister Isabella. She's as sweet as can be and a little feisty. Reminds me of you, sort of. And I even kind of like Serena, believe it or not. She's not half bad, especially now that I know all that I thought was true about her wasn't. She's got a little pissy streak in her, in a good way. And she can be pretty bawdy too, for a blueblood."

"So what's it like having people wait on you hand and foot."

"Sometimes it's amazing. I mean like never having to wash a dirty dish is so not a bad thing. I could truly get used to that. Actually I have gotten used to it. Actually I haven't. At meal times I go to clear my dishes only someone else clears them before I can even think to. Sometimes I feel a little pampered. Okay I feel really pampered. It's just amazing."

"And your royal wardrobe?"

"So get this: they come to me. I mean if I want to shop at stores I can, but I can also have people bring me clothes. Stylists and designers. Considering the fanciest I ever got was J. Crew or Anthropologie, and that only rarely, this is way out of my league."

"And you and Adrian?"

Emma's eyes got all swoony and her face Dalai Lama-serene. "It's amazing, Caro. *He's* amazing. Never could I have imagined being so happy with someone. I am absolutely over the moon."

Caroline smiled, finally. "It couldn't have happened to a better person. I'm so happy for you, Emma. So, so very happy for you."

And she was. Although she wished right about now she could make crank phone calls to Darcy like the kind they used to make back in sixth grade. Maybe one of those *I hear you have Prince Albert in a can. If so, you'd better let him out!* type of calls. Though they'd have to change it to Prince Adrian. Gah! Anything to get his attention. To hear his voice with that dreamy accent. To enable her to take the pulse of the situation. To understand why it was that they had gotten along so well and their chemistry was pretty darned electrifying and then all of a sudden he dropped off the face of the earth. It didn't make any sense, and things that were senseless made Caroline crazy.

But the fact was, she couldn't be making long-distance phone calls to Europe. Nor did she want to come across as desperate. If he wanted her, he'd have reached out to her. And clearly he had moved on. So what that when she showed up at Emma's wedding he was going to be best man to her maid of honor, and they'd likely be paired up and have to fake it that they even wanted to look at one another, let alone that they might have almost cared about each other. Because by then she wasn't going to care. Not one whit. And if Darcy wanted her, he was going to have to crawl to her on all fours. Better yet, slink. Like one of those royal ermine. Skitter and slink right back into her heart, damn him.

Chapter Two

DARCY rubbed his eyes hard with his fingertips as he plunked down into that darned uncomfortable chair yet again, weary from days by his father's side in the hospital. The beep-beep-beep of heart monitors and whatever else was taking the pulse of his father's fading body had started to really wear on Darcy, a constant reminder that soon those beeps were going to fade away altogether. While he was more than a little tired of that electronic medical metronome, he knew the silence would be worse. He cherished his father, and rued the day he'd no longer be here.

Darcy, his sister Clementine and little brother Edouardo had been taking turns alongside his mother, Charlotte, holding vigil as the family patriarch slowly made his exit from this world. Darcy's father, Lord Hubert (please, people, pronounced with silent "h" and "t") was a remarkable father who balanced managing his impressive estate with being a very involved and quite down-to-earth father. Some of Darcy's best times were spent in the company of his father, hunting, fishing, even traveling to exotic locales like the African continent. His father lived life to the fullest, so it was with at least a small amount of gratitude Darcy acknowledged he'd had plenty of time to fulfill his dreams. And at some point dreams must come to a close. Something Darcy was realizing all too factually now.

During some of the late nights in the contemplative dark of his fathers hospital room, Darcy marveled that only a few weeks earlier, he was, truly, footloose and fancy-free, feeling none of the burden of the family patriarchy that he'd known, deep in his heart, would someday be something with which he'd have to deal.

Wasn't it only Christmas time when he was traipsing across the States on the heels of Adrian, his runaway charge? It seemed his only care — other than ensuring Adrian's safe return — had been his burgeoning friendship (if he could call it that) with that cute, rowdy redheaded friend of Emma. And now that was about the last thing he could dream about dreaming about, even if maybe he did find himself occasionally revisiting some of the high points of his time with her. Including that little encounter on the beach, despite the frigid weather, and yeah, the after-party in their cheap hotel room that night.

But now he had the family sandbag weighing down his shoulders, the knowledge that it was up to him to ensure the family name and tradition continue on, to upkeep the property and holdings of his fathers financial empire to last long past even his own heirs.

Heirs. Now there's a funny one. Darcy hadn't given a fair thought to a serious relationship in, well, ever. He didn't need to. He wasn't in charge of a country, or even really anything. He was Adrian's best friend and thus evolved into being his equerry after a shared boyhood at boarding school and years together at university. He was Adrian's right hand man, he knew him as if a brother, and he loved being there for his friend. Until now, Adrian's priorities took precedence over his own. Who knew what twist this relationship would take now that Adrian was settling down.

Of course Adrian would still be traveling, though likely less so, but now, more often than not, Emma would join him. Emma would, undoubtedly, take over many of the roles that Darcy had played. Which was fine. It made sense. Adrian was moving on. And, like it or not, Darcy would have to move on, to adopt a more serious role running the family estate. Which would leave little time for travel with Adrian, anyhow, and less still for personal indulgences like flings with feisty American firecrackers named Caroline.

Chapter Three

CAROLINE was finishing up a workout on the elliptical machine—okay, actually, she was catching up on the *Real Housewives of New Jersey* while barely breaking a sweat—when her phone rang.

"It's me," Emma said.

"Princess! To what do I owe this honor?"

"Stop with the princess. It isn't even an accurate term for me yet."

"Fine. How about princess-in-waiting?"

"Why are you breathing so heavily? Am I interrupting something? What's his name? Oh, God, sorry—I'll call back when you're not, um, indisposed. At least you've gotten over Darcy."

"Oh stop it," Caroline said. "I'm at the gym. And no, I haven't gotten over he-who-shall-not-be-named."

"Wait a minute. *You*," Emma said, pausing, "are working out? The woman who said she'd rather die fat and happy than set foot on a treadmill?"

Caroline shrugged. "Yeah, well, this is what happens when my best friend moves away and I'm superbored and my job is gone and the guy I was just getting to know has evaporated from my life," she said. "I think I'm sporting biceps."

"Biceps are good. Better than soloceps."

"I don't even know what that is. Sounds like a dinosaur name."

"I think you're thinking triceratops."

"Well, I definitely am not sporting any triceratops, thank goodness," Caroline said, glancing at her arms to be sure. "To what do I owe this pleasure, Your Highness?"

"Seriously, don't call me that. I don't know if I'll even eventually be referred to in that way, but I'd be totally embarrassed if you called me all the wrong things in front of Adrian's family."

"Considering I'm about, oh, an eight-hour flight away from his family, I think we're safe from any awkward royal gaffes from *moi*."

"*Au contraire*, my friend."

"Huh?" Caroline's interest was piqued with that comment, enough so she turned off the volume on the show just as someone's hair was about to be pulled hard. And she hated to miss the good stuff.

"See, I just can't plan a wedding without my best friend. I need some input. Plus, the queen is giving us a home. More like a sprawling estate. That's in addition to an entire wing of the palace—the royal apartments, they call them. And I'm going to have to decorate and staff it all. Staff. Can you imagine? Here I always thought of staff as an infection you get from dirty razor blades."

"Pretty sure that's spelled differently."

"Whatever. Don't you see? Now staff is my friend! As in people, working for me! And they'll work in my home. I keep pinching myself—I can hardly believe this is real. But I need some help. And sound advice. And someone who knows me and my tastes. And someone who will call it like they see it, and the only person I know who fits that description is—"

"Yours truly?" Caroline said, treading as slowly as humanly possible on the elliptical, hoping someone wasn't about to kick her off since her hour time limit was finished. "Shucks, Ems, I'm honored and all, but there's that little bit about the cash flow and all—"

"About that cash flow," her friend said. "There is no flow issue anymore. See, I spoke with Ariana—"

"*The queen*," Caroline interrupted. "Please. I need to have 'Her Royal Highness' drummed into my head or I'll start calling her Ariana at your wedding. And I'm pretty sure one of those guys with the big furry hats and the epaulets and brass buttons and really shiny shoes and super long rifles and swords will come at me for calling the queen by her first name."

Emma laughed. "Tell me about it. I've always thought it would be superweird addressing any in-laws by their first name. Which I figured wasn't going to be a problem since I wasn't planning to get hitched anyhow. But now here I am marrying into royalty and—*awkward!*—I can't begin to tell you how to address half these people, all of whom have a slew of names and titles. I go around feeling like a complete doofus for not knowing what to call any of them."

"Yeah, you're like, um, hey there, uh, sir, er, um…"

"Practically. Thank goodness I'm being coached on protocol."

"Seriously? You have a protocol coach?" Caroline said. "So that 'the rain in Spain falls mainly on the plain' rolls off your tongue in a most pleasing way?" She added that last bit with a Continental accent.

"More like so I don't stab someone with the seafood fork when I've realized I have no idea what a seafood fork even looks like."

"Violence is not the answer, Emma."

"Joking. It can be a little bit daunting, trying to get up to speed on all this information that took Adrian a lifetime to absorb."

"So don't rush it. All in good time. Rome wasn't built in a day. For that matter, I'm sure Porto Castello wasn't built in a day."

"You've got a point there. This nation's capital has been here for hundreds and hundreds of years. I suppose I need to build up my knowledge base one brick at a time," Emma said. "But in the meantime, I could use your help. Which brings me to what I was going to surprise you with before we got off on a tangent. Pack your bags, sistah."

Caroline was silent. In front of her on the tiny screen, one of the housewives was throwing a full glass of red wine against a fireplace.

Heir Today, Gone Tomorrow

"Caro? You still there?"

Caroline took a deep breath. "I thought you just said something about packing my bags. And I'm terrified to get my hopes up in case it doesn't mean what I hope like hell it means. Because if it means I just won a weekend at a timeshare in the Ozarks, I'm totally going to cry. But if it means I might be en route to see my BFF, well, oh, crap, I am so not going to get choked up—"

"Wow. You've gone soft in my absence. Since when have you cried over anything other than spilled wine?"

"Point in fact, I just witnessed spilled wine on the little television screen I'm looking at. So there."

"*Your* spilled wine."

"Okay, so I'm not really weepy. Well, maybe just a bit. I need more information before a full-out bawl."

"So you remember that amazing, amazing, incredible jet that flew us to Monaforte at Christmastime?"

Caroline shook her head. "No. I totally forgot about it. I had to purge it from my memory because I'm so far removed from that luxury now."

"In that case, good. Because you're not going to fly on that," Emma said. "Sorry, but Prince Enrico is off somewhere with that plane. But we're going to fly you commercial. Hope you don't mind."

"Business class, maybe?" Caro asked with a hint of hope in her voice.

"Better still. I've got you a one-way first-class ticket with the first-class cabin instructed to treat you like royalty," Emma said. "Will that suffice?"

Caroline thought for a second about how she'd eaten stale Rice Krispies for breakfast and how she knew the milk was on the verge of turning but she didn't want to waste a drop because it costs a fortune these days and who can afford to throw that down the drain? And she contrasted that with the notion of her flying as if near-royalty back to Monaforte. And her breath hitched as she tried to speak.

"I don't think I even know what to say," she said. "It's too amazing to believe. Here I've been trying to figure out what to do with myself, and now you're handing me a project on a silver platter." Caroline stared at the mess the housewife had made of the place, broken glass everywhere and blood-red stains all over the taupe-colored walls. And she imagined what it would be like to be able to toss your dishes away like that, not to mention expensive wine. Well, it was a fake show, maybe it was dyed water. But even then, staff was going to clean it up. And staff—wow, Emma has staff. And now Caro was going to sort of be staff.

"Am I going to be one of your staff?" Caroline asked. "I mean not like I don't want to be, but I'm not sure how I feel about being a minion."

Emma laughed. "You are the weirdest person I know. No, you are not staff. Consider yourself my advisor. My royal advisor, if you'd like to add that to the title. Do we have a deal then?"

"As long as you promise I can be on the first plane out of here."

"Well, the first one has left already. Will the next work for you?"

"Today?"

"No time like the present."

Caroline looked down at her sweaty shirt. "Oh, man. I've got some serious work to do to get myself into a presentable state."

"You won't be alone then," Emma said. "We can work on that together."

"I am so going to pilfer your new wardrobe."

Want more? Get Heir Today, Gone Tomorrow now!

The complete *It's Reigning Men* series:

Book 1: Something in the Heir
Book 2: Heir Today, Gone Tomorrow
Book 3: Bad to the Throne
Book 4: Love is in the Heir
Book 5: Shame of Thrones
Book 6: Throne for a Loop
Book 7: It's Getting Hot in Heir
Book 8: A Court Gesture

I hope you've enjoyed getting to know the characters in the *It's Reigning Men* series! I had so much fun with the royals in Monaforte that I decided to spin it off into another series called *The Royal Romeos*, featuring the winemaking Romeo family from the Chianti region of Italy. The series begins with *Red Hot Romeo*.

You met Alessandro Romeo in *A Court Gesture* (or you will!) and I hope you'll read on to see what's been happening with Sandro since you met him in Milan with Luca....

Read on for a sneak peek:

Red Hot Romeo

Chapter One

ALESSANDRO Romeo was enjoying a beautiful sunset, sipping his Negroni, neat, on the terrace of his winery's palazzo that overlooked his family's vast estate when he noticed a fat curl of dark smoke trailing skyward on the other side of the sprawling Tuscan manor home. Quickly setting his drink aside, he raced down the terrace steps, rushed through a gauntlet of tall, narrow cypress trees and across the Italian garden in front of the palazzo as the acrid smell of smoke grew stronger and blackened clouds of it enveloped more of the once melon-colored late-day sky.

In the distance, he spotted a tiny white sports car racing down the estate's long, cypress-lined driveway just as he finally came upon the source of the now choking smoke: his beloved Lamborghini *Aventador Superveloce*—a cool half million dollars of premier driving pleasure—sizzling away with the crackle of fire and lick of flames that were embracing his dream car and turning it into a veritable conflagration.

"*Aiuto!*" Sandro shouted, calling for the farm hands to help, if not to salvage his burning car, then at least to keep the vehicle from exploding and injuring anyone. "Help! Bring water, *prontissimo!*"

The *Cantine dei Marchesi Romeo* was a vineyard with many

employees still working into late afternoon trimming back grape leaves, so within a minute several workers had arrived, directing hoses and buckets of water to try to douse the fire until all that was left were the charred remains of his beloved sports car. Sandro felt grateful that at least they'd stopped the fire before the car exploded.

"*Vaffanculo, si strega,*" Sandro said, shaking his fist in rage toward the now long-departed car he'd seen racing away from the scene. *Fuck off, you witch.* It didn't take much to deduce who'd torched the thing: he'd just seen the taillights of his hot-tempered on-again/off-again girlfriend Gia Sandretti's convertible trailing down the long drive. The woman had already resorted to plenty of other extreme ways to express her irrational jealous rages, including recently impaling him with the heel of one of her Manolo Blahniks—which resulted in five stitches to his arm—so he knew immediately this bore her telltale fingerprints.

He'd tried to extricate himself from the relationship more times than he could count at this point; it hadn't been but a few months into dating her that he knew she had a streak of green running through her like a river of toxic waste. Alessandro couldn't so much as inadvertently glance at another woman, even in a magazine, without Gia flipping out on him, which meant the usual stream of foul language spewed at him alongside crazed accusations and the occasional hurled glass object or other breakables.

By nature a genial and fun-loving guy, he'd put up with it, thinking that eventually she'd find her way to another man to harass, but as much as he tried to let her go gently so as not to trigger her impetuous fury, she simple wasn't getting the hint.

Sure Gia, a stunningly statuesque dark-haired brunette, was gorgeous, but he hadn't taken to calling her Crazy Gia for nothing. And the last thing Sandro needed in his life was a drama queen fashion model with no self-control who acted more like a secret police interrogator than a lover.

Sandro had met Gia at one of the many social functions he normally attended as principle of the world-famous Cantine dei Marchesi Romeo winemakers. His was an Italian family with a history of six hundred years of wine-making and roots that reached back to the days of Italian nobility and the famed house of Savoy. His family had immediate ties to the royals of neighboring Monaforte as well, as his uncle Enrico, Duke of Santo Miele, was married to that country's Queen Ariana.

Officially Alessandro's title was Marchese Alessandro Romeo, but he tended to downplay that archaic terminology except when necessary at official events, where the cachet of the royal title helped with his family business. Or as was more often the case in the past: when it helped him pick up beautiful women.

No doubt it's what drew Gia to him in the first place, aside from his handsome good looks. He wore his thick, wavy dark hair to near his shoulders, often pulled back in a ponytail, and sported a neatly-trimmed goatee beard and moustache that proved irresistible to many women. His sincere, brown eyes caused them to swoon even more. Throw in a royal title, a famous family name, and plenty of wealth, and Sandro was a delicious catnip that most women simply couldn't resist. Except when it came to nutters like Gia, who seemed to want to push him away all while clinging desperately to him as if he was a gangrenous appendage. But this was the last straw with her; this time he would file a police complaint and ensure that she was no longer allowed anywhere near him or have anything to do with him. Enough was enough.

A week later…

Sandro dusted off his hands and placed them on his hips, beaming as he gazed at the object of his near-undivided attention for the past six years: the design and building of a massive new headquarters for Romeo wines, a place that would house the offices of Marchesi Romeo wines but also become a tourist destination for wine lovers the world over. It had been Sandro's dream to create this destination venue, something he'd imagined for several years prior to actually implementing the plan.

He and his family had collaborated with one of the top Italian architects to envision the one-of-a-kind design of the building, constructed with local materials, intended to keep in harmony with the landscape while remaining environmentally-friendly, energy-efficient, and ultimately to serve as a veritable work of art in the Tuscan countryside. And in a few days, others would finally be able to share in Sandro's dream-come-true, at the grand opening gala. Guests who would attend included celebrities, political leaders, prominent local officials, and of course family and friends.

Sandro had reached out to his favorite cousin, Luca, the youngest of the Monaforte princes, to ensure his attendance. Monaforte was a small European principality on the Mediterranean with strong ties to Italy.

"You know, I'll disown you if you don't show up," Sandro said, teasing his good friend. "I'll cut off your vino supply—hit you where it'll hurt most."

Luca had for a long time been Sandro's social sidekick, but last year had settled into a relationship with a European-based American reporter named Larkin Mallory, and now it was as if he barely left the comfort of his living room. Sandro hated how complacent men became once they got "whipped": always at the woman's beck and call, never free to do as they pleased.

Now that Gia was out of the picture, he was going to make sure he didn't allow a woman to cloud his judgment and create hassles for him ever again. *No thank you.* The loss of his expensive sports car was a small price to pay to learn that lesson.

"I'd be crazy not to show up at this one," Luca said. "It's the event of the season, I hear. Even homebodies like me will be there."

"Homebodies," his cousin said with a grumble. "Whatever

happened to the man I knew who partied till dawn and couldn't be bothered with such things as commitment?"

Luca laughed. "You know that was ninety percent urban legend anyhow," he said. "It's not like I really caroused that much."

"Yeah well sometimes the legend is as true as fact."

"That's what's wrong with this world."

"You've become a grumpy old man."

"Not grumpy. Happily settled is all," Luca said. "You should give it a try some time. No more out on the prowl, hoping to get laid without catching any communicable diseases. It's a good thing."

"Hell no," Sandro said. "You do know about Gia's latest— and final—batshit crazy maneuver?"

"Of course," Luca said. "I always suspected there was something off about that one. Even when you first started dating, she was irrationally demanding. Like when you dragged me to that godforsaken fashion show she was in just so she would have an audience."

"Tell me about it," he said. "Yet one more reason I will never cross paths with a fashion model again. Ever. Those women are the worst. I think they get hangry from lack of food and they get totally *pazzo*."

"Hangry?"

"It's a combination of hungry and angry," he said. "All the worse for Gia, because she's an Italian girl who can't eat pasta. *Mamma mia*, what kind of life is that? Who wouldn't be crazy like that?"

"Well in that case I'd better apologize in advance because Larkin is bringing along her friend Taylor to your gala, and, well," he said, lowering his voice to a whisper. "She's a fashion model."

Sandro shook his head, even though Luca couldn't see him protesting physically. "No, thank you. I'll take a pass," he said. "You can have her all to yourself. If that's your thing."

"If what's my thing?"

"If you want to hook up with her."

"Are you crazy? I'm perfectly happy with Larkin. Not looking to add anyone into the relationship," he said. "I was thinking maybe you'd like Taylor. She's beautiful, of course. But she's really sweet as well. Completely down to earth."

"No. Models. Ever, dude," he said. "Ever."

"Fine, go ahead and punish yourself," Luca said. "But trust me, you'll regret it. You'd be lucky if she'd have anything to do with you anyhow."

"No doubt," Sandro said. "But do me a favor, just keep her far, far from me. I want nothing to do with any of those crazy women, and this is a night I want to completely avoid erratic women with bad tempers. So whatever you do, spare me."

"Fine," he said. "I'll respect your wishes. But trust me, you'll regret it."

"To the contrary, *mio cugino*, it's for the best," Sandro said, even though his curiosity was already getting the best of him as he Googled supermodels named Taylor to see exactly what she looked like. Old habits, after all, were hard to break.

Chapter Two

TAYLOR McFarland loved a good black tie party, she thought, taking a final sip of champagne as her plane was about to land in Florence. She'd get to dress in yet another amazing designer gown, and hot men in tuxedos would be plentiful. It was so up her alley. It was why she was on her way to Italy, and this one promised to be particularly fabulous—a spectacular venue in an architecturally-creative structure built into the hillside at some Italian guy's vineyard. And the wine would be flowing freely.

What's not to love? Plus she was joining her good friend Larkin, and Larkin's boyfriend Luca, and she always had fun with the two of them. Talk about opposites attracting: Larkin had been such a quiet little mouse of a woman when they first met, and Luca, well, he's a prince, a bit of a bon vivant, and used to the limelight. It was lovely that the two of them found each other, albeit after some struggles. Taylor had helped to spruce up Larkin's appearance a bit, steering her away from the clothing-as-camouflage manner of dress, and Larkin had taken to it with a vengeance, and had now practically achieved Taylor's level of clothes-craziness.

Luca had invited Taylor to join them and to stay at the palazzo owned by his winemaker cousin whose vineyard supposedly made a one of the most famous wines in Tuscany. Luca had promised her that he was a lot of fun, but really, Taylor wasn't on the prowl anyhow. She was over dealing with men who were nothing but a pain in her butt, thank you. She was perfectly happy to just go and browse the merchandise without making a purchase. Besides, she didn't have time for dalliances right now; she had much more important things to do than having to tag-team a long-distance relationship anyhow.

Taylor had recently started a charitable organization called *Rags to Riches*, to help children who couldn't afford to buy clothes piece together outfits that would allow them to not feel like such outsiders. Having grown up in a household with a single mother who struggled to pay the bills each month, Taylor knew what it was like to show up to school in the same threadbare outfits all the time: it was demoralizing, and kids loved to taunt the ones who looked like they'd just come in off the streets. If she had a dollar for every time kids called her white trash, she'd have had plenty of money to clothe herself as she was able to now that she had become a famous fashionista. So it was particularly gratifying to be able to help out other children. It might seem like a superficial thing, providing decent clothes to a kid, but having come from those very circumstances of lacking, she totally got what it meant to them and knew that even a little bit of window-dressing could make a difference.

She figured a lot of powerful people with money would be in attendance at this event, and they were her favorite type to strong-arm into making fabulous donations. A Christie Brinkley lookalike, with gentle blond sun-bleached waves and soft blue eyes, the American supermodel was not beyond using her looks and stature to get what she wanted, if it helped others in need. She knew wealthy men in particular would never turn down a gorgeous woman in a slinky evening gown soliciting them for funds. Just as long as they didn't presume she was soliciting anything else.

After a smooth landing, Taylor was off the plane quickly and through customs in no time at all. As she exited the security area with her luggage, she saw Larkin and Luca practically entwined on a bench near the entryway, oblivious to her existence while they made out like a couple of horny teenagers.

She wheeled her bag up to them and cleared her throat.

"Ahem," she said, crossing her arms and tapping her toe, staring at them both, her brow arched.

Larkin detached quickly and blushed. "Oh, Taylor! So sorry! Luca and I were just, uh, getting re-acquainted after being apart for a few minutes while I ran to the restroom." She grinned as her boyfriend swiped his finger along her lips to remove some excess saliva. Gross. She stood up and gave Taylor a warm embrace.

"Please," Taylor said, shaking her head as she hugged her friend. "I'm totally used to PDA when I'm around you two. I would have expected nothing less. I'm just impressed you kept your clothes on." Larkin gave her a playful smack.

It did make her laugh how Larkin had gone from such a wallflower to apparently a wild ass. It was nice to see her come into her own.

"I was merely expressing my affection for Luca like any true Italian would."

"Only you're not Italian."

"When in Rome then?" she said.

"We're in Florence, duh," Taylor said.

"It doesn't matter," Luca said, reaching for Larkin's hand. "Soon she'll be an official member of the Monaforte royal family. And that means she'll technically even have some Italian ties, being that my father is one hundred percent hot-blooded Italian. She'll nearly be Italian herself." He winked.

"Oh, my God!" Taylor said with a squeal, pulling Larkin into a hug. "You two are getting married? What? When? How? And I won't ask why, because, well, that's obvious." She grabbed her left hand and lifted it up closely to inspect the three-stone crown-set ring with a center ruby surrounded by old European-cut diamonds.

"It's from Monaforte's crown jewel collection," Luca said. "I consulted with my mother before choosing this, which belonged to the only other blond member of the royal family, a very distant great-, great-, great-grandmother or something.

Mum thought it would be fitting for Larkin to have this ring."

"It's stunning, Larks," Taylor said, holding her hands up to her face in surprise. "I'm just so overwhelmed about this! But I want to know all of the details!"

"So we just spent a few days in Venice," she said. "On the last evening, before a breathtaking sunset on the Grand Canal in front of *Piazza San Marco*, we were being serenaded by our gondolier when Luca got down on one knee and asked for my hand!"

"I can't even believe it," Taylor said. "Fairytale perfect. Wow. I'm so glad there are still romantic men in the world. I was starting to think they all died in the Pleistocene era."

Luca laughed. "Were there humans back then? Or we were still mollusks?"

Taylor rolled her eyes. "I think humans were just getting started then. Nothing personal, but men are still mollusks, if you ask me."

He gave her two thumbs up. "Thanks for that vote of confidence."

"Aww, poor Taylor has plenty of reason to be sour on men," Larkin said, squeezing her friend's hand. "What's it been, like five guys in a row who ended up only wanting to be with you because you're a model? And when they found out you actually did things with your life other than look beautiful and decorate their arms, then they walked away? I think the problem is you've got to find the right man, and not the Troglodytes you've been dating."

"Yeah, no more men who want to drag me by the hair back to the cave so that I can prepare a fat brontosaurus steak for him."

"I don't know about you but all this talk of prehistory is making me hungry," Luca said, rubbing his stomach. "In fact, a good, bloody Florentine steak sounds awesome."

"I'm with you," Taylor said. "I had just enough champagne on the plane to remind me I haven't eaten since my measly croissant at breakfast."

"Perfect," Larkin said. "We've got reservations for dinner in Florence, and we'll drive down to Sandro's afterwards."

Taylor scrunched her nose. "Speaking of Troglodytes. I know you guys want to fix me up but really, I am so not interested."

"Oh, stop," Larkin said, waving her hand dismissively. "He's a really sweet guy once you get to know him. I thought he was a jerk at first too but really, I think you'll like him."

"Wow. There's a ringing endorsement," Taylor said, arching her brow. "At any rate, you're sure it's okay with me tagging along? I mean I'm happy to come to this big fête, but I don't want to be an imposition."

"First off, you, my dear, would never be an imposition," Luca said. "Secondly, my cousin Alessandro won't even know you're there, the place is that big. It's a palace, literally. A gigantic Renaissance palazzo. It could be days until he knows if any of us are there. Plus I'm sure he's going to be at the new building overseeing the finishing touches anyhow. So no worries."

Taylor shrugged. "Okay, if you're sure. I'd just hate to have the man be mad that I'm invading his space."

Luca shook his head. "Not at all," he said. "Besides, he's always had a thing for models."

Taylor rolled her eyes. Yet one more reason she would have exactly nothing to do with that man.

Red Hot Romeo

Available now.

All books by Jenny Gardiner:

Contemporary Romances Available from Jenny Gardiner

It's Reigning Men series:
Book 1: Something in the Heir
Book 2: Heir Today, Gone Tomorrow
Book 3: Bad to the Throne
Book 4: Love is in the Heir
Book 5: Shame of Thrones
Book 6: Throne for a Loop
Book 7: It's Getting Hot in Heir
Book 8: A Court Gesture

The Royal Romeos series
Book 1: Red-Hot Romeo
Book 2: Black Sheep Romeo
Book 3: Red Carpet Romeo
Book 4: Blue Collar Romeo
Book 5: Silver Spoon Romeo
Book 6: Blue-Blooded Romeo
Book 7: Big O Romeo

The Falling for Mr. Wrong series:
Book 1: Falling for Mr. Wrong
Book 2: Falling for Mr. Maybe
Book 3: Falling for No Way in Hell
Book 4: Falling for Mr. Sometimes
Book 5: Falling for Mr. Right

Other Contemporary Romances:
Accidentally on Purpose
Compromising Positions

Single Titles:
Slim to None
Anywhere but Here
Sleeping with Ward Cleaver
Where the Heart Is

Memoir:
Bite Me: A Parrot, A Family and a Whole Lot of Flesh Wounds

Essay Anthology:
Naked Man on Main Street

About the Author

Jenny Gardiner is the author of #1 Kindle Bestseller *Slim to None* and the award-winning novel *Sleeping with Ward Cleaver*. Her latest works are the *It's Reigning Men* series, the *Royal Romeos* series and her new *Falling for Mr. Wrong* series. She also published the memoir *Winging It: A Memoir of Caring for a Vengeful Parrot Who's Determined to Kill Me,* now re-titled *Bite Me: a Parrot, a Family and a Whole Lot of Flesh Wounds*; the novels *Anywhere but Here*; *Where the Heart Is*; the essay collection *Naked Man on Main Street,* and *Accidentally on Purpose* and *Compromising Positions* (writing as Erin Delany); and is a contributor to the humorous dog anthology *I'm Not the Biggest Bitch in This Relationship*.

Her work has been found in Ladies Home Journal, the Washington Post, Marie-Claire.com, and on NPR's Day to Day. She was also a columnist for Charlottesville's Daily Progress for over a decade, and is the Volunteer Coordinator for the Virginia Film Festival.

She has worked as a professional photographer, an orthodontic assistant (learning quite readily that she was not cut out for a career in polyester), a waitress (probably her highest-paying job), a TV reporter, a pre-obituary writer, as well as a publicist to a United States Senator (where she first learned to write fiction). She's photographed Prince Charles (and her assistant husband got him to chuckle!), Elizabeth Taylor, and the president of Uganda. She and her family and menagerie of pets now live a less exotic life in Virginia.

Visit Jenny at her website at www.jennygardiner.net where you can sign up for her newsletter, visit her blog, or find her on Facebook and Twitter. And every blue moon she'll post adorable pictures of her pets on Instagram as @thejennygardiner.

CPSIA information can be obtained
at www.ICGtesting.com
Printed in the USA
LVOW13s1427010618
579256LV00018B/466/P